PACIFIC BLUE TATTOO

LISA SILVERTHORNE

A felon with an artificial conscience,
An immortal tattoo artist,
And a rookie cop hunt a serial killer in...
PACIFIC BLUE TATTOO

Convicted felon, Kip Thorpe had no conscience until the government gave her one. As a sociopath, she knew how to recognize others.

Like the one collecting and killing blonde, tattooed women in downtown Seattle—including Kip's missing sister.

Rookie Seattle detective Tristan Bowker is the last person Kip wants in her life. But he's the last cop listening. And the last complication she needs.

Shadowed by Bowker and Persephone, her mysterious tattoo artist coworker claiming to be queen of the underworld, Kip fights a one-woman war against this deadly street predator. *Before her sister runs out of time.*

PACIFIC BLUE TATTOO
Lisa Silverthorne
Copyright © 2021 by Lisa Silverthorne
All rights reserved.

Cover Layout Copyright © 2021 by ElusiveBlueFiction.com
Cover Art Copyright © 2021 eAlisa, leolintang/DepositPhotos, Brusheezy

Based on the short stories, *Permanent Ink* and *The Spirit House* by Lisa Silverthorne.

This work, or parts of this work, may not be reproduced in any form without prior written permission from the publisher, except brief quotations for review purposes.

This is a work of fiction. Any resemblance to actual persons, places, or events is merely coincidental.

Novels by Lisa Silverthorne

Standalones:

ISABEL'S TEARS

REDISCOVERY

LANDFALL

PACIFIC BLUE TATTOO

A Game of Lost Souls series:

THE CINDERELLA HOUR

THE PRINCE CHARMING HOUR

THE EVER AFTER HOUR

THE FALLEN HEARTS SEASON

THE RISING SPIRITS SEASON

THE ETERNAL SOULS SEASON

THE ROYAL WEDDING HOUR

THE HEAVENLY HONEYMOON HOUR

Haunted Portraits series:

BEAUTY: CAPTURED AND FRAMED

SCIENCE FICTION WRITING AS L.S. SILVERTHORNE

Experiencing True Purple series:

RECOMBINANT, Book 1

HELIX, Book 2

COMING SOON!

A Game of Lost Souls series:

The Divine Newlyweds Show, Book Nine

The Celestial Couples Show, Book Ten

The Enochian Apocalypse Show, Book Eleven

The Angelic Anniversary Hour, Book Twelve

A Game of Lost Souls—Angelic Hearts:

Muriel's Spark

Kesien's Fire

Anahera's Flame

Azrael's Embers

Haunted Portraits series:

Monster, Loose and Unhinged, Book Two

Harmony: Recaptured and Under Glass, Book Three

SCIENCE FICTION WRITING AS **L.S. SILVERTHORNE**

Experiencing True Purple series:

Splice, Book 3

Cipher, Book 4

Renascence, Book 5

1

1:56 AM, August 31st
   Somewhere north of Seattle, WA

GRASS SWISHED, sliver of moonlight pale through the blindfold, crystalline in the indigo darkness. Sarah Thorpe's breath beat hot against the spit-soaked gag, heartbeat in time with the man's footsteps as he dragged her across the ground.

Toward what?

Her throat was raw from screaming, but no one heard. *Oh, God— somebody please hear me!* She couldn't form words, but the noise, if only someone heard the noise.

His breath stank of Jim Beam as he sang to himself, angry staccato notes that twisted and slurred words.

"Never lettin' go...forever mine to hold...sleep, baby, sleep... forever mine to keep..."

Cold fear bored through her and again, she struggled, but his fist slammed into her chest. Sliver of moonlight blurred then sharpened again, stabbing her burning eyes. Whatever he'd put in her soda made her so groggy. Everything so hazy.

And nobody in that club had noticed, nobody tried to stop him. All she could do was stare up at the blur of passing faces, a pleading expression on her face. She couldn't react, couldn't stop him from shoving her into his van.

Pain throbbed into her shoulders, arms so tired and aching from the twine wrapped around her. She was so tired. Tired of fighting against him. So tired of the icy fear slicing through her. Her eyes dripped more tears. He was going to kill her now. And she was powerless to stop him.

Her body slammed against the ground, falling...falling. She screamed—as loud and as long as she could. *Why won't somebody hear me?* But no one came. No one heard.

He'd taken her someplace no one would ever find her. Her chest heaved as she clawed at the twine, trying to free her hands.

She thought about her mom, how devastated she'd be. And her sister. She felt guilty, knowing Kelly would hunt this guy down. And it would send her back to prison. She'd hoped to reunite the whole family, but without her to mediate, Kelly would just drift further away.

"Sorry, Mom...Kelly," she whispered. "I'm so sorry."

He stood over her, tearing the blindfold away from her face. Gone was the sling on his right arm and the clumsy helplessness that had gotten her to carry that box inside for him. His cruel stare pierced her, making Sarah shake all over again.

Her body seized at the jagged memory of his body against hers, over and over. The stink of him, the weight of him taking whatever he wanted and she was too groggy to fight him, too confused to react. Tears flooded her cheeks as she stared up at his leering face, shock of hair and wild blue eyes.

Above his head, the sliver of moon hung high, tall fir trees rising into the night. In the distance, wind chimes rang like shattered glass.

Tires whispered against pavement. She concentrated on the moon.

But the ground was so cold, so shallow. She gasped, feeling the fresh earth around her, wood slats on either side.

No, a coffin, she at last realized.

Not like this, please. I don't want to die like this.

"No, please!"

Reaching into the box, he cut the twine around her right shoulder and jerked her right arm free. Camera flash blinded her. He gripped a handful of her blonde hair and the camera flashed. Again, and again, it flashed as he snapped several pictures. Of her hair, her face, the butterflies tattooed on her shoulder.

But why? Why?

"Why are you doing this?" She tried to swing at him, but his grip was too tight, the box too cramped.

"Sleep, Sarah, sleep," he sang in a half-whisper, grinning as he raised a wooden lid from the ground. "Like a picture, forever mine to keep."

"No! No, please! Don't lock me in here!"

The lid slammed down on her, blotting out the moon and the trees. Her body jolted. And the air!

She slammed her twine-wrapped body upward, her shoulder smashing against wood, but she couldn't stop him from nailing it closed. Like gunshots, a nail gun closed her into darkness.

"Don't do this! Don't do this!" She beat the lid with her fist.

A sliver of light filtered into the blackness, from a hole at her right shoulder. But a wide, plastic pipe quickly filled the hole.

Scritch, plunk. Scritch, plunk. The horrible sound of dirt hitting the wooden lid. Burying her alive.

"Kelly, help me! Kelly!"

She pounded the lid, shouted, fought, but the sounds were lost beneath wind chimes, falling dirt, and that horrible song.

2

11:01 P.M., August 31st
Downtown Seattle

PERSEPHONE STEPPED outside the tattoo shop for coffee, the night ripe with heat. The pavement smelled hot and oily, the whisper of cars and flash of headlights on the dark streets as she stood near Colman Dock, looking out at Elliott Bay, wishing she belonged somewhere, with someone.

She'd taken off her red Versace blouse, wearing only a black Von Furstenberg camisole and skirt and the heat felt good against her bare shoulders. She glanced down at her black Prada's, remembering how her friend, Kip commented on how they sounded the same on pavement as her discount shoes.

It was frivolous, she knew, but sometimes, wearing nice clothes eased the loneliness she felt at times here with humans. She'd lived lifetimes among these mortals, watching designers and their popularity rise and fall with the centuries—as their clothes got more and more casual.

Luxurious clothing connected her to simpler times in Greece so long ago. When she was a child at Demeter's side, playing in those ancient fields, plucking wildflowers, and chasing butterflies.

But the screech and rattle of Hades' chariot still haunted her, his overwhelming strength as he plucked her from that field in Eleusis eons ago, carrying her into the underworld's greyness.

A goddess, born in the light—taken to his world of death and darkness.

There had been youth and wildness about Hades then. He had never forced himself on her, but he'd wooed her—delicately. Gently. Lovingly. Over time, his passion and strength made her fall deliriously in love with him, enough to swallow the six pomegranate seeds that forever bound her to him and his realm.

Queen of the Underworld. But for only six months of the year, when the earth slumbered in winter greyness—thanks to Hecate's negotiation on her mother's behalf.

The other six months, she returned to the light, to the living, and roamed this world freely, free to do or be whatever she wished.

But only for six months.

At times, she hated Hades for what he'd made her into—for what she'd become. A permanent visitor in two realms, never feeling part of either, never connecting or living.

This spring, when she'd left the Underworld for Hecate's crossroads, she traveled on a mortal ferry in the Puget Sound. Seattle's light and darkness attracted her, making her feel at home. She loved Seattle's misty piers, brightly lit walkways, and dark streets. And the feeling of permanence she'd felt when she stepped into Pacific Blue Tattoo and saw the art adorning skin.

All of it—especially the human mortals here—made her feel comfortable. Connected.

As a tattoo artist now, her ancient knowledge of the arts and things lost allowed her to create art that mortals had never laid eyes on since before Christ. She was intrigued by the commitment mortals made when they chose to permanently mark their bodies with her artwork.

For the first time, she'd even marked her own body, portraying those imprisoning pomegranate seeds on her stomach. Ruby red and glistening, they were a symbol of her slavery to a god who had grown weary of his promise to love and cherish her for eternity. A man who barely spoke for days on end, who spent more time with his three-headed dogs than the woman he'd fought so hard to make his own.

She missed his passion, the fire that had driven him to carry her off to the underworld and woo her. The passion that had brought him to his knees, sobbing with joy when he first saw those pomegranate seeds on her bare belly.

It had been so long since they'd made even love, him knowing all the while that soon, she'd have to leave him again for six months. When she'd left through Hades' gates this last time, he hadn't even given her a gentle peck on the cheek or said goodbye.

Was he even aware she'd left at all?

Would he even notice when she failed to return this time? Would he understand exactly what would happen in the mortal world when she didn't return to the Underworld?

Autumn wouldn't come.

The leaves would never fall. A chill would never touch the air. The world would remain in perpetual summer.

A warm breeze brushed her face and her long black hair. She closed her eyes, leaning into the wind, a hot mocha in a To-Go cup clutched in her right hand.

Seattle's heatwave was her doing. And it would remain until she left the mortal realm. She regretted that, but it was unavoidable. She wouldn't return to a man that only tolerated her presence now.

Besides, Kip Thorpe needed her help—the help of a goddess.

She took a sip, the scent of coffee and chocolate warm as the heat slid down her throat and into her belly and turned away from the bay.

Tourists walked along the piers in their white pants, white shoes, and fanny packs, cameras slung around their necks and cell phones clutched in their hands. Like little rabbits hopping along the edge of a dark forest, not seeing the wolves' red eyes staring out at them.

Like all the major cities of the world, Seattle had its share of wolves and rabbits, both living peacefully side by side, but tonight, she felt a human predator connected to Kip. One that stood out as twisted, vicious, and deadly. Despite her status as Queen of the Underworld, as a goddess of yesterday's magic, she had no power to stop this mortal.

But she could help Kip Thorpe hunt him.

Not a grand hunt like Artemis would have led. Just a quiet, desperate little search. But the stakes were so high for Kip. It made Persephone's chest ache. Kip knew this type of predator better than anyone, but she was human. As susceptible to death as the other women he'd killed.

Persephone held no power over the living or the dying, only the dead. But she would use yesterday's magic to help Kip find this killer. Kip had no one and Persephone had a weak spot for anyone lost and alone in the darkness.

She knew that feeling well—especially now.

Humans lived such short lives, but the passion that burned in them was brighter than anything Persephone had ever seen among the gods (except for Hades once).

Maybe that was why many gods and goddesses envied them? Even her.

She took another long, slow drink of coffee, glanced at her watch, then headed back to the shop. She had one last appointment—three hours of tribal designs from a race long dead. Symbols of eternal life. A shame that those symbols were all that had survived. She looked forward to sharing them with others who would appreciate them.

Unlike the monster that hunted in Seattle's streets. A monster that worshipped death.

3

4:06 P.M., August 3 1st
Downtown Seattle

ANOTHER DEAD BODY. The fourth one since April.

Kip Thorpe trudged down the rain-soaked sidewalk, past the downtown alleyway, her gaze unblinking at the red flash of sirens and white-draped form.

Crime scene tape.

A million bad memories rushed back from a past she wanted to forget as she stood at the edge of the alley. Six years ago. Another body in another Seattle alley. All for twenty bucks and a lousy credit card.

She hadn't pulled the trigger (Donny had), but she'd ganked the guy's wallet. Five years in prison and a year of community service hadn't been as hard as the artificial conscience she carried around in her head now. She'd agreed to the fingernail-sized microchip implanted in her brain. It was part of her rehabilitation.

It branded her a monster.

She'd been responsible for that guy's death and every day she lived with the reality of her actions.

Lived with it? She sighed. *It ate at her like acid.*

Cops crawled all over the place, picking up stuff and dropping it in plastic bags, searching the ground with flashlights for clues, measuring distances, taking pictures. Anything to catch a killer.

She hated cops.

Took them nearly a year to find her and Donny. Wincing, Kip closed her eyes, sickened at the memory and her guilt.

Cops were power hungry control freaks, that thin line barely separating most of them from the rage and hunger that drove two-legged animals to prowl. But some felt a little lost and confused every time a predator racked up a body count. Most cops didn't understand these monsters, so they couldn't really feel it enough to track sociopaths and worse.

No, a few still gave a shit about other people, about the law or some other highbrow stuff too far up from the gutter for Kip to see. But no matter how hard the cops tried, they couldn't understand that lurking darkness.

But Kip did. She'd embraced that void once, knowing nothing else. Now, her artificial conscience lifted her above it, but she always saw its shadow beside her. It was always there. She understood it well.

And she never wanted to go back.

Gravel crunched above the hush of rain and whispers on the sidewalk. For a moment, it had that cathedral feel to it, that hushed sense of reverence you got when you walked into St. Somebody's or a funeral service. But it was only a moment.

The air smelled dirty as a handful of people in rain ponchos and fanny packs—tourists—gawked like the crime scene was some movie set. Something to brag about.

Hey, the missus and I saw a crime scene when we visited Pike's Market! Wanna see pictures? I posted them online.

Kip scowled, shoving past the yellow tape and growing crowd. And *she* needed an artificial conscience?

She thought about the person under that sheet and the people they'd left behind. It made her gut ache (always the tale-tell sign that her artificial conscience was working).

Two investigators—a woman and a man—in blue rain jackets flooded the alley with camera flash, photographing the body from every angle. King County Medical Examiner's Office was printed on the back of their jackets. The guy put a tag on the dead person's ankle while the woman wrapped the hands in paper bags. Small hands. Female.

They collected stuff around the body, too, sealing it in plastic bags before unfurling a nylon body bag. Carefully, they laid the body inside, but one arm slipped free of the folds. Drama masks in bold purple and teal peeked out from a woman's paper-white forearm crisscrossed with red marks.

Kip frowned. She'd seen that tattoo before—at the shop.

The investigators zipped the bag and loaded it into the back of a black van parked against the curb.

Her brain went back to the tattoo. Drama masks.

Cold stabbed Kip's chest, her skin clammy as she wrapped her arms around her middle, finally remembering where she'd seen it. Shit. Her friend, Carolee had a tattoo like that. She worked at a nearby club, called 86 or something like that.

Aw, dammit, Carolee.

Kip slumped against a brick wall, surprised by the needle of pain that momentarily stabbed through her numbness. She didn't realize she was sinking until someone grabbed her arms.

A tall, black-haired woman with black-rimmed eyes and pale skin. Persephone—her friend from work. Kip's body went slack again.

"Kip? You okay?" Persephone asked, her large blue eyes intense against the smudged blackness lining them. She wore a short jean skirt and cuffed white blouse beneath a grey duster. "I saw the lights flashing on my way in."

Seph had one of those weird gazes, that calming *everything's-gonna-be-fine* expression like she'd seen it all before. Like even the worst trauma would end soon. She had an oldness about her, too. Not in some wise ass way, but a smart kind of way. Like she'd seen and done it all. Or she no longer cared. Kip was never sure.

Persephone glanced around then nodded toward the van. "What happened?"

Kip shrugged. "They found another body," she said, standing up straight.

She pulled away from Persephone, trying to act unfazed and brushed dust off her faded jeans and blue Henley. Through Persephone's thin white blouse peeked the outline of ruby pomegranate seeds like teardrops on her stomach. She'd tattooed them herself. Kip pointed toward the body bag and exposed forearm.

"Seph, I think that's Carolee Eddleston."

Seph didn't blink, even though she'd done the drama mask tattoo on Carolee's forearm. Her mouth flattened into a taut line, her jaw line sharpening. "She was coming by the shop soon," said Seph, her gaze settling on the body bag. "Tragedy needed more teal."

The pain in Kip's gut made her lean against the bricks again. Poor Carolee didn't deserve this. Like Kip, she was ragged like a busted beer bottle, but once you got past those jagged edges, Carolee was sweet and cared about things. Like leaving her tuna salad for the alley cats or giving some old beggar her bus fare. Like it'd somehow save somebody. Maybe she knew it'd buy some crack or a bottle of Night Train, but to her, she was helping someone.

Everybody has two masks, Carolee told Kip once while Seph was tattooing those drama masks. *The trick is to see the one underneath.* Looked like Carolee saw the wrong mask on somebody last night.

A thin man in a brown leather jacket stood on the sidewalk flashing a badge and jotting notes on a damp yellow note pad. He looked dark and smoky, a little bored and a little angry as he talked to gawkers and freaks who claimed to have seen everything. Anything for their fifteen minutes of fame. He kept glancing at her and Seph then scowling.

Beside the man was an intense, sandy-haired guy with a badge and stubbled jaw, his dark pants and white shirt damp as he listened to information and drew on a notepad. Wiry and lean, he didn't have that almost dead stare of the first cop.

No, he seemed hell-bent on saving the world, one faceless witness at a time.

His face was a mixture of passion and innocence, kinda like riding the Tilt-a-whirl at the fair for the first time. Plenty of movement, but not enough spin yet to make him hurl. The other cop had been on this ride before and he'd definitely been spun too much.

For a brief moment, Kip admired the other cop, even if she didn't quite understand why. But she'd seen that look on his face before, in the eyes of people she used to care about (her sister Sarah, and her case worker, Mary Margaret).

Even in her own mother's eyes once, before she got tired of all the bullshit.

It was an attractive gleam and Kip felt like a moth to flame as she stared at the man's handsome face. Yeah, he was hot, too. And there was something deep behind those eyes. He gave a shit about something, someone. Maybe she would too, again?

Like static before a storm, his gaze connected with hers. Defying his optimism, she met his stare with the emptiness she'd carefully cultivated all these years, but dammit, her artificial conscience was starting to fill that void. No matter if she wanted it filled or not. It was making her want to care.

He didn't look away, his gaze enveloping her. What did he see there? Which mask played across her thin face and pale eyes? Did he see the monster? She bit her lip. He was a cop; he had to see it. They all saw it, sniffed it out like bloodhounds.

Kip looked away. "Let's go," she said to Seph, grabbing her arm. "We're late for work."

Persephone swung her long black hair off her shoulder as she moved down the block. "Not that Nick would say anything." She smirked. "He knows I'm his best tattoo artist."

"I'm sorry, Carolee," Kip muttered, turning away as they loaded Carolee's body into the ambulance.

She walked beside Seph toward Pike Place. Nobody did tribal art and ancient drawings like Persephone, but receptionists were easy to replace and Nick would find a new one if Kip didn't show. She cast one last look behind her, at the chalk line, yellow flutter of police tape, and the hot, wide-eyed cop then shut out the images. It was better that way.

PACIFIC BLUE TATTOO was in this really cool old building on Pike Place with tall, narrow windows and high ceilings. Its bright white lights and blue neon were like a lighthouse in the grey Seattle streets. Persephone's stiletto boots pounded the sidewalk and she never looked around, her chin always high like she knew she was untouchable. Kip liked her *don't even try it* attitude. Seph pulled open the bright blue door and stepped inside the shop.

The autoclave hissed above the steady hum of needles and ink against skin as Kip slid into the empty desk chair at the front desk. The maple wood was cool against her forearms, smell of antiseptic strong in the air. Seph slipped off her duster and hung it on a hook at her station. Okay, so it was two bookcases and a coat rack surrounding an old barber's chair, but it got the job done. She rolled up her sleeves as she sat down and checked her needles.

Kip looked over the appointment book, but her thoughts drifted back to Carolee, the drama masks an afterimage in her head. It made her stomach hurt. Donny knew a guy once, really twisted, used to pick up women all puttied up with makeup and blue eye shadow. Said he was an Elvis freak. He was only half right.

Elvis didn't kidnap women and lock them in his basement.

Someone cleared their throat and Kip glanced up. Good cop bad cop from the crime scene stood at the desk. The really tall, angry, smoky-eyed one shoved a badge in her face. She recoiled. She'd been around enough cops to last a lifetime.

"Seattle Police Department, Miss," said good cop, the sandy-haired guy she saw in the alley. Her breath caught. He was much hotter close up. "I'm Detective Bowker and this is Detective St. James."

"You seemed awfully interested in what happened a few blocks from here," said bad cop, still in her face. "Why was that?"

Kip scowled. "I'm no drive-by tourist. I was on my way to work."

"Which corner?" muttered bad cop.

Kip rose from the chair, leaned her palms on the desk and glared at Detective St. James. St. James? A funny way to spell asshole. His hair was dark and regulation straight, no rings on either hand, looked really conversative and narrow-minded. With his head up his ass.

"Here for a tattoo?" she asked St. James. "We've got some great flash of jackasses that'd be perfect for you. Which cheek?"

Snickers rolled through the shop. Even Persephone was laughing. Dull pain drifted through Kip's stomach, but she ignored the artificial conscience. She'd done her time. She wouldn't put up with any more cop hassles.

The sandy-haired cop stifled a laugh, pulling back his partner. A tiny diamond stud winked from his left ear. It was sexy as hell.

"Look, I'm sorry for my partner's bad behavior. We're interviewing witnesses and bystanders who might have seen something, heard something. Any information you could offer would be a great help."

Kip's gaze didn't soften. Bowker wasn't total saccharin, but she wasn't in the mood for nice, polite bullshit either. St. James made it clear how he saw her.

"Fine," she said, nodding toward the dark-haired guy. "Just keep him on a choke chain. All I did was walk past that alley. I saw chalk lines and a white body bag. Hope you find her killer."

Bowker's expression changed subtly as he glanced at his partner. St. James rushed around the desk and grabbed her arm.

"We kept the body covered," he said, his breath smelling of coffee. "How'd you know it was a woman?"

His face was almost touching hers now. He stunk like expensive cologne and new leather. Kip wrenched her arm free and pushed St. James backward.

"Because I saw the tattoo when they loaded her into the van. Carolee was a friend of mine, okay? She didn't deserve that!"

The pain in her stomach was sharp now, gnawing at her gut in a mixture of sorrow and rage. She hated these intense emotions; she wasn't used to them and they hurt. She bit her lip. She wouldn't let these cops see her weakness.

"Kip, everything okay up here?" Seph asked, moving toward her.

Nick was behind Seph, his face all tight and pinched, like he was pissed off. Again. He wore a faded black Foo Fighters t-shirt and torn jeans.

This wasn't her fault. She hadn't called these jerks inside.

Kip shrugged and rubbed her arm, still glaring at the dark-haired detective.

"Miss..." said Bowker, his hazel eyes almost sad. "Kip. You'll need to come to the precinct and answer some questions."

Seph crossed her arms and leaned against the desk. "Then you'll have to take me in, too."

"A pleasure," said St. James with a smile. Persephone was tall and beautiful. Kip wasn't surprised by the guy's reaction. It pissed her off, but she wasn't surprised.

Bowker's brows furrowed. "Did you know the victim, too? Miss—"

"Hadis. Persephone Hadis." Her blue gaze met St. James' dark eyes. "Because I saw exactly what Kip saw. That tattoo? It was my artwork. Carolee was coming in this week for a retouch."

The two detectives exchanged looks. It was a chance to break this downtown killer case. Kip had seen the news online. Carolee hadn't been the first body found downtown. Whatever happened to her was connected with three other downtown murders. Kip was certain of it.

Kip cast a knowing gaze at Bowker which sent a ripple of surprise across his face.

She sighed at what might have been, knowing that in a few minutes they'd run her name and instead of the receptionist, she'd be a monster again. Her boss, Nick knew about her past. She'd told him everything up front and he hired her anyway. No, Bowker would quickly transform into bad cop like St. James. Her stomach ached. She didn't care. Bowker was just another pretty face, like those old oil paintings in museums. She could look up at them on the wall, but never eye to eye.

Detective Bowker swept his arm toward the door, opening a path for Kip.

Kip hesitated.

"Please," he said in a hushed voice. "Help us catch your friend's killer."

Her lips parted in surprise. He believed her.

He wouldn't much longer, but seeing trust looking back at her for even a moment was a good feeling. She hadn't seen that look of trust since her case worker, Mary Margaret died. Cancer sucked.

Kip nodded at him and stepped around the desk.

"See me when you get back, Kip," said Nick, walking away from the door.

Kip groaned. Kiss this job goodbye.

"We will," said Seph over her shoulder as she followed Kip out into the damp air.

A dark Charger sat beside the curb and Bowker ushered Kip into the backseat. St. James helped Seph into the back then climbed into the driver's seat. Inside the dark car, red and green lights flashed and pulsed, a scratchy radio muttering numbers and street names. The car smelled like Burgermaster, home of the best burgers in Seattle. Kip tuned out St. James as he radioed ahead and the car pulled away from Pacific Blue Tattoo, headed for West Precinct.

WITH ITS CONCRETE walls and black grid-work, West Precinct looked like a prison. Kip's skin crawled as she entered the building, the wave of past images overpowering. Sometimes they were freeze frames of moments she most wanted to forget: the moment Donny pulled that trigger, the moment when she could have stopped him and didn't. The frenzy of flashbulbs and sirens, handcuffs biting into her wrists, the sound of the cell lockdown and the awful dark hours until morning.

"Kip, he's asking for your name."

Persephone shook her shoulder. Kip sucked in a quick breath. The green and grey office felt like the interrogation room where she'd once spent hours, days. The air smelled like stale coffee and dust. Her gaze traveled across the table to Detective Bowker who still smiled politely. St. James leaned against the wall, arms crossed, dark eyes boring holes through her.

"It's Thorpe," she said with a shrug. "Kelly Thorpe."

Bowker started typing on a laptop.

Kip jumped up from the chair and pointed at the notebook. "And before you rake up all my dirt, yeah, I've got a record! But I did my time."

This brought St. James off the wall and at her shoulder. "Sit down. Now!"

Kip matched his glare with one of her own, challenging him to take this farther. She hadn't done anything and she wouldn't let him treat her like a criminal. Not again.

"Dammit, Keith," Bowker growled. "Chill! This isn't an interrogation. She's not a suspect."

"How do you know?" St. James shouted, pointing at Bowker. "You haven't even seen the rap sheet yet!"

Kip slammed her hand against the table. "He doesn't need a rap sheet to know that crime was committed by a guy! Probably the same guy who killed those other three women."

"Five years for robbery and manslaughter," said Bowker. "One year in Experimental Rehab." Bowker's eyes widened as he looked over the laptop screen at her. "Holy shit! You really got a chip in your head?"

Bowker seemed more fascinated than repulsed, but the fight left Kip.

Freak. Monster.

The words played in her head as she sagged into her chair, not wanting to face Persephone or St. James' ridiculing stare. The monster was loose again.

She nodded. "They say I don't have a conscience without it." Her voice was quiet this time.

St. James thrust his hand at her. "See! There ya go! It was probably a rob-and-roll, same M. O."

"You're way off, so drop it," Bowker snapped at St. James.

Kip wanted to wipe that smug smile off St. James' face. What an idiot to try and connect a stolen wallet with a psychopathic killer!

"But you forget I was with Kip the entire time," said Persephone, looking smug as she crossed her arms.

St. James' face pinched into a frown.

Seph patted Kip on the sleeve. "Kip did her time. She's here to offer information as a witness, nothing more." Her gaze fixed on St. James and his anger seemed to float away. "So, treat her like a witness."

Bowker smiled and rose from his chair. He eased St. James back out of the way and dropped on his haunches beside Kip.

"Kelly," he said in a respectful tone.

She glanced at his face, into his steady hazel eyes. She couldn't tell what he saw her as now, but the fact that he still looked at her was enough.

"Please. Tell me what you know about our victim? So, we can find her killer."

No one had called her Kelly in that tone since Mary Margaret at the hospice in Coupeville. It sounded kind of nice on his lips.

"Carolee was just out of high school, not sure if she graduated or not. She was a good kid, paying her way through beauty school by working nights at some downtown warehouse club. Think it was called 86—something like that. Nick let her trade haircuts for piercings or tattoos."

Kip remembered Carolee trimming her hair once in the backroom of Pacific Blue. She looked like a very blonde Natalie Portman. She'd been all excited about a guy she'd met. Said he loved her tattoos.

"Wait a minute," said Kip, rising from her chair.

Bowker stood up with her.

She felt cold all of a sudden, like somebody had opened a freezer door.

"Two weeks ago, she met some guy. He was crazy about her tattoo, a unicorn on her shoulder blade. So, for him, Carolee was getting the drama masks on her forearm." She glanced at Persephone who nodded.

"Yes, I remember that!" Seph laid a hand to her chin. "Carolee was gushing about her new guy as I colored the drama masks."

"Where'd Carolee meet this guy?" Bowker asked, his intense gaze moving to Seph.

Persephone scrunched up her pale face, shaking her head. "She didn't say."

"Kelly?" he asked, turning back to her.

God, he was looking at her like an actual person. She resisted the urge to reach out and touch his face. It was a handsome face—strong jaw, smooth chin.

Bowker stepped closer. "Think. Where'd she meet the guy?"

He smelled like soap and rain and his closeness was intoxicating.

Kip squeezed her eyes closed, fighting to call back anything Carolee might have said that night. A word, a phrase —something that might help.

"The Midnight Hour," she blurted out finally, remembering Carolee talking about some new fancy club.

St. James moved over to Bowker, his face pale. He whispered something Kip couldn't hear.

"Ladies," said Bowker, "you were an immense help. That's all the questions we have for now." He reached into his shirt pocket and retrieved a business card. His gaze fell onto Kip as he extended the card. "If you remember anything else, please call us right away."

Kip took the card from Bowker's hand. His fingers were strong and smooth, steady, not delicate-looking like St. James' almost manicured hands. She glanced at the card as the two detectives led them into the hallway and toward the exit. Detective Tristan Bowker. It was kind of girlie, but she liked it. If she remembered anything at all, like the capital of Washington State, she'd call.

It was Olympia.

The four of them walked outside into the damp night. As they moved toward the Charger, Kip stopped and tugged on Bowker's sleeve.

"He hunts them near that club," she said in a quiet voice.

Bowker's lips parted as he cast a sideways glance at his partner.

"Why do you say that?" he asked, his brow creasing.

She and Donny always kept to places that were familiar. Wallets were easy to snatch when you knew the escape route. They had the power in those places. It was their world and everyone else was a tourist. That's what this guy was doing, too. It was familiar ground. Kip brushed hair out of her eyes.

"Because your killer really knows the downtown streets. He hunts where he has the power. He's connected to that club in some way."

For a moment, all Kip heard was Bowker's steady breathing in the dusky street.

"Yeah, he hunts," Kip continued. "To him, we aren't people. We're playthings. Toys that he gets tired of, but he's gotta have more, y'know? A collector."

"We haven't revealed any details about those murders," said St. James, his voice sounding all suspicious and angry. Kip sighed. The idiot still thought she was a suspect. St. James might be a good cop if he just paid attention.

Kip turned toward him. "You didn't have to. Some of my best friends were psychopaths." She turned back to Bowker. His kind face was much nicer to look at. "I saw Carolee's arm and the marks. He tied her up for a long time. Kept her somewhere else. Didn't he?"

Bowker winced, casting another uncomfortable glance at his partner.

She felt sorry for him. It was like he felt all of it inside him somehow. Not sensitive exactly. Empathy. Yeah, that was it, what the judge told her she didn't have. Six years ago, that was true, but with this chip, she felt some of it too, now. Down deep like part of her wanted to curl into a ball and shake. St. James kept moving too fast to let that stuff hit him in the face, but not Bowker. Yet, here he was still doing the job. God, she admired that.

"I uh, might have more questions—for you later," said Bowker as he opened the car door. He watched Kip with renewed fascination as she crawled into the back seat after Persephone. "Is it the chip?"

Kip frowned. "Chip?"

Bowker climbed into the front seat as St. James got into the driver's side and started the car. Bowker turned toward her again. "Does it give you some kind of...new insight?"

She nodded. "What being human feels like. But I know the flip side of that feeling, too."

He was silent as the car drove away from the curb. Kip reached out and touched his left sleeve. She wasn't even sure why she did it, but it was important that somebody else understood. To her surprise, he laid his hand against hers—just for a moment—then let go.

"It's awfully dark in that other place, a place I never wanna touch again," she said in a low voice that only he could hear. "But it scares me that I still know the way."

4

NICK WAS SULLEN when Kip and Persephone returned to the shop. He glared at Kip as he called her to the back office. Sighing, Kip walked across the creaking wood floor, past the four tattoo artists' stations. Ross and Taku glanced at her a moment then returned to their clients as she stepped into Nick's cramped, well-lit office. Nick's station was empty.

He was kind of a messy guy with piles of papers all over his desk. His walls had all these pictures of framed flash art from tattoo artists he admired. One picture of some columned building in Greece, done by Seph, was his favorite. That one hung over his desk. He was so hot for her. Everybody in the shop knew it, but Seph didn't like him like that.

Nick motioned her toward an old, red wooden chair and she slouched into it. He sat down in his desk chair, stringy brown hair in his eyes. He laid his fingers against his dark Van Dyke beard and didn't quite look Kip in the eye, instead looking at Seph's art on the wall. The room smelled like Ivar's chowder from the half-eaten container ringing last month's Tattoo Artist Magazine.

"I know I told you when I hired you that your past's your business." He licked his thin lips and glanced at her once then back at the walls. Whatever. She didn't like people who wouldn't look her in the eye. "But I've got a reputable business and if people see cops here—especially with all the downtown murders—well, it's bad for the place."

Kip stared unblinking at him. "If you're gonna fire me, the least you could do is look me in the eye and do it."

She sighed. She was really hoping this job would work out.

He glanced at her, the tale-tell flicker of fear in his brown eyes. Like she was connected somehow to that psycho killer. That made her angry, but she bit her lip to force it down into her stomach. What next? Peasants with torches and pitchforks?

"Kip...I'm sorry, but—"

"But what, Nick?" Seph asked from the office doorway. She swept into the room to stand beside Kip. "Did Kip tell you about our customer, Carolee? They found her dead in an alley near Third. The cops have asked for our help in the investigation."

Nick shook his head, glancing at Kip then back at Seph. "We hadn't got that far yet," said Nick. "Look, Seph, this is private."

Kip nodded at Persephone. "He was halfway through firing me. We'll be done as soon as he looks me in the eye and tells me why." She turned her gaze to Nick who was running his fingers over and over his chin. Like he always did when he was nervous—or around Seph.

Persephone frowned. "Firing Kip? Why?" She crossed her arms.

"We—we don't need cops coming and going when four women have been murdered. It's bad for business."

"So is a client being murdered. Kip and I saw the same thing out there, so if they aren't talking to her, they'll be talking to me." She shrugged. "Guess we're both fired. Come on, Kip. I'll get my jacket."

Humming softly to herself, Seph clacked across the floor toward her station and slipped on her duster.

"Persephone, no!"

Nick jumped up from his chair and clomped out after her.

Kip rose from the chair and moved toward the reception desk to grab her backpack. She usually left it there in case she bought groceries on the way home, but she'd better take it now. Looked like she wasn't coming back this time.

"Seph, please!" Nick hovered around her, flapping his arms. "You're my best artist! You just mean for the season, right? Until April?"

"No, for good. Bye, Nick."

Seph's boots echoed through the very quiet shop. Not a single tattoo was in process now, even the autoclave had gone silent. Everyone stared at Nick and Seph.

"Seph!" Nick shouted. "Seph, don't!"

"Ready, Kip?" Seph asked with a smile.

Kip nodded and slipped the empty blue pack onto her right shoulder. When she opened the door, Nick shouted her name.

"I didn't take anything that wasn't mine, Nick," Kip called over her shoulder.

"Kip, I'm sorry," he said through gritted teeth. "I—"

"Jumped to conclusions?" Seph offered, somewhere behind her.

"Yeah, yeah—I did and I'm sorry. Can we all just get back to work and forget this?"

Kip allowed the hint of a smile on her lips as Seph winked at her.

"Thanks," said Kip in a quiet voice. "I owe you one."

Seph slid off her duster and turned back toward her station. "Forget it. You paid for your mistake. It's time to move on, y'know?"

"What'd he mean by you leaving for the season?" Kip asked.

"Every year, I leave on September first and come back in April. But this year, I think I'll stick around."

Kip nodded, careful to keep the emotion out of her face. Seph was cool and she liked hanging with her, but she didn't want Seph to know that. Pain always came when she cared about something, someone. She'd learned that when her mom dumped her on Dad and moved to Idaho with Sarah, Kip's little sister.

Looking back, Kip kind of understood why. She'd been impossible to control. She wouldn't let anyone control her. Her eyes stung.

Damn chip. She let the thought go and moved back to the desk as Seph's 6:30 P.M. appointment walked in from the rain.

CAROLEE'S MOTHER lived up north, in Lowell. Kip remembered her saying once that she was going up there to see her mom. Carolee and her mom were tight. Maybe she could tell her something helpful? Right. The cops had probably already gone through all of her things and found out everything her poor mother knew. Kip hated to intrude on the woman's grief, but it was the only way she could help Carolee.

She picked up one of Nick's maps and studied the bus routes, trying to find a way out to Lowell. She'd get there. She had to.

Around 10:30 P.M., the tattoo shop phone rang. Kip set down her coffee mug and picked it up.

"Pacific Blue Tattoo, this is Kip."

"Kip? It's Mother."

Kip bristled at the cold voice from her past. Why would that woman call her now, after all these years? Mother. Kip scowled. She hadn't gotten so much as a Christmas card from the woman since she was twelve.

"How'd you find me?" Kip demanded, trying to keep her voice low.

"Your parole officer." The condemnation dripped from her voice. "It was the only way to reach you. I need to get in touch with Sarah. Can you get a message to her to call me?" The icy distance in her voice made Kip cringe.

"What are you talking about?" she replied, unable to chip away that hard edge in her voice. She and Sarah emailed each other all the time, but Kip hadn't seen her little sister in years.

"Look, just have her call me, all right? I don't know why you're trying to scare me like this."

"Scare you? She's not here," Kip said, her voice rising. "Why are you calling me?"

An angry sigh hissed through the phone. "Of course, she's there! She took a bus out to visit you on the thirtieth."

A chill danced across Kip's heart. Sarah had her address and knew where she worked. Maybe the bus had gotten in late or she'd gone to stay with friends?

"Maybe the bus had a flat or something? Have you checked with the bus line yet?"

Heavy silence pressed against Kip's ear. "I just expected she'd be there by now," said Kip's mother, her voice tight and filled with worry. "She was supposed to call when she got there. I've called her cell phone dozens of times, but it just goes to voicemail."

"Okay, there's no reason to panic," said Kip, a dull grinding pain drilling into her stomach. "Call the bus line and the cell phone provider. Find out what you can. Give me her route numbers and I'll check with the station here."

Kip's mother rattled off the routes and her phone number. "Call me if she shows up or you find out anything," she said hurriedly. "She was going to surprise you."

"Surprise me?" Kip's stomach burned. Sarah had come out to see her as a surprise? She smiled at the thought, but it fled quickly. Long, pale blonde hair (new color), huge grin, and skinny jeans, twenty years old. She and Sarah had shared some pictures in Snaps and texts. In the last year, she and Sarah had gotten close. Kip had been saving money for a trip to Idaho, but Sarah beat her to it.

"I can't wait to see her! What was she wearing when she left?"

"She's wearing a red jacket, pink t-shirt, and jeans," said her mother. "Call me when you hear from her, okay? And tell her to call me."

"Will do." Kip hung up the phone, feeling sick inside.

Where was Sarah? Kip hoped the bus had just been delayed, but something told her it was worse than that. Much worse. Had Sarah and Carolee's paths crossed? At the hand of some psycho who'd killed four other women.

Tomorrow. Somehow, she'd get up to Lowell tomorrow morning and talk to Carolee's mother. She needed information and she needed it fast. Kip swallowed hard. Sarah needed it fast.

5

11:39 P.M., August 31st

DETECTIVE TRISTAN BOWKER stood in line behind his partner, Keith St. James and waited for a latte as he tried to block out today's crime scene. Even at this hour, Puget Sound Café was crammed with customers. The drone of conversation was a low roar above the gurgle of steamed milk, the scent of hazelnuts and roasting coffee beans wasn't enough to distract him as his mind went back to the woman in the alley.

And Kelly Thorpe's disturbing and deadly accurate portrayal of her killer.

Milk-pale skin, blue eyes empty and fixed on the grey sky. Like a doll thrown in a dumpster, unmarred except those angry red crisscrosses marking her half-nude body, carefully posed as if she was reclining. Pine nettles and lacy white flower petals clung to her blonde hair.

This time, the bastard dumped the body just blocks from West Precinct in blatant challenge.

Taunting them with the killing.

Tristan pinched his eyes closed, wincing at the memory and the hint of rose perfume that still lingered on her torn blouse. He sighed. His first serial murder investigation and the whole thing made him queasy.

He'd only been on Seattle's police force two years and these streets were a lot meaner than his former Illinois precinct. Less than twelve hours into the case and no leads. He was exhausted, but there wasn't anything else he could do tonight. Besides, he had to be back in at six. While he grabbed a couple hours of sleep, he prayed the lab or eyewitness reports would give them a lead to follow, something to grab hold of and pursue.

The more time that passed, the less likely they were to find this guy. Every cop knew how important those first forty-eight hours were in an investigation.

His drink sat on the counter for several minutes before Keith snatched it up and thrust it at him.

"Come up for air, Tris," said Keith with a frown.

"Huh?" He took the To-Go cup from Keith's hand. "Oh, thanks."

Keith scowled at him. "Don't know how you can ruin good coffee with all that milk." He sipped his black coffee as he palmed a Danish, tossing it onto a corner table that had just opened up. He plopped down in a chair and Tristan sat across from him.

Tristan took a smooth sip of coffee and tuned out Keith's bad mood. Was it over the dead ends they'd already hit on this case? Or maybe Keith just liked to complain? Sometimes, he wasn't sure. Keith was usually angry about something or somebody. Tristan wondered where he got so much energy to get that worked up all the time. Keith was a good guy and a good friend, but sometimes the attitude got to him. Like today at the precinct.

He couldn't help but smile though, remembering how Kelly Thorpe put him in his place. At six foot four, Keith could be a scary guy, too, but Kelly handled him like a pro. With her intense brown eyes and rich brown hair, she was very nice to look at, too. But he wanted to know the whole story about her—the manslaughter and armed robbery conviction.

Maybe this case was just getting to Keith? Tristan rubbed his forehead. Like him.

God knew how it hung onto him when he went home at night. Four women murdered and no suspects. Two other women with descriptions matching the four victims were also missing, one taken before Carolee Eddleston. He took another sip of coffee, tired but not anxious to fall asleep. For months, he'd hated what stared back at him from his dreams. And after seeing the Eddleston woman's body, he felt a new level of sickness hang in the back of his throat. Not to mention the terrible anger that ached through him. He wanted to get this guy, hurt him like he'd hurt those poor women.

Keith took a bite of Cheese Danish. "Why so quiet? Long day?"

"No shit," Tristan snapped. Had he actually managed to forget the image of that woman in the alley?

"Crime scene gettin' to you?"

Tristan's hazel eyes narrowed. "Shouldn't it?"

Keith patted him on the shoulder. "Dude, you gotta get as far away from that stuff as you can. Leave it at work or it'll drive you crazy."

"Like you," Tristan said with a smirk.

Keith laughed. "Stick with me, Bowker and I'll show you how to become a callus bastard before the year's out."

Tristan cringed. Keith was right about not taking it home with him, but he never wanted to reach a point where a death didn't affect him. He squinted at Keith, at those dark eyes he could never read, and wondered if the job affected him more than he let on.

With a sigh, Tristan set down his cup and leaned his elbows on the table, steepling his fingers. "I just want to get this guy, Keith. Bad." He gritted his teeth, gripping his fingers into a fist. "Before he kills another one."

Tristan had learned about unsolved murders at an early age when his father was gunned down one summer night. A Midwest boy, he hadn't expected a drive-by shooting in his small northern Illinois town. What his six-year-old ears mistook for firecrackers had been shots fired and it wasn't until the next morning that he found out his father was never coming home again. The shooter was never caught.

"We all do, buddy," said Keith in a soothing tone. "All I'm saying is don't let it ride around in your head." He poked Tristan in the shoulder with his fist. "And get some sleep tonight. You've been looking grey around the edges all week. Leave it at work, okay?"

Finally, Tristan nodded. "I'll do my best." But how did he leave those images at his desk?

"Do better than that, man. Seriously. It'll eat you alive if you don't." Keith reached over and picked up Tristan's latte. "Isn't it illegal for a guy to order a latte?"

"Bite me, St. James," said Tristan, snatching the cup from his hand.

Keith smirked at him as he rose from the chair. "Sorry to cut out on you, but I've gotta get home. We've got an early call tomorrow, so get some sleep."

"Early call?" Tristan stared at him. "What are you talking about? I'm going to be at my desk by six."

"Some surveillance, buddy. That Thorpe chick knows more than she's telling. She's still a person of interest in my book."

"Would you get off that already!" Tristan shouted. "You're way off base. Besides, the M.E. will have the autopsy results tomorrow morning. I need that report."

"Dude, she knows case details that no one else could know," said Keith, setting down his coffee cup. His dark eyes narrowed. "The tattoo fetish, the twine-wrapping, the collecting...how do you explain that?"

Tristan gripped the edge of the table. "I can't, but my gut says she had nothing to do with it. And I want those lab reports."

Keith poked his stomach with his thumb. "Well, my gut's telling me she's probably involved with guy who's doing it. You'll get the reports soon enough tomorrow."

"You're crazy!"

"Am I?" Keith leaned toward him. "I saw her rap sheet, man. She was hot and heavy with the trigger man. It's not a huge leap to make that call in this case."

She'd been involved with that cold-blooded killer, Donald Evan Wiese? The thought made Tristan shudder, but something about that didn't ring true. He leaned back in his chair, crossing his arms.

"So, we're surveilling Kelly Thorpe tomorrow?"

Keith nodded and tossed his empty cup into a nearby waste bin. "Follow the rabbit down its hole and see where it leads us."

Tristan let a smile touch his lips, remembering her classic good looks and a strength that he admired. But her darkness attracted him in a way that made him uncomfortable. She had a record...armed robbery and assault, and a smile that burned through him. But she was deeper than that, filled with remorse and determined to walk away from her past. He understood that kind of resolve. And it was sexy as hell. But her insight into this killer both disturbed and fascinated him.

"Okay," he said, leveling his gaze at Keith. "We follow Kelly Thorpe around and see who she talks to, where she goes." He'd welcome another look and maybe she'd even blur those sharp-edged images in his head.

Keith clapped him on the shoulder. "Pick you up at 6 AM," he said and headed out into the Seattle night.

"G'night, Keith," Tristan called and finished his latte. He laid his head against the wall, closing his eyes a moment.

Carolee Eddleston stared back at him, past him, milk-white face spattered with rain, blonde hair—turning dark at the roots—pressed against her cheek. Camera flash strobed through the darkened alley, rain pinging against metal, the air smelling like wet cardboard and decay. Flash. Empty-eyed drama masks. Flash. The medical examiners' silhouettes. Flash. Body bag rustling in the horrible cold silence.

Tristan's eyes snapped open as he lurched forward, grabbing hold of the table.

The roar of conversation buzzed like crosstown traffic, squeals of laughter, rumble of deep voices. Oblivious to what had happened only hours ago. He stared at their faces, wondering if one of them was his killer? He ran a hand across his face and reached for his cup. Empty. He needed more caffeine.

With a shudder, he rose from the table and moved to the sales counter. He ordered another Grande latte, hoping it would keep him awake until morning and made his way to the parking lot. But the alley echoed through his head as he started his car and pulled away, heading north toward Ballard.

The wind was soft—soothing—through the pines when reached his apartment complex. Pine needles brushed across his jacket sleeve and clung to his Merrell's as he walked across the lot toward the doorway. Nettles and small white petals twined in her hair...petals?

None of the others had petals in their hair. What did it mean? Something to throw them off track? Like the Dramamine in her system?

He took a sip of his latte as he climbed the stairs to his second-floor apartment. Tomorrow he'd check with the lab, but tonight he'd hope for a break in the case. And a way to clear those images from his head.

6

8:37 A.M., *September 1st*

KIP PRESSED the cell phone against her ear, anger rising as the automated system informed her that Sarah's bus had arrived on time. Last night, she'd scoured Sarah's texts and emails for names, anyone she knew in Seattle, any hint of someplace she might have gone first.

The system dumped her into the hold queue and Kip paced, waiting to talk to someone—anyone. Classical hold music filled her ear as her impatience rose.

Minutes and Mozart trickled away.

Carolee hadn't been much older than Sarah and both women had blonde hair. Long legs and Barbie doll looks. She remembered the surprised—no, astonished—look in Bowker's eyes (hauntingly beautiful eyes) when she'd described the killer back to him. Her instincts were spot on and he knew it.

This guy was killing blondes, she realized, blondes with that uncommon, doll-like beauty most women envied. But how did the tattoo fit in—why the tattoo? A chill danced down Kip's spine, her stomach tightening. She had to find this guy. Fast. But she needed more information, starting with Carolee's mother.

Bach trilled in the background. Answer the fucking phone!

Disgusted, Kip slammed the phone closed, but the knock on her door surprised her. She hurried through the dim lit studio apartment, wooden planks creaking, and opened the door.

Persephone stood there wearing jeans and a tight pink t-shirt that said goddess in faded white letters.

"What's wrong, Seph?" Kip asked, motioning her inside. She stepped inside, her stiletto boots clacking against the old wood floor. Seph wasn't a morning person, so this had to be important or urgent.

"Nothing," she said with a shrug. "Just thought you could use a ride." She crossed her arms and glanced at the Nirvana poster above Kip's green couch.

Kip squinted. "A ride? What are you talking about?"

"I saw you looking at maps on your phone last night. Trying to get to Lowell, right?"

"Yeah. So." Why was she being so nosey? Nobody knew about Sarah.

"Why?" Seph asked.

A burning pain gnawed at Kip's stomach and she turned away from Persephone, so she wouldn't see her face. Of course, she felt bad about Carolee and the other women. Didn't need this damn thing to magnify what she already felt.

"Carolee's mom lives up that way. I need to talk to her, see what I can find out."

Find her killer and stop him from killing Sarah or anyone else.

She closed her eyes a moment, knowing the grim reality: there *were* others. He had them right now, somewhere, and soon, he'd kill them like Carolee.

She remembered this guy (a friend of Donny's) who saw women as trophies, playthings for his amusement. He kept two and three at a time—runaways and junkies—locked up in his house until Kip made an anonymous call to the police. The guy was convinced that any woman in tight clothes was playing the game. *His* game of rape and confinement.

Now, he was confined for life in Walla, Walla. Couldn't have happened to a nicer guy.

But this tattoo killer...it wasn't a game to him. It was power, collecting—playing God somehow. Finding the perfect woman.

"I want to help, okay?"

"So do I," said Seph, seeming satisfied now. She laid a hand on Kip's shoulder, turning her around. It was a gentle gesture that Kip appreciated. "Okay, let's get going."

Kip smiled. "Just like that?"

"Just like that," Persephone answered and moved toward the door.

Kip grabbed her jean jacket and purse off the back of a chair and followed Persephone into the narrow hallway that stunk of cooked onions and stale beer. She slid on her jacket over a green t-shirt as the warm air touched her face. It was already too warm for a jacket, but just in case.

She shoved her cell phone in her jacket pocket and stopped in front of the pale-yellow Volkswagen at the curb. She climbed into the passenger seat as Seph revved the motor and pulled away.

THE DARK GREEN sedan stayed with them through the express lane and Persephone's frequent lane changes. Kip kept glancing in the rear-view mirror, watching the sedan's movements and the distance it stayed back. She squinted, unable to stop the sour expression from curling her lips. Two men.

Idiot cops! They were tailing her. She rolled her eyes.

"What are you looking at, Kip?" Seph asked, turning the radio down.

Kip leaned back in her seat and crossed her arms. "At the cops who've been following us since Third Avenue."

"What?" Persephone's gaze jerked up to the rearview mirror. "Which car?"

"The dark green sedan."

Seph's eyes narrowed. "Let's find out." She sped up and swung into the fast lane, passing a white Dodge truck and a beat up, red Nissan. Ahead, she nudged her VW into a tight spot between an Eclipse and a Suburban. Kip stared at the mirror, waiting for the sedan to move up.

"I don't see the sedan anymore," said Seph with a shrug. "Maybe they were just tailgaters?"

Kip shook her head. "Just wait. You'll see the sedan back in reaction range shortly."

"They're gone, Kip. Relax, okay?"

"You'll see," said Kip, slouching in the passenger seat.

In about ten minutes, the green sedan edged back into the mirror.

"Uh, Seph?" Kip poked her shoulder and motioned toward the mirror.

"They *are* following us," she said, glancing out the back window. "This is crazy. Our exit's coming up."

"Drive your butt off toward the nearest mall," said Kip, snapping up in her seat. She'd turn the tables on whoever was following them.

"The mall?" Seph's gaze was piercing. "You planning to pick up some pumps or a shotgun?"

Kip laughed. "Didn't your mom teach you to scream loud and hard in a public place if you were being followed?"

Seph frowned. "No. That might have come in handy though."

Kip glanced out the window as the exit sign for Lowell slipped past. Her heart rate quickened. She'd better figure out something fast. The last thing she needed with Sarah missing was cop hassles. The cops already had their interviews with Carolee's mom. Now, it was her turn.

"There's a huge outlet mall right off I-5."

"Perfect. Head there."

Seph cast a sideways glance at Kip. "What are you going to do when we get there?"

Kip shrugged. "I don't know yet. But I will by the time we get there." She hoped so anyway. She hated crowds and it was time she got rid of the one following them.

The outlet mall appeared on the right side of the highway and Seph waited until the last minute to turn. Tires screeched on pavement, across yellow lines, and finally onto the I-5 turn off. Kip watched the rearview mirror as the road wound right and onto another road. As the VW turned right, she caught sight of the green sedan on the off ramp.

"Quick, turn here!" Kip shouted, pointing left at the nearest mall entrance.

Seph cut across a lane of traffic into the turn lane then turned left across the highway into the mall parking lot.

"What now?" Seph asked.

"Head for that packed row of cars and let me out. Then circle around like you're trying to park."

"Let you out? Kip, what if they aren't cops? What if—"

Kip reached for the door handle. "I'm getting out whether you stop or not, Persephone."

Seph frowned, shaking her head slightly. "What's gotten into you?"

"Just stop the car, Seph!"

Persephone hit the brakes and Kip shoved the door open. She climbed out and motioned the VW on through the parking lot. She rushed into the lines of parked cars and crouched behind an SUV, watching for the green sedan to enter the row.

In the next row, Seph's yellow VW lurched forward as Seph pretended to look for a space. Kip's heart pounded against her ribs.

It seemed like forever until the sedan rolled past the SUV, following the bug at a careful distance. The windows and windshield were dark with tinting, so Kip couldn't see who drove the car.

She waited until the sedan reached the end of the row then turned left in Seph's wake.

Move! Now!

Kip glided across the parking lot and into the next row of cars, watching the sedan stop behind a car pulling out of a space. It followed the car down the row and then turned right after Seph's car.

Kip ran down the aisle in the opposite direction, straining to reach the end just as the yellow Volkswagen turned left into the next crowded aisle. With head down, she hurried across the aisle into the next row of cars. She held out a hand for Seph to stop near the end of the aisle.

Seph put on her right turn signal, pretending to wait for another car as Kip moved left, away from the VW and crouched behind a Taurus as the green sedan approached. When the sedan stopped behind Seph's car, Kip walked up to the sedan and pounded on the driver side window.

"You're made, so give it up!" she shouted as the window rolled down.

Glaring at her, Detective Keith St. James slapped the steering wheel. She gazed past him and saw Detective Bowker in the passenger seat. Laughing. My God, he was laughing like a banshee! She kept the smirk on her lips.

"Told you she made us downtown, dude," said Bowker.

Cold fury burned in St. James' face as he stared at her.

Kip folded her arms against her jean jacket. "So, why the tail?"

Seph rushed up beside her after parking the car. She nodded at St. James.

St. James' fingers curled around the steering wheel, his knuckles turning white. "You're still a person of interest in this case," he said in a gruff voice, not looking at her.

Kip sighed. This guy was into being hardcore wrong. "Fine. You wanna follow me into Victoria's Secret? They're having a thong sale. Might even have your size."

Her gaze met Bowker's and he was doing his best not to burst out laughing again. He bit his lip. She saw the laughter crinkling around his eyes and the quiver of his mouth.

She wanted to press her lips against his and run her fingers through his sandy hair. To explore the laugh lines around his eyes, touch the gentle curve of his jaw.

Shaking away those thoughts, she turned away to refocus on Sarah. What had that bastard already done to her? Kip balled her hand into a fist.

Seph motioned Kip away from the car. She snickered and ran a hand across St. James' shoulder as she walked away.

"We can bring you back one if you want to wait, Detective. Just tell me your color."

Kip waved goodbye and followed Seph toward the mall entrance.

"Let's grab some coffee," said Seph, boot heels clacking against the pavement as she opened the glass door. "And when they're gone, we'll head back toward Lowell."

"Works for me," Kip replied, her skin crawling at the crowds of people pulsing around her. Herds of people rushing around in shorts and tank tops. Kip pulled at her collar. It was hot in here!

She waited at the door, watching the sedan pull out of the parking lot and onto the I-5 on-ramp. She'd scan the parking lot when they went back to the car.

Seph nudged Kip, a worried look on her porcelain face. "Why would you take a chance like that? What if that hadn't been St. James and Bowker?" She shook her head. "This life is so short without taking that kind of risk."

Kip turned away from the door and leaned against the wall, bowing her head. There was so much Seph didn't know about her. Most of it was a waste of breath, but not Sarah. No one knew about Sarah's disappearance and she wasn't in the mood to share.

Seph grabbed Kip's arms and her probing gaze surprised Kip. "Talk to me! I want to help, but you've gotta be straight with me."

"Straight with you?" Kip wanted to pull away but couldn't. Seph's gaze was mesmerizing. "I didn't ask for your help!"

She wasn't afraid of this psychopath, but she was terrified for Sarah. And artificial conscience or no conscience, she'd personally destroy the bastard if he harmed her little sister. That's what everyone including her parole officer was expecting, wasn't it? Waiting for her to screw up and go back to the joint. The criminal justice drones were against the experiment from the beginning, convinced it would fail. Once a convict always a convict.

"Maybe you should just tattoo it on my forehead in big black letters?"

Seph squinted. "What are you talking about?"

She gestured toward the parking lot. "Felon—convict! You're just like St. James! You think I'm involved in this sicko's game."

"You're high!" Persephone shouted. "If I thought you were involved, I'd be long gone, believe me."

She let go of Kip's arms and paced a few steps toward the nearby jewelry store. After a moment, she turned around, her boots clicking, and pointed a finger at Kip.

"You're not telling me something, something that made you blindly face down that sedan." Her hands snapped to her hips. "I'm your friend, Kip. Talk to me."

How did she do that? How had Seph figured her out so fast? Kip was a master at bricking out the world. Being sized up so quickly like that unnerved her. Sighing, Kip shoved her hands into her pockets.

"Look, I'll buy you a coffee and we'll head back to Lowell."

Seph shook her head. "I'm not going anywhere until—"

"I'll tell you on the way! Okay?"

Seph stared at her a moment and finally, a smile brightened her face. "Cool."

KIP TOOK a long sip of her mocha and glanced at Seph who merged the VW into I-5 traffic. She'd studied the parking lot and the cars around them, satisfied that St. James had given up his witch hunt for today at least.

"There's more to this than Carolee, okay?" said Kip, setting the coffee cup in the nearest cup holder.

"All of that falls under *duh*. You can do better than that."

"I'm getting there. Just let me talk."

Seph nodded for her to continue.

"My sister's missing, okay?" Kip focused on her hands as she twisted the edge of her jean jacket. "She came out here on a surprise visit and no one's seen her since she got off the bus in Seattle." It felt like somebody had punched her in the kidney. She sucked in a breath.

Seph's face went all pale like she was going to faint or something.

"Kip, I'm so sorry."

Kip stared at her hands again, biting her lip to keep it from quivering. "It's worse than that. See, Sarah has those Barbie doll looks like Carolee...and she has a tattoo of a butterfly on her shoulder." She looked up from her hands and met Persephone's shocked expression. "I think he's collected Sarah, Seph. That's why I've gotta talk to Carolee's mom. Find out anything I can to track this bastard."

Seph reached out and squeezed Kip's shoulder. "Don't you worry. We're going to find her alive."

The bitter taste of bile burned Kip's throat as she clutched her hands into fists. Gritting her teeth, she kicked the floorboard. "If I don't, they're gonna find the guy who did it in pieces. I swear it, Seph."

The car went all quiet and Kip felt bad for making everything so awkward. But Seph had to know where she stood. Seph had to know what she was planning. No one spoke until Seph pulled into a neighborhood of single-story cracker box houses packed together like boxes in a moving van.

"What's the address?" Persephone asked, brushing a lock of black hair off her shoulder.

Kip gave her the number. A little tan house just up the tree-lined street. A grey Ford sat in the driveway. After Seph parked the car on the curb, Kip climbed out and walked up the cracked driveway, past a drooping rose bush and up to the doorstep. The air smelled sweet with fresh cut grass. She rang the doorbell, hearing Seph on the walkway behind her.

In a few moments, an ashen-faced woman with short blonde hair opened the door. She looked like someone had taken a deep breath and sucked the life out of her.

"Yes?" the woman asked.

"Mrs. Eddleston?"

The lines between her brows furrowed as the woman glanced from Kip to Persephone.

"Yes?"

Kip sighed, sliding her hands into her back jean's pockets. "I'm a friend of Carolee's and I uh wanted to talk to you if I could."

"I told the police everything I knew," said Mrs. Eddleston in a hard tone, closing the door.

"Wait—please! I wanna get this guy!"

The door whispered open again.

"*You* want to get this guy?" Her red-rimmed eyes widened. "How do you think I feel?"

Kip laid her hand on the door. "Then help me! Look—I'm not a cop or a reporter. She was my friend and she didn't deserve this." Kip drew in a sharp breath. "And every minute this bastard's loose, other women are in danger."

Mrs. Eddleston's puffy eyes filled with tears. "I already told the police everything I knew. I don't know what else I can say."

"Could you tell it one more time?" Seph asked. "Please. It's important."

Mrs. Eddleston wiped tears from her face and opened the door wide, motioning them inside.

The family room had a familiar-looking beige sofa, the kind Kip had seen many times. Pale blue carpet and cream-colored walls. Smelled like vanilla and cooked beef. She and Seph sat down on the beige sofa. Mrs. Eddleston, wearing a black jogging suit, sat down in a burgundy easy chair and laid her hands in her lap. The suit's material rustled every time she moved.

"Mrs. Eddleston, I'm Kip Thorpe and this is Persephone Hadis."

The pained look in her eyes softened a bit. "Call me Annette. Carolee's mentioned both of you before." Her bottom lip quivered as she motioned at Persephone. She fished a rumpled tissue out of her pocket and pressed it to her nose, sniffing. "You did the drama masks, right?"

Persephone nodded. "She was so proud of them."

"Annette, who was Carolee seeing? The one who liked her tattoos."

A stony expression tightened her face. "He's trash. She could have done so much better. He talked to her like a dog, knocked her around sometimes."

Kip's eyes narrowed. "Do you have his name?"

"Marky Burk," Annette practically spit his name. "Works in some auto repair place in Seattle—Eric's Body Shop. Carolee used to drive him everywhere because he didn't own a car. Have you ever heard of such a thing? Works in a body shop and doesn't have a car?"

Kip planned to pay Marky a nice visit this afternoon. Maybe Seph had a tire iron in the trunk—in case she needed visual aids?

"What do you know about Carolee's day, on the day she disappeared?" Kip cringed. She was starting to sound like St. James. "She called me at the shop to make sure Persephone would be there to touch up her tattoo. Said it'd be after work." Kip sighed. "When she didn't show up, I just figured she changed her mind."

Annette nodded, daubing her eyes with the tissue. "Carolee got out of beauty school at four o'clock that day. She was supposed to work downtown at that club. Oh, what was it called?" She closed her eyes.

"Was it 86?" Kip asked.

"No, it was something...something with time in it. Hour Time, no—"

"Midnight Hour?" Kip blurted out.

Annette's eyes snapped open. "Yeah, that's the place. Downtown Seattle. She was waiting tables until ten that night."

Persephone nodded. "The shop didn't close until eleven that night, but Carolee never showed up."

"One of the bartenders saw Carolee around nine forty-five. That's the last time anyone saw her." Sobs rippled through Annette, her hands shaking. "She stayed here the night before, in her old room. After supper, she—she said it was too long a drive, so she slept here." Tears streamed down her face. "I didn't know that was the last time I'd ever see my little girl."

With tear-filled eyes, Persephone moved over to Annette's chair and slid an arm around her shaking shoulders. "I'm so sorry about Carolee," Seph said in a half-whisper.

But Kip didn't feel that need to comfort. All she felt was anger—cold, clinical rage. And she longed to inflict this pain back on the one who caused it. At the edge of her perception, Kip felt a deep sense of sorrow. From her artificial conscience, she knew, but she couldn't handle that rush of emotion, so she kept it at an extreme distance. Her hands trembled and she clenched them together so no one saw. It had taken her a lot of time to get over her friend, Mary Margaret's death from cancer. The pain of losing her was the worst thing she'd ever felt. She wasn't about to get that close to anyone again. But she thought of Sarah and knew it was already too late.

After a few moments and more tissues, Annette Eddleston pulled it together. Kip admired her strength.

"Did Carolee leave anything behind that night?" Kip asked, rising from the couch. "Anything the police thought worth investigating?" She paced the room, the raw emotions too much.

"They took her backpack and cell phone—that's it," said Annette. "They weren't interested in seeing the room."

"Could *I* see it?"

Annette nodded and motioned her forward. "Down the hall on the right."

Kip followed the short hallway toward a bathroom. Family pictures lined the wall: a brother's football game, Carolee in pigtails and front teeth missing, graduation pictures.

To the right was a room with yellowing white furniture and lavender walls. Blue and white pompoms hung on one wall, posters of Ashton Kutcher and Usher on the other wall. A navy sweater, white smock, and white pants lay at the foot of the lavender and green comforter.

Annette Eddleston appeared at the doorway as Kip stepped inside, Persephone behind her.

"I left it just like she did," said Annette.

Kip picked up Carolee's smock and looked in her pockets. A tube of lip gloss, pack of Trident bubble gum, a band-aid. She glanced at the lip gloss: Sheer Desire. It looked almost homemade with a laser printed label.

"Seph, do you recognize this brand?" Kip asked, holding up the silver tube.

Persephone's nose wrinkled as she took the tube from Kip. She turned it over a couple of times, finally shaking her head.

"It's not from a drug store. Not designer makeup either. Maybe one of those home sales brands?"

Kip took the tube from her hand and held it out to Annette. "Do you recognize this brand?"

Annette shook her head. "No, but Carolee always has beauty products I've never heard of—from those beauty supply stores, I'd guess."

"Can I keep this for a while?" Kip asked.

"Sure, if it'll help."

Kip looked in the closet, on the dresser and in the night stand beside the bed. A small black purse hung inside, on the closet door knob. Kip picked it up.

"She was carrying that purse when she came for supper. Left it behind the next day."

Kip frowned, exchanging a surprised look with Persephone. "Why didn't the police take it with them?"

Annette shrugged. "I don't know. They just seemed interested in her backpack."

The little black purse was barely a four-inch nylon square. Kip opened the flap, finding one pocket and a zippered compartment. In the pocket, she found a bank card, bus pass, a business card, and three dollars. She glanced at the silver business card: Freida Mason, Sheer Desire beauty consultant. All it had was a phone number and a web address.

She unzipped the compartment and found a book of matches that read, *The Midnight Hour*, a box top for palest blonde hair color, and two receipts: two packages received from Northwest Parcel Pickup. The slogan read, *Seattle's best bonded courier*.

She checked the dates: August 11th and August 20th.

Kip moved back to the closet and peered inside. Underneath a pair of hiking boots sat a small cardboard box with a pale blue and white sticker that read, *Northwest Parcel Pickup*. Kip lifted a box flap. Inside were several small silver boxes. She slid a narrow one out of the box and written on its side was *Sheer Desire*. Opening the box revealed a tube of clear lip gloss like the one in Carolee's smock pocket.

"What did you find?" Seph asked, peering over her shoulder.

Kip held out the lip gloss to Annette. "Did you know that Carolee was selling this makeup?"

Annette shrugged. "She mentioned something about a new makeup line. She was thinking about being a beauty consultant for it, but hadn't made up her mind yet."

Kip pulled the cardboard box out of the closet and set it on the bed. "Apparently, she decided to go ahead with it."

"Did she find out about the makeup at beauty school?" Persephone asked, glancing from the box to Annette.

"No, not at school. At work."

"Work?" Kip said with a frown. "The Midnight Hour?"

Annette nodded. "Somebody she worked with showed Carolee some sparkly lip gloss and Carolee went crazy for it."

The business card. Kip glanced at the business card again. Freida Mason—did she wait tables like Carolee had? She planned to contact this woman after she talked to good ol' Marky.

Detective Bowker seemed thorough enough. He'd probably talked to Marky already, but she wondered if they went through Carolee's purse. Maybe the investigators missed it? Or maybe they missed the fact that Carolee had stayed here the night before she disappeared?

"Can I borrow these things for a while?" Kip asked, holding out the business card, matches, papers, and lip gloss. "It'll help me dig deeper."

"Of course, but be careful," said Annette, sounding so tired. "They haven't caught this guy. I don't want this happening to anyone else's daughter."

Kip swallowed hard. Neither did she. That's when she saw the silver box in the bottom of the larger one. A long, thin box underneath the smaller ones. Kip picked up the box and opened its flap, tilting it downward. Dozens of small, resealable plastic bags fell out into the bigger box.

Frowning, Kip picked one up, seeing the all-too familiar white powder. She turned the box on its end. Printed in black letters, the box flap said Arctic Nights body talc.

Annette and Persephone both stared at the packets, mouths open in shocked silence. This stuff wasn't talcum powder. Kip cringed.

Carolee was dealing coke.

7

2:03 P.M., September 1st

KIP STEPPED out of the pale blue Volkswagen, heading toward a run-down body shop in south Seattle. Wait a minute... She squinted at the VW a moment. Hadn't it been yellow? Had she just imagined it was yellow?

The day had gotten hotter than she'd expected, especially for September. She left her jacket in the car, but even her long-sleeved t shirt seemed too warm.

She walked toward the grimy shop's glass front door. A long time ago, this place must have been a gas station and the concrete and glass building hadn't aged well. Its red neon sign, with two letters out, read, "Eric's Bod hop." Grass and weeds threaded through the cracked, pocked concrete. Except for the lit neon sign, the place looked abandoned.

Persephone followed behind her. "What are you planning to do once you get inside?"

Kip shrugged. "Depends on his attitude." And hers, she didn't say out loud. If Marky didn't cooperate, her attitude would be less than polite.

Seph seemed pleased with her response and she was glad. Still, she felt a twinge of guilt jabbing at her insides, but she did her best to ignore it. Someone like Marky Burk didn't deserve her remorse.

A bell rang as Kip shoved open the door and walked toward the counter. The brick red tiles were scuffed and blackened. The air stunk with burnt oil and that gaggy-smelling cherry air freshener. Some scruffy teenager in dingy grey coveralls stood at the cash register, cleaning his hands with a dirty rag.

"Help you?" said the kid, looking up through a tangle of blond bangs.

"Marky around?" Kip asked, leaning on the counter.

The kid looked Kip up and down then Seph. Finally, he nodded his head toward the door to his right. "Sure. Go on back."

Kip and Seph entered the noisy garage, metal clanking against metal, a motor revving off to her left. In the back office, a curly-haired guy leaned against a desk, his back to the door. Kip opened the office door just as the guy snuffed up a line of coke. He slammed the lid on a red lacquer box that sat on the desk and wiped at his nose.

"Hey, no customers allowed back here!" he shouted, running his hand over his nose again, brushing away any trace of powder.

"Relax, Marky," said Kip, closing the door behind Seph. "We just want a few minutes of your time."

"Who are you?"

"I'm Kip and this is Persephone." She motioned toward Seph who smiled briefly then leaned against the wall. "We're friends of Carolee's."

"So." He took a menacing step toward Kip, but Kip didn't move.

She put her hands on her hips and shook her head in disgust. "You look really torn up about Carolee's death."

"Carolee was a good time, but life goes on, y'know? So, what do you want?"

This guy was scum.

"I want to know if there's anything you might remember that could help us catch the lowlife who killed her."

"What are you? Cops?"

Kip gave him her best *are you insane* look and rolled her eyes. "Just talk to me, Marky. It's nothing to you. Tell me something about that club she worked at, the one where she met you. Who she hung out with there? Who might have been obsessed with her?"

This piece of trash didn't even care if the guy who killed his girlfriend got caught. Kip glanced at the lacquer box on his desk. Marky Burk was a user. He used people and Carolee was no exception. Carolee probably didn't even know those drugs were in with her cosmetics. Had she been selling an item, thinking it was blush or face powder, when it was really filled with cocaine? Like that woman on the business card or the weird courier listed on the boxes. Maybe Marky wasn't the only person involved in this little drug ring? Did this whole operation originate at The Midnight Hour?

He smirked at her. "Why should I tell you anything?"

Kip glared at him, getting right in his face. He was five ten to her five seven, but she didn't care. Any excuse to pound this guy was a good one.

"Because you're amped on flake, dude. So, tell me, how long was Carolee your mule? Bet the cops'd be interested in knowing that little detail."

"You're nuts!" Marky shouted, shoving her backward.

Kip rushed at him, shoving him hard enough to hit the desk. "I've got the box of makeup, dude. The one with the special face powder. It's got your name on it."

Okay, so his name wasn't on the box, but what the heck! She was on a roll. A dull ache quivered in her stomach, but she ignored it.

"Bullshit!" Marky's face flushed deep red, fury in his dark eyes.

She shook her head. "You wish. The box's from Northwest Parcel Pickup. Just how tight are you and Freida?"

"She's with Rudy, you stupid bitch!" He went immediately quiet, his face pale, a dark expression in his eyes.

She grinned. Coke boy finally came through with a detail she could use. "Who's Rudy?"

Marky lunged at her, but Kip slammed the heal of her hand upward, smashing it against his nose. With a scream, Marky crumpled beside the desk, holding his nose. Blood trickled between his fingers. A good shot, right on target.

"You broke my fuckin' nose!"

Kip slapped the edge of the desk, glaring at him. "I'm just getting started, so talk to me, Marky. Who's Rudy?"

"Weatherford. Midnight Hour's his club. Now, get outta here!"

Kip leaned over him. "Did he have a thing for her?"

Marky kept silent.

"Answer me or I'll aim lower!"

"Yeah! He was hot for her, okay? She wasn't interested though. Now, get out before I call the cops."

Yeah, right. He probably had hundreds of dollars' worth of coke in that box. That was the last thing he wanted.

"Nice talking with you, Marky," said Kip, turning toward Seph.

Seph opened the door and they stepped out into the noisy garage. Ahead, the door into the waiting room opened and through it walked Detectives Bowker and St. James. Kip let her breath out in a hiss. Had they been following her again?

"What are you doing here, Thorpe?" St. James shouted, that familiar suspicion all over his face, burning in his eyes.

"Same reason you're here," she replied.

Bowker smiled at her, but the smile slid off his face when he saw Marky Burk rolling on the floor clutching his nose.

"What happened?" he asked.

Kip shrugged. "My bill was too high."

She and Seph kept walking toward the door. With a smirk, Kip turned around and found Bowker still staring at her, but he was also still smiling. She nodded toward the office.

"That guy's a waste of time. But just so you didn't waste a trip, check the red lacquer box on his desk."

Kip laid her index finger against one nostril and sniffed at the air. Bowker frowned.

Kip got close enough to smell Bowker's mint gum. She wanted to taste it on his lips, but resisted the urge. "I think our boy in there was using Carolee as his mule," she said with a sigh. "She carried around his coke to buyers and didn't even know it. And he doesn't even care that she's dead."

"What a loser," he said, shaking his head. "Anything else?"

Kip nodded. "A lead. Rudy Weatherford. He owns The Midnight Hour club. He was obsessed with Carolee. She wasn't interested."

"That's a good motive for murder," Bowker said with a hiss, those hazel eyes lighting up like embers. "Thanks for the tips, Kell. I appreciate you being so forthcoming despite my partner's behavior." He ran his hand through his hair. "I'm really sorry about this morning. I—"

Kip waved him off. "Forget it. I know St. James has issues."

Bowker laughed, his teeth so white and straight. God, he was attractive.

"See you around," he said as St. James shouted at him.

She certainly hoped so. And soon.

He motioned toward Marky Burk who had a cloth to his nose and his head tilted up as he talked to St. James. "I'd like to talk to you more about this sometime." He lowered his voice. "Off the record, if that's possible?"

"Anytime, Detective Bowker," she answered, holding back a grin.

"Tristan," he said in a half-whisper. "It's Tristan."

"Anytime, Tristan," she said and laid her hand on his forearm.

It felt like pure electricity running through her fingers, up her sleeve, and into her heart. She wanted to spend some time looking into his eyes, but with Sarah missing, the thing she wanted most was someone to trust. She hadn't had that before. And she needed to trust someone. Sarah's life was at stake. And at last, Kip had some direction, something that might lead her to Sarah's abductor. And Carolee's killer.

Right now, though, she had one question: how close was the bus stop to The Midnight Hour?

8

8:43 P.M., September 1st

THE TELEPHONE at Pacific Blue Tattoo rang, startling Kip. It hadn't rung in over thirty minutes. She picked it up and pressed the receiver to her ear, repeating the same canned greeting she gave every time.

"Kip, it's Mother."

Her fingers turned to lead at the familiar voice, the desperation quivering in the woman's tone. Kip sucked in a quick breath.

"What'd you find out?" Kip asked.

"Sarah's bus arrived around 9:40 P.M. that night. Their records showed that Sarah got off the bus and picked up her bag." A sob interrupted her a moment, followed by sniffling. Kip's stomach tightened into knots. "My God, what could have happened to her! Are you sure you haven't seen her?"

"If I had, I'd have already called you." Kip sighed. "Did you file the missing person's report?"

She replied yes through another crying jag. The woman was bordering hysterics and Kip had nothing to say that would calm her. If she knew about the serial killer loose downtown, she'd lose it. Kip had no love for the woman, but she wasn't cruel. She'd keep that part to herself for as long as she could. It wouldn't help anything if her mother knew.

"Look, I have a friend who's a cop here in Seattle. I'll see what he can do to help." She had no intention of asking Tristan for help, but maybe that would calm her down enough so she wouldn't freak out or something.

"*You* have a *cop* for a friend?"

Kip gritted her teeth against her mother's acidic tone, trying to hold in the anger. She was at work. Besides, she wouldn't give Nick any more reasons to fire her.

"Yeah, even people like me can have cops for friends," Kip replied in a sharp but quiet tone.

The line went silent for a moment. "I'm sorry. I didn't mean it like that. You've just never liked cops, that's all."

Kip let some of her anger go. "I guess you're right. But this one's different. He listens and he wants to help people. He's a good cop." And he looked damned fine in a pair of Levi's, too.

"I hope he can help us find Sarah."

"Me, too," said Kip, her throat tightening. "I don't know what I'd do if—"

Suddenly, Kip choked up, unable to say anything.

"Kip, you there?"

"Yeah," she answered finally. "I'm here."

"You sound...different. Not like yourself."

Kip sighed. "I'm not that person I used to be. And Sarah means a lot to me."

The phone crackled with silence. "I'm glad," said her mother finally and Kip heard the smile in her voice. "I miss my Kelly."

Her Kelly? Had the woman ever really thought of her in that

way? She couldn't remember that far back. There had been too many hard years, too much pain between them.

"So do I," said Kip in a half-whisper.

"Call me after you've talked to your cop friend."

"I will," she said. She and her mother said awkward goodbyes and hung up the phone.

With the missing person's report filed, it would no doubt end up on Tristan Bowker's desk (and every other cop in the city). Would he make the connection, she wondered, and help her find Sarah? She didn't know if she could trust Tristan yet. She barely knew the man.

Fear turned cold in her stomach and she shook her head. No, she couldn't take that chance. She couldn't put Sarah's life in someone else's hands, not when she didn't fully trust them.

TEN MINUTES BEFORE CLOSING, the shop door opened. Kip looked up from the magazine she was staring at (she couldn't manage to concentrate on anything but the pictures), expecting some half-drunk college kid wanting a tattoo. She couldn't stop the smile that curved across her face. Detective Tristan Bowker entered the shop, wearing an army green Henley and Levi's. No dress pants and shirt. He was off duty. He offered her a faint smile and stepped over to the desk.

"Finally decide to get that tattoo?" she asked above the drone of fans cooling the stuffy shop. August had been hotter than hell. Looked like September wouldn't be any different. Totally weird for Seattle. She set down the dog-eared copy of *Wired*.

He shook his head, looking kind of distracted. His sandy hair was all windblown and almost scruffy, his sexy jaw stubbled with the first day of beard. "I need to talk to you." He glanced at his watch. "What time do you close?"

"Eleven," said Kip.

"I don't want to get you in trouble with your boss," Tristan replied, glancing around the shop.

Kip waved him off. "Nick and the others left at ten. It's just Seph and me now and the place is empty."

The silence seemed so strange. No buzzing of needles or drone of conversations, not even the hiss of the autoclave whispered tonight. It was like everything was sleepy.

Seph walked up to the desk, the clack of her heels echoing. Seph liked expensive clothes, her clunky black shoes—Prada's or something. On the sidewalk, they didn't sound any different than the two-for-ones at Shoe Corral. Seph wore a short black skirt and thin red blouse, the new *Cosmo* under her arm, and a steaming mug of Chai in her hand. Tristan's gaze widened then returned to Kip. Kip and her Old Navy layered tanks (purple and yellow tonight) and faded bootcuts. She hated skinny jeans. A hint of a smile touched his lips, lit his eyes, and she couldn't help but smile.

"I'll watch the desk if you want to go in the back, Kip. It'll be more private than sitting in this picture window."

"Thanks, Seph." Kip led him through a doorway behind the desk that led to the supply/break room.

He sat down in a straight-backed wooden chair that stood beside a huge, wire spool table. Kip sat down in the chair opposite him. He ran his fingers through his hair, straightening it. The shadow of stubble on his chin made him look strong. Or exhausted. She wasn't quite sure.

This investigation was changing him, she realized. Each time she saw Tristan, she noticed little bits of pain building in his eyes, some of the shine wearing away. What would he be like at the end of this thing? Would it burn him out forever or make him stronger, harder—jaded? Like St. James. God, she couldn't let that happen. She felt an overwhelming need to protect him. He was everything she'd hoped to be one day and she wouldn't let him be this killer's final victim.

"So, what did you need to say?" Kip asked, unblinking.

He leaned on the table, studying her a moment. His jaw line was sharp, his mouth a tight-lipped frown. He had bad news. She felt it, a cold nervousness that made her shiver inside.

"Something's wrong," she said.

Tristan nodded. "'Fraid so." He looked down at his hands and cleared his throat. "Are you any relation to a Sarah Thorpe?"

Her stomach fell, her heart hammering into her throat. Please let it be the missing person's report.

"You got the missing person's report," she said.

She'd expected that report to lay around for weeks in some guy's inbox, but Detective Bowker had gotten it and acted on it immediately. She was scared and impressed as hell.

His lips parted in surprise, his eyes widening. "I just got that report about two hours ago. She fits the profiles of the other victims. You're connected to her, aren't you? That's why I came."

Kip twined her fingers together, pinching her eyes closed a moment as she gathered the courage to tell him, to trust him, to make herself vulnerable for a little while. She nodded.

"She's my sister. Disappeared from a Seattle bus stop two days ago. She was coming here from Moscow, Idaho—to surprise me with a visit. I haven't seen Sarah for eight or nine years." Kip bowed her head. "Not since I was fourteen."

"And you think there's a connection between her disappearance and our serial killer?"

"I'm almost sure of it."

His jaw tightened again. "That's why you went to see Annette Eddleston this morning."

Kip nodded. She knew he'd already figured that out after seeing her at Eric's Body Shop.

"Did you find anything that would connect Carolee with your sister?"

"Not yet."

He laid a hand on hers. Sparks shot through her fingers. God, his touch felt good.

"Maybe she just stopped off to visit friends or see the sights first? Maybe hit some clubs?"

"Not Sarah," Kip snapped. "She doesn't know anybody in Seattle but me. And she's only twenty. Don't know if she has a fake ID yet, but she didn't go to clubs alone. Sarah's a little shy of that scene."

Tristan studied her face again and Kip bristled, wondering what judgment he was making about her sister.

"You said you haven't seen your sister for eight or nine years," he said in a steady voice, without any attitude like his partner would have given. "How well do you know your sister? I mean, could she have changed a lot since you last saw her?"

Kip shook her head. "Sarah and I've been texting and Skyping for about a year or so. We've talked about a lot of stuff. No, Sarah's got her head on straight. Graduated near the top of her high school class, a sophomore in college now. She wants to be a doctor."

Tristan pulled a small notepad and a pen from his jacket pocket. "Can you describe your sister for me?"

"She's about my height, maybe taller now. Blonde hair, green eyes."

He glanced at her then kept writing and Kip felt the distance increase between them. She felt a coldness come over her when he slipped back into cop mode.

"Any distinguishing marks?" he asked, glancing at her briefly then returning his gaze to the notepad. "Birthmarks, scars—tattoos?"

Things they'd use to identify a body. The words stuck in Kip's throat as it tightened. She was so scared for Sarah.

Tristan looked up from his notes. "Marks?" he repeated, but his gaze instantly softened. He took her right hand in his and squeezed gently. "I know how tough this is, but the more you tell me, the better I can help you."

Did he really know how tough it was? Had he seen his friends shot on the streets or self-destructing at some shelter? Had he ever slept in a cardboard box? He looked so white-bread, so Midwestern polite—did he really have what it took to think like a killer, enough to bring one down?

Kip stiffened. She couldn't risk Sarah's life on that kind of long shot. Or him.

"What's that look about?" Tristan asked, his brows pressed into a frown. He let out a sigh and leaned back in the chair. "Look, I know how hard this has gotta be for you. It's not like you've had a lot of reasons to trust cops. You did your time. It's in the past now."

Was it ever in the past? She knew better. It was as much of the present as it had been six years ago.

Kip crossed her arms. "You and I both know it'll never be in the past. As long as it comes up on a computer screen somewhere, somebody'll dredge it up over and over again."

Tristan laid a hand to his chest. "I'm not everyone. You're not a monster, Kelly. You were young and you made some poor choices."

Her eyes stung at those words, words she'd hoped someone would say to her. He didn't see her as a monster. She leaned forward and laid her hand against his arm, fighting the quiver in her bottom lip. "Thank you for that," she choked out.

He reached out a hand to her face, gently brushing wisps of brown hair out of her eyes. "I meant it. And I'm so grateful you decided to help us with this investigation. Your insights have made a huge difference." He grinned. "And they've royally pissed off Keith because you're ahead of him on his own investigation."

Kip laughed then fell silent for a few moments. "I've gotta find this guy, Tristan. Before he gets tired of her."

He cocked his head, frowning. "Tired of her?"

She nodded. "He was tired of Carolee. He'll get tired of Sarah, too—and the others. It's the hunt, the collection that excites him. He doesn't care about them individually." She squinted at him. "He likes some better than others, keeps some longer than the rest. Were the victims found in order of capture?"

When Tristan's lips parted slightly and he swallowed hard, Kip knew she was right.

"I'm right, aren't I?" she said finally.

Tristan shook his head. "You know I can't answer that."

But what made this guy get tired of them? How hard the women resisted him? Their attitudes toward him? Was it something physical? He collected the women, but something made him get rid of them for others. A prettier catch? More tattoos? She needed to figure out what that something was. Somehow.

"We need to figure out what makes him dump them. Is it their looks? Similar tattoos?"

Tristan set down his notepad and drew Kip's chair closer until their knees touched. With a sigh, he propped his elbows on his knees, pressed his hands against his face, and stared so deep into her eyes that she felt it in her toes.

"I could lose my job over this," he said in a husky half-whisper. "But whether you know it or not, you're an extraordinary profiler, Kelly. You're my best hope for solving this case."

He bowed his head a moment and steepled his fingers, turmoil sharpening his features, the struggle against protocol and the right thing. Finally, he looked up, laying his hands against his knees.

"I trust you, Kell. Swear to me you won't communicate any of the details I'm about to reveal to you."

Pain hovered in his eyes and she could only stare at him. All this time, she'd been struggling to trust him and he'd been fighting the same battle. He needed her help as much as she needed his. He was the first person to see the mask few people had ever tried to see. That alone made her trust him. She nodded and held up her hand.

"I swear it, Tristan," she said then laid her hand on his. "I'll say nothing."

A smile warmed his face, those hazel eyes lit with fire, but then it disappeared beneath his cop look again, all serious and business. He was Detective Bowker again.

"You're right. The victims weren't killed in order of disappearance."

Kip nodded. "I knew that already. Go on."

"They've all been blondes with tattoos—"

The ring of his cell phone startled Kip as it echoed through the store room. Sighing, he pulled the phone out of its clip and looked at the display a moment. Then he flipped it open. "Bowker."

His cheeks hollowed, the color fading.

"Where?" he asked in a grim tone and Kip's stomach churned. "You're kidding. All the way out there? When?" She gripped the edges of the chair, waiting for him to say something. "On my way. Be there in fifteen," he replied and closed the phone.

He jumped up from the chair then cast a sick look at Kip. "Another body."

"Where?" Kip demanded.

"Ballard. I've gotta go."

Kip grabbed his arm, cold fear pounding the pit of her stomach. "A blonde? With a tattoo?"

He nodded. Of course. Stupid questions—they'd all been blondes with tattoos.

"A butterfly, on the—the shoulder?"

When Tristan bit his lip, Kip's heart fell into her stomach as her knees sagged. He slid his arms around her, holding her against him, and she felt his hot breath against her neck.

"It's gonna be okay," he whispered.

She couldn't help herself. She wrapped her arms around him, wanting—no, needing that closeness.

"I know how you must feel."

She pulled back from him. "Do you? Do you really, Tristan?"

Nodding, he set his jaw, his hands still on her arms. "My dad was murdered when I was six. Shot right in front of the house." He sucked in a breath through gritted teeth. "Nobody was ever charged with his murder."

Pain cut through Kip's middle like a knife and she grabbed hold of her stomach. He caught her before she sank and steered her back to a chair.

"Kelly? What is it?"

"I'm sorry," she struggled to say. "I stupidly assumed you had a perfect life. But my artificial conscience reminded me nothing's perfect."

"Forget it," he said, stroking her hair. "We all do stupid things we're sorry for. Being sorry and being stupid are critical to being human. I'm a specialist in stupid."

"Me, too," said Kip with a smile, the pain fading. "I'm sorry about your dad."

"Thanks," said Tristan, nodding. "He was a good guy."

Kip rose to her feet, Tristan's hand still on her arm to steady her. He could have left it there forever and she wouldn't have cared. He laid his hand on the small of her back as they walked out front. From the front desk, Seph rose from the desk chair and pointed toward the door.

Detective Keith St. James stood inside the doorway, a scowl on his jaded face. He glared at Kip.

"I've been calling and calling you? Then I find you here. What gives, Tris?"

Tristan's eyes narrowed as he let his hand drop to his side. He moved to stand in front of St. James.

"I'm working," he snapped. "I left a report on your desk —a missing person's report. Did you read it yet?"

St. James glared at him, looking exasperated. "A missing person's report?" he shouted. "I don't have time for missing person's—"

"Guess you'd better make time. Partner." Tristan clapped his hand against St. James' shoulder. "It's another possible."

"What?" he asked, frowning.

Tristan gestured at Kip. "Her sister arrived in Seattle two days ago—surprise visit. She's vanished without a trace."

"*Your* sister?" St. James replied.

Kip nodded. "Twenty-year-old. Long blonde hair. Green eyes. Tattoo of a butterfly on her shoulder."

St. James cast an uneasy look at Tristan. "No shit."

"I need to find her before..." Kip's voice trailed off and she turned away from both men. She couldn't say the words.

Tristan was beside her again, stroking her hair. "I'll call you later," he whispered in her ear.

"You don't have my cell number," Kip whispered.

"Hey, I'm a cop," he whispered. "We'll be in touch soon," he said out loud and stepped away.

The front door creaked open then closed as warm air wafted in from the balmy night, smelling like hot asphalt until the ceiling fans caught it and stirred it into a cool breeze.

Kip fanned herself. "When is this heat gonna end?"

Seph clacked over beside her. "Sorry about that."

"It's not your fault," said Kip, wrinkling her nose.

She shrugged. "Actually, it is. See, I'm normally gone this time of year. I've delayed autumn, but I wanted to stay and help you. You've made me rethink a lot of things, Kip."

"What are you talking about?" Kip asked. "How could you—or anybody—delay autumn?"

Seph stared down at her Prada's for a moment. Kip had never seen her at a loss for words before. "Look, there's a lot you don't know about me. Things you probably wouldn't even believe. Let's just say I've decided not to go back to my husband for the season. Which complicates things."

Kip's eyes widened. "Like the weather?"

Nodding, Seph folded her arms against her chest and through her thin red blouse, Kip saw the pomegranate seed tattoos on her stomach.

"So, you're married...why aren't you going home for the season?" Kip asked. "He knock you around? Try to make you sleep with his friends?"

"No, no—nothing like that. He's a good man." Her voice trailed off a moment and she ran her fingers across her belly.

This didn't make a lot of sense, but much of the time, Seph didn't make sense. She was just different, that's all. Of all Nick's tattoo artists, Seph's designs were the most unusual. There was an oldness about her mythic designs, a realness about the symbols she drew. Authentic, that's what Nick called them. And the awards and certificates that lined her station walls proved it. Nobody captured the soul of mythic designs better than Persephone Hadis. Nobody. She'd let the autumn comment go.

"Let's just say I'm tired of the commute," she replied. There was a tiredness in her voice that Kip hadn't heard before. "Six months here. Six months there. It's just too much."

"Where's your husband? Back east or something?"

Seph grinned. "More like south."

"You mean like Texas?"

She laughed out loud and paced around the desk. "Much farther, I'm afraid." Then she sighed. "I guess I'm just tired of being a transient."

Kip nodded. She understood that feeling. She felt that way most of the time. Now, all she wanted was a small place of her own. Nothing fancy, just someplace where people didn't walk like crazed elephants on her ceiling or blare the television next door at six in the morning. No hallways that smelled like old piss and cigarettes.

"Everything is so temporary. Disposable plates, mops—clothes. Even the people are disposable. They change spouses like coats." She patted her stomach. "Here for an instant then forgotten. That's why I like tattoos. They're a message of permanence. Like these pomegranate seeds. They're a symbol of my marriage, of its permanence."

Kip shook her head. "I don't get it, Seph. You're talking about leaving your husband and everything being temporary in the same breath. Which is it?"

"I'm not leaving him," said Seph, her brow furrowing. "Just the arrangement. I'm tired of the back and forth." She touched her stomach again. "These seeds are a symbol of forever. Of lifetimes ago, lifetimes to come." She sighed, a faraway smile on her face. "I remember Athiniai and her pervasive blue. Always so blue—warm, tropical blues, deep blues, pale blues. It's the only thing that really lasted about the old age."

"That's way too New Agey for me," said Kip, holding up her hand. "The only lifetime I'm concerned about is the here, the now."

The ones in danger.

"Of course," said Seph. "I couldn't help overhearing the conversation, despite St. James' oh so quiet voice and calm demeanor. They found another body?"

"God, I hope Sarah's okay." She glanced at the clock on the wall. Four minutes after eleven. Time to go—she had plans.

"I hope so, too," Seph replied in a quiet voice.

Kip nodded toward the clock. "It's quitting time. I'm taking off now."

"I'm going to stick around. I've got a design to finish. I'll lock up, okay?"

Kip retrieved her purse from under the desk. "Sure. Seeya tomorrow."

"You got plans?" Seph asked, walking her to the door as she jangled a set of keys.

"I'm going to check out the bus terminal and what's around that club, Midnight Hour."

Seph squeezed her shoulder. "Just be careful. If you need anything, call me on my cell." Seph paused in the doorway, door still open, letting in the hot air.

"It's okay," said Kip stepping out into the steamy night air. "I'm not blonde."

"Some people get their hair done because they like the pampering more than the styling," said Seph.

Kip stopped in the middle of the sidewalk, staring into the dim-lit streets as Seph's words hit home. What a funny comment to make.

"And tattoos?"

"Some people get a rush from the pain, the violence. Or a release. It's not the picture. It's the process."

Seph turned off the blue neon sign and locked the door. Kip

watched her disappear behind her bookshelves as her own thoughts burned through her brain at light speed.

This killer craved the process of confining, of killing. What else about his process turned the bastard on? Were the tattoos somehow a message to him that these women liked to be hurt?

9

11:05 P.M., September 1st

SEATTLE'S EMPTYING streets burned with heat, the air heavy, the night darker somehow. Kip walked up Pike Place and headed up Stewart Street toward the bus terminal, watching for signs, something —anything—to stand out. Anything that might lead her to a killer.

Sarah had walked down this street, backpack on her shoulder, excitement blinding her to a predator. Pacific Blue Tattoo was only half a mile from the Greyhound station. Did she even make it this far?

Kip winced. Was it Sarah's body that Tristan had gone out to Ballard to photograph like today's special? Wrapped in a white sheet like butcher's paper?

She gritted her teeth, balling her hands into tight fists as her stride lengthened.

For the first time since her artificial conscience had been implanted, Kip felt rage. The same white-hot fury that had launched her at all the wrong people and all the wrong places. It was the one thing she and Donny had in common. Until tonight, her artificial conscience had held it in check, but now—she wanted it to run wild.

It'd take a monster to track a monster. She was ready to let down her mask and set it free.

But pain burned after it, made her constantly aware her artificial conscience was there. That was the idea, right? Keep everything in check, so she didn't act on it?

Not this time. Her rage was familiar. It was rightfully hers and she needed it right now.

She stopped in the middle of the sidewalk, causing three men in business suits to nearly run into her, and stared at the white lights that glittered four blocks away. Blinking the words, *The Midnight Hour*, at her.

Daring her to come find it.

The air had a smoky scent tonight. Not a factory kind of smell, more like a bonfire, real burning wood. The air seemed charged. She half expected to hear the distant rumble of thunder.

Kip stepped over a crack in the sidewalk and turned right toward the glowing sign.

Had Sarah taken the same steps, walking past a crack in the sidewalks toward the comfort of those lights? Or had she been looking for a Metro stop? A taxi? Anything to get out of the big city night.

Kip swallowed a hot breath. Or get away from someone who'd made her uneasy. Approached her. Threatened her.

She glanced around at the dark storefronts and nearly deserted sidewalks.

Had he grabbed Sarah right here? Or followed her somewhere, taken her quietly? Yeah, quietly, she knew.

It was about the charm, the lure.

First, he'd have gained her trust. He probably even had a charming smile, nice hair, a way of making her feel comfortable. Maybe he'd even played the victim? Limping and dropping papers. Looking lost and trying to find the bus stop. Middle aged and harmless.

Knew the area like a pro. Probably lived or worked nearby, so he knew the streets blindfolded.

This guy was all about smooth. And gaining their trust. It was part of his game. He got off making them go willingly with him. Made him feel superior.

Hell, it made him feel like God.

Her gaze caught the Midnight Hour's lights again. Maybe he'd taken her in here for a drink? To use a phone. To ask directions. All the time, probably telling her he worked at Pacific Blue Tattoo or lived in Kip's building. She cringed.

Dammit, Sarah! She knew better.

She wouldn't have gotten inside the club though. She was only twenty. They'd have carded her.

Or would they? Letting pretty girls in was good for business. Especially if she came in with a regular or a guy with lots of presidents in his pocket.

Kip felt a cold chill dance along her spine.

Like this club would ever tell the cops if Sarah had been in that night—a twenty-year-old—and have Excise all over them for selling alcohol to minors. Not a chance.

If Sarah had been here that night, the cops would be the last to know.

Kip pulled her phone out of her pocket and opened a picture of Sarah. On prom night. Taken at the house. A strapless pink dress and roses at her wrist, Sarah looked twenty-one. Twenty-one enough to pass around her picture in a dark bar and ask questions.

They wouldn't talk to Tristan or St. James, but they'd talk to her.

Two blocks from the club's front door, Kip walked past a black delivery truck, pale blue evergreen on the side, the letters Northwest Parcel Pickup in small letters flowing around the branches. Just like the shipping labels on Carolee's boxes, the ones with the Sheer Desire makeup.

Kip reached the corner when a metal door slid open behind her.

Dull footsteps against pavement, softer on the sidewalk. Moving toward her.

A car turned at the corner and she waited for it to pass. Headlights passed across her, steady orange wink of turn signal. Still, footfalls echoed.

She brushed the back of her hand across her forehead, wiping away a sheen of sweat.

Steady, rhythmic steps continued behind her. Measured. Even.

Bring it on, Kip thought, turning around, hands on her hips.

Ready to face whoever moved toward her.

A man approached. Black pants. Black t-shirt. Pale blue evergreen over his heart. Tall. Stringy bangs, tanned face, thick arms.

He began whistling as he got within a few steps of her, pausing at the corner. Glancing sideways, he mumbled a quick hello, nodding at her, then crossed the street, clipboard in hand, and moved toward The Midnight Hour.

Kip watched him disappear beneath the wash of white light into the club. The place where Carolee met Marky. The last place she'd been seen alive. Had Sarah met the same fate?

Exhaling sharply, Kip crossed the street and followed the sidewalk to the warehouse club, The Midnight Hour.

A burly guy with tattooed sleeves and shaved hair stood beside a battered metal door. Red. Rusting. He wore a silver nose ring, orange t-shirt and skinny jeans. She hated skinny jeans. He smelled like mildew and cigarettes.

He motioned at her.

"ID."

Kip fumbled her ID out of her wallet and handed it to the guy who shined a small flashlight on it and then her face before handing it back. He opened the door. It squeaked, rasping against concrete as he motioned her inside. Shoving her ID back into her wallet, she stepped over the threshold. Into noise and dizzying lights.

A dance club.

The place throbbed with bass, a tangle of people gyrating and spinning. The constant beat pulsed deep in her breastbone, against her teeth, her eardrums thrumming.

It made her want to dance.

A cavernous warehouse with two rows of concrete posts, a DJ spinning tunes at the far back of the room. Spray painted tarps and strings of lights and chains draped the walls. On her left, a long, L-shaped bar wound around the wall's edge, track lights casting all kinds of spotlights. Several oil drum barstools lined the front and they were all occupied. To her right, black pleather booths covered the other wall, tables in front of them.

The rest of the place was dance floor. All dance floor.

The whole place smelled sweet and sweaty, a hint of clove smoke coiling its way through the room, above the acidic bite of cigarette smoke and skunky weed. Kip walked around the edge of the dance floor and sat down in a booth.

Waiters and waitresses, dressed in tight black leather rushed past, carrying trays of shots and mixed drinks. The men wore vests and women wore halters. Showing off snake tattoos, eagles, Celtic knots and butterflies as they hurried past.

Across the room, by the bar, Kip saw a man in an expensive grey suit, white shirt, and polished black shoes. His dark hair, thin and wavy, was slicked back and his long face made him look like a possum. He looked like he owned the place.

Rudy Weatherford. It had to be him. He motioned at the bartenders, pointing, and nodding as they rearranged glasses and bottles.

The guy from Northwest Parcel Pickup stood beside Weatherford, holding out his clipboard. With quick slices of the pen, Weatherford signed something. On the bar set several little silver boxes beside a larger cardboard box.

Kip was on her feet, moving toward the bar, toward the Northwest guy and the little silver boxes. She worked her way around the tangles of the flailing bodies, around lit cigarettes, until she'd gotten close enough to see the little boxes better.

Sheer Desire swirled across the boxes in white script.

One of the waitresses, tall and leggy, Wal-Mart blonde hair, and a tattoo of a butterfly spread between her cleavage, rushed up to Weatherford and threw her arms around his neck.

The Northwest guy (and two others at the bar) gave the woman a visual grope as the woman bounced around Weatherford. She was early twenties, a little cheap looking but model quality looks. Kip felt her mouth go dry.

Barbie doll looks. Tattooed. Like Carolee and Sarah.

The delivery guy turned away, moving toward the exit. Dammit —not yet! She needed to see his clipboard.

Kip rushed forward, colliding with the guy. She grabbed hold of his arm and the clipboard, pretending to lose her balance. Quickly, she stole a good hard look at the signature as he helped her stay on her feet. Illegible.

But the printed name below it said Rudy Weatherford. Ching!

"Hey, wanna dance?" Kip asked the guy, smiling as seductively as she could.

Pretending to be a little drunk.

He flashed her a charming smile and patted his clipboard. "Love to, but I'm still on the clock."

"Some other time then," said Kip.

He nodded, then moved toward the exit.

Kip kept moving toward the bar, toward Weatherford and his latest Barbie doll. One of the oil drums opened up as she approached, so she hurried toward it, plopping down before a guy with pierced eyebrows and chin could grab it. He wandered off toward the tangle of dancers, spilling his Red Hook as he staggered.

"What'll ya have?" asked one of the bartenders, a woman with dark hair and a darker tan.

"Seven and seven," said Kip.

Kip fished a twenty out of her purse and listened to Weatherford and his plastic doll carry on.

"A present for me?" the woman squealed. "Oh, baby, you're the sweetest!"

Kip glanced left at the woman with her arms around Weatherford's neck. Clutched in her left hand were two slender Sheer Desire boxes.

"First one's always free, baby," he said, his possum face stretched into a grin.

The woman waved him off and he patted her on the butt as she grabbed her tray and hurried toward the booths.

"Fourteen dollars."

Kip turned back to the bar and held out her twenty. The bartender gave her six ones back. Kip handed her three back.

The woman smiled. "Thanks very much. Let me know if you need anything else." Her gaze lingered on Kip for a moment. Finally, she nodded toward the waitress. "You know her?"

Kip hesitated, a twinge of guilt in her gut. She'd have to twist the truth a bit. "Not very well. That's Carolee Eddleston, right? She was missing for a while, right? I'm glad she's okay."

The woman's eyes turned all watery and she bit her lip.

"No. Carolee's dead."

Reaching for her own deeply buried emotions and images she'd seen, Kip played out the news with shock and horror.

"My God ...dead ...how?" She grabbed her drink and took a big swig.

The woman reached out a hand and steadied Kip's arm.

"Take it easy, it's okay. I'm sorry I blurted that out like that. It gets worse though. See...Carolee was murdered."

Kip dropped her head into her hands. "Murdered?"

When the woman moved out from around the bar and laid a hand on Kip's shoulder, Kip fought down the urge to flinch it away. But she needed a contact in this joint, somebody who'd give her the straight story.

"Take it easy. Deep breaths, okay?"

Kip pretended to hyperventilate a little, but she took another hit of her seven and seven, letting the warm feeling calm her.

"Johnny, take over for me a few minutes," the woman said to a guy behind the bar.

"Sure thing, Denise," the guy called to the woman as she took hold of Kip's arm and her drink. "Let's get you to a booth. It's a little more private."

Kip let the woman called Denise lead her through the maze of people and back to the booths. She slid her into the booth and set down her drink. The bass still thrummed, but it seemed a little quieter than the rest of the club.

"Thanks," said Kip, staring down at her hands. "I—I don't know what to say. Carolee didn't deserve that."

Denise pulled a lighter and cigarette out of her pocket and lit it. She took a long pull then exhaled the smoke through her nose.

"She was a good kid. It wasn't fair."

"I came here—hoping she could help me." Kip set her phone on the table and showed the bartender a picture of Sarah. "See, my—my sister's missing and she might have been in here the night she disappeared. I thought Carolee might recognize her."

Denise laid her cigarette in the ashtray and glanced at Kip's phone. The woman frowned, the lines on her forehead deeper now.

"She's awfully young," said Denise, glancing from the printout to Kip. "She looks a little like Carolee. Awfully young though."

Kip nodded.

"When would she have come to the club?"

"August thirtieth, sometime after nine o'clock that night. She'd just gotten off a bus on Stewart. From Idaho. Never been to a big city alone before. I think she had a drink with someone here, or came in with someone."

Denise continued to stare at the printout. "I worked the bar that night." She closed her eyes, tilting her head down like she was trying to call up that night. "I remember that night well." Her eyes opened and she fixed her gaze on Kip. "That was the night before they found Carolee's body."

Kip winced.

"Diet Coke," Denise said, sitting up.

"What?"

"Yeah, I remember now." A smile brightened the woman's over-tanned face. "Diet Coke. This guy was with a young blonde and no matter how hard he tried to convince her, she wouldn't order anything but a Diet Coke. Greg waited on them."

Kip's heart skipped a beat. "Guy? What guy? What'd he look like?"

She smiled. "Real cute. Brown leather jacket, nice pants, white shirt. Looked like a professional. He's been in before—once or twice when I was tending." Her smile faded as her gaze got all faraway again. "His arm was in a sling that night," she said finally. "And he had a briefcase or a box with him. The blonde carried it in for him."

Kip wanted to scream. The bastard had lured her inside, pretending to have a bum arm so she'd help him carry something.

Denise picked up her cigarette and took a drag from it. The smoke trailed up in a slithering coil into the darkness and flashing lights.

"Come to think about it, she didn't look twenty-one to me. Evan's always screwing up at the door, but I'm usually too busy to notice. Excise cops have fined Rudy twice for underage drinkers on the premises, so I was glad she ordered a Diet Coke."

"Then what happened?"

Tapping ashes off her cigarette, Denise took another quick puff, and laid it in the ashtray again.

"She seemed really sleepy, so he helped her up from the chair and they left."

Bastard roofied her! Kip swallowed hard.

Of course, this guy was a coward. Immobilizing them to even his odds, to get them into his car or truck or whatever without a struggle.

Capturing them in plain sight, in a room full of people. He got off on that, too.

"How sleepy? It's been a long day kind of sleepy or I've been drugged kind of sleepy?"

The woman's face went pale. "Drugged? Oh, God. It never crossed my mind."

"Think. What else do you remember about him?"

She squeezed her eyes closed, struggling to remember and Kip took a hard drink of her Seven and Seven. Please, something—anything—any clue she could follow. Something that would get her to Sarah before it was too late.

"The box," she said, her eyelids sliding open.

"What about it?"

She shrugged. "It was just kind of odd. He left it in the booth."

"What was in it?" Kip asked.

"An old phone book. That's it."

"What happened to it?"

Denise smudged out her cigarette. "It's in the office—in lost and found."

"Show me," said Kip.

"Be right back."

The woman disappeared for several minutes. Long enough for Kip to down her Seven and Seven and wonder if the woman had blown her off.

Finally, she came back with an awkward-looking box. She set it on the table. It looked like a really tall pizza box, plain brown cardboard. Kip turned it around, turned it over, on its side. That's when she saw the white and blue remnant of a label cut off the box. A feathered, light blue edge hugged a sliver of white. The edge of an evergreen, she realized.

Northwest Parcel Pickup. Their label was unmistakable.

Her gaze darted to the front door and the man she'd ran into, the man with the clipboard.

Had she just spoke to Carolee's killer?

She needed to do a little research about this company. It was a regional company, she knew that much. Whoever left with Sarah that night may be connected in some way to Northwest Parcel Pickup.

Kip reached into her purse and slid out a twenty-dollar bill. She pushed it across the table at Denise.

"Thanks for your time," said Kip, rising from the booth. "If the cops come in asking about Sarah, make sure they get that box, okay?"

Denise nodded. "Good luck."

Kip turned away toward the dance floor, moved between the wall of people, and escaped into the solitude of Seattle's streets.

She traced her steps back to Stewart and walked toward Elliot Bay and Third Avenue. And her apartment. The streets still sizzled with heat and by the time she'd walked the two miles to her apartment, she was drenched in sweat and shaking.

She shucked off her jeans and tank tops, tossing them into the bathroom hamper and ran the shower. The one thing she'd looked forward to after getting out of prison was a private shower. Even now, she relished the warm spray of water against her skin, not having to look over her shoulder or be out in three minutes. Here in the haven of her apartment, she took a long shower, trying to scrub away the grit. No matter how much strawberry shampoo or vanilla shower gel she used, she never felt clean enough.

When her muscles stopped aching, Kip turned off the water, wrapped her hair in a towel and dried off her body. She slid into grey sweats and a short white T-shirt.

Her cell phone rang.

Her heart pounded into her throat as she rushed out of the bathroom, across the dark living room to her phone lying on the round, glass coffee table. She snatched it up.

"Bowker?"

"Yeah, it's—it's me, Kelly."

His shell-shocked voice, his stuttery words made her skin crawl and all the air explode out of her lungs.

"What is it?" she demanded. "What's the matter?"

"The body—it's...it's...Kelly, I'm sorry."

"No," Kip snapped. She gritted her teeth against the raw pain spreading like food poisoning through her stomach. "It's not her. It's not Sarah, Bowker."

"God, I hope not," he said in a soft, almost choked voice. "I need you to uh, come down to the morgue though. Identify the deceased, if possible. I'll pick you up."

"No!" She couldn't hold back the animal cry that wrenched out of her throat. She didn't want him to see her like this. She couldn't let him see her weakness. "No," she said, calmer this time. "I'll get there myself. Give me the address."

"I'll meet you there," he said in a soft voice and gave her the address.

"Okay. Be there in fifteen, twenty minutes."

Kip ended the call, shoved it in her sweatpants' pocket, and slid into her black Converses.

Dread wore a hole in the pit of her stomach as she grabbed her house key and stormed into the hallway of old piss and stale beer.

Heading to the morgue.

10

12:53 A.M., September 2nd

BOWKER STOOD outside the door of the King County Medical Examiner's office.

He looked pale, dark circles framing tired hazel eyes. He stared out at the occasional whisper of cars that drove past the medical center, hands in his jeans pocket, pacing.

The air still smelled warm, oily from a newly paved side street. It felt heavy against Kip's skin as she approached him, arms folded against her white T-shirt. Everything felt heavy, her arms, legs, a weight sitting on her chest as she walked toward him and the grey building's glass doorway.

It reminded her of a cell block.

She shuddered. She couldn't think about Sarah lying in there, naked, cocooned in a body bag.

He looked up when her Converses squeaked against the sidewalk.

"Kell," he said, moving toward her, an arm outstretched. To comfort.

She wanted to shrink away from that touch, that tender kindness that was so much a part of him—and so vacant within her.

His worried hazel eyes looked so deeply into hers, the concern that burned so clearly—for no one else but her. She couldn't push him away. But at the same time, she didn't understand it.

How had she earned such significance to him?

He barely knew her, yet she couldn't ignore her attraction to him any more than she could deny the cold fear that fanned out through her entire body. It trembled in the pit of her stomach. This time, she wanted a kind touch, a concerned gesture.

When his arm wrapped around her shoulders, her trembling intensified. She couldn't stop it.

Bowker didn't say a word. He pulled her against his side, his arm sliding around her waist and she leaned into him. The faint scents of antiseptic and soap clung to his skin. His closeness was a comfort—she admitted it.

And she needed right now.

"I asked if they could use a monitor—"

"No TVs," Kip said, staring up at him, her jaw tight, her teeth chattering. "I'll see her in person."

She pressed her lips together to keep her bottom lip from quivering.

He laid a hand against her cheek, studying her eyes a moment. Two.

"I won't second guess you. If you need it done this way, then that's how it'll go down."

Kip slid her hand into his for a moment, squeezing. Strong fingers, squared palm, smooth skin.

"Thank you." She sighed, her breath razor-sharp against her lungs, then nodded him toward the door.

Bowker keyed in a code and the door lock clicked. He opened the door and Kip stepped inside. An empty grey hallway, fluorescents brighter than she'd expected. Bowker led her to an elevator that opened immediately. They stepped inside and he flicked a button. The elevator descended into the basement and Kip stiffened.

When the doors hissed open, Kip hesitated. She glanced at Bowker, twisting the edge of her T-shirt, wishing this was all a bad dream.

He reached out and smoothed the hair out of her eyes.

"Ready?" he asked.

Kip nodded and he led her down a narrow hallway. Tan walls.

The floors were unpainted concrete, clean, the room ahead well-lit. Lots of stainless-steel, including the desk ahead where a skinny guy with a soul patch and chestnut hair sat. He wore a blue scrub shirt over a white T-shirt and faded jeans, an ID clipped to his sleeve. Bowker slid his badge out of his back pocket.

"Detective Bowker. There's been a change of plans," he said, tight-lipped. "Ms. Thorpe would prefer to see the deceased in person."

"In the cooler?" He kind of winced. "You sure?" His gaze flicked from Bowker to Kip and he looked sad, like he really cared about how this thing affected her. "It's easier on the monitor."

Kip shook her head and gestured toward the door behind the desk. "If that's my sister back there, I want to be at her side, not watching her like she's the six o'clock news."

The guy nodded then gave Bowker a sympathetic glance. "Either way, it's tough." He rose from the desk, keys jangling in his hand, and opened the door. "This way."

The back room was bright and spotless, stainless-steel tables and sinks shiny. It smelled like some kind of cleanser, not stinky room spray or dried blood. The guy took her and Bowker toward a glass door to the left.

The cooler. Her heart pounded faster.

The guy keyed in a code and the door snapped open. He led her inside and Bowker toward two columns of stainless-steel drawers, slowly pulling open one on his left. She felt instantly cold and folded her arms against her stomach.

Her feet felt like twenty-pound weights as she stepped toward the drawer. Her breaths fogged the air like little escaping ghosts, taking little bits of her strength and apathy with them.

A white nylon body bag lay inside the drawer. The guy stared at her, looking for some kind of sign that she was ready for him to unzip the bag.

Maybe he was expecting her to yak right there or pass out? She shifted her weight, her breath quickening.

Bowker's hand pressed against her back as she sucked in a deep breath then nodded at the guy to unzip it.

The zipper growled through the silence, the white nylon parting like a blooming lily. Revealing a face.

Kip stared past it, unable (or unwilling) to recognize it.

Skin as white as chalk. Blonde hair so stark against the slender face, dark roots showing. She averted her gaze.

To the monarch butterfly tattoo, its vibrant orange and black against the pale, pale skin. Angry crisscrosses cut across her chest and upper arms.

Kip froze, closing her eyes, unable to look into the face.

Freeze frame.

A man slumped against an alley wall, the stink of gunfire burning her eyes. The thin haze of smoke floated like a breath of cold air.

His frozen eyes stared at her, pleading why as he slid down the wall. Why?

She held his wallet—twenty dollars, some old photos, and a credit card—as the life emptied from his eyes with a quietness that disturbed her more than the sound of the gunshot.

It'd been so easy for Donny to pull that trigger. So easy for her to stand there and watch. Even now, she remembered the faces in those photographs.

How many lives did they destroy that night?

She felt her chest rise and fall, trying to pull in air that wouldn't come. Why hadn't she stopped Donny? Why?

She wanted to lie to herself and say it had all happened too fast, but God, it had been so horribly slow, each unbearable moment lasting hours and still she didn't even try to stop it.

Even when the gunshot popped in her ear, she hadn't believed she'd heard it until the man fell against the wall.

She couldn't look at this young woman's face. It was her fault. Her payback for that horrible night she could never take back. Sarah had paid for her crime. It was wrong. So wrong!

The wetness on her face made her eyes snap open. Tears?

She hadn't cried since she was eleven. But seeing the image of that poor guy's face—those smiling faces in his pictures not yet knowing he was dead—made the tears burn down her cheeks.

Bowker's hand slid up her back, around her shoulders, down again.

One last time, she stared at the Monarch butterfly with wings spread as if it could actually take flight.

After a few moments, she let her gaze travel past the bruises and large gash on the pale, white neck to the face. Masked by death. She sucked in a deep breath.

The face.

Her whole body trembled, a flood of weakness turning her into a ragdoll.

Her knees buckled.

"Oh, God..."

"Kell?"

Bowker caught her before she fell, holding her up. She launched herself into his arms, pressing her face against his shoulder. He smelled warm like cedar, clean and safe like soap and the solidness of his body, steady rise and fall of his chest against hers made her feel alive and protected.

"It's not her!" Her voice cracked. "Oh my God, Bowker—it's not her!"

He wrapped his arms around her and she felt his smile against her hair. "It's okay now. Everything's okay."

He was quiet for a moment.

"Kell, look at the tattoo. Does it look like any of the Pacific Blue artists' work? Anyone's you'd recognize?"

Kip turned back around and stared at the brilliant golds and burnt oranges, the gentle sweep of the butterfly's wings. No, Taku's strokes would have been bolder, Ross' lines thinner. Seph's would have had more shadow, more dimensions and animation. And Nick's would have been grungier, edgier somehow.

She shook her head. Pacific Blue hadn't done this tattoo.

When she turned away again, she heard the body bag zipped back up and the drawer close as the strength came back into her knees. She wished Bowker was right, that everything was okay.

She let go of him, shivering, and walked out of the cooler. She stepped into the hallway toward the elevator. Bowker followed a step or two behind.

"As soon as we've got a cause of death and a positive ID, Bowker, we'll contact you," said the guy, returning to his desk. "Glad it was a negative."

"Me, too. Thanks, Jerry," said Bowker with a wave as the elevator door slid open.

He started into the elevator then stopped, turned around.

"Jerry!" he called.

"Yeah?" the guy answered, turning back around, his keys jangling.

"Did you guys find any flower petals in this Jane Doe's hair? At the scene?"

The guy's face scrunched. "Flower petals?"

The elevator dinged, but Bowker kept his hand on the door so it wouldn't close.

"Lacy white flower petals. Check the report on Eddleston, Carolee. Let me know if you find anything similar, okay?"

"Will do, Bowker."

"Thanks," Bowker called, letting the doors slide shut.

Outside in the thick air that still smelled hot, Kip stared past Bowker. Sarah was still out here somewhere and the clock still ticked away the minutes with its deadly little second hand.

He reached out and brushed brown hair out of her eyes.

"You okay?" he asked.

She nodded. "What'd you mean about the flower petals back there?"

He shrugged, staring at his feet. "Nothing yet. Just something I noticed at one of the scenes." With his right hand, he rubbed her shoulder. "Take you home?"

She nodded again, feeling drained. She didn't want to think anymore, didn't want to worry and wonder anymore. Not tonight. Not ever.

His blue Toyota RAV4 was parked in the lot. He unlocked the doors and she climbed in on the passenger side. The car smelled almost new, the faint smell of coffee from the Anchorhead coffee cup in his cup holder. He climbed in and started the SUV, pulling out onto Ninth Avenue.

The whole ride back to her apartment was a blur and she didn't speak, but she felt Bowker's concerned gaze the entire time. He constantly glanced from her to the road.

Maybe he just didn't know what to say or maybe he didn't want to intrude on her silence?

He pulled against the curb of her apartment complex and turned off the motor. The sudden silence left her alone in her thoughts, one place she didn't want to be right now. She grabbed the handle and pushed open the door, ready to flee, but couldn't. Glancing back at him, she felt an almost panic well inside her.

For the first time in her life, she didn't want to be alone.

"Tristan?" she asked in a quiet voice. "Would you mind...I mean, could you um—come up?" She sighed. "I sound like an idiot. Dammit!" She leaned her forehead against the half-open door, unable to look at him, her breath fogging the window. "Look, I just want to be with somebody who understands this stuff, okay?"

A smile curved across his face as he closed the driver's side door and walked around to her side. He opened the door wider and leaned into her, resting both hands on either side of her legs, his face so kissably close. She smelled his warm breath, hint of coffee, trace of cinnamon.

"That really hurt to ask for help, didn't it?" he asked, almost smirking.

Kip frowned, her eyes narrowing, the irritation rising. "I'm used to taking care of myself, Detective. I don't need anybody's help."

He laid his hand against hers. "It's okay to need help, Kell. We all need it from time to time. And I care about you. Is that such a terrible thing? To ask somebody you care about for help? For comfort?" He slid back, straightening up, sighing. "God knows I could use some myself. I was first on the scene tonight."

His eyes flickered with hints of pain and sickness, of an almost soul-weary tiredness. He was tired of scenes like the woman in the morgue and she wondered if he'd burn out before this case was solved.

He was like watching a Fourth of July sparkler, all bright and fire, eating its way to the end of that silver stick, left dark and smoldering in less than a minute. Nothing about Tristan Bowker was a slow burn, but having this predator still loose in his city was eating him alive.

Her chest tightened, thinking about him finding the body just like the killer had left it, not cleaned up and sanitized like just now.

Raw and violent, like that guy in the alley. No, worse—much worse. She had to understand that.

She reached out and laid her hand against his cheek, cupping his chin. "I'm sorry. You must have seen terrible things tonight."

He nodded.

"It's just that all my life, everything's been a fight. I'm not used to having someone on my side."

He slid his arms around her shoulders. "Get used to it. I'm not going anywhere." He smirked then nodded toward the building. "Except in there."

Kip slid out of the SUV and closed the door. She slid her arm around his waist, his warm soapy scent burning through her. It cut through the stink of the lobby's mildewed carpet and old cigarette smoke until she was inside her studio apartment with him.

He walked toward the midnight blue couch, staring at Kurt Cobain. You could almost hear Cobain's urgent voice straining out "entertain us" above the growl of guitars.

"Want a drink?" Kip asked, moving across the beat-up maple wood floor to the small kitchen.

"Got any Pyramid?"

Kip smiled. Her favorite.

Kip grabbed two bottles of Hefeweizen out of the banged up, gold refrigerator. She handed him a beer. He sat down on the couch, twisting off the cap, and leaned his head against the wall, eyes closing. He looked exhausted. She tossed her own bottle cap on the coffee table and lit the half-burned stick of sandalwood incense in its wooden tray. She sat beside him, rubbing his shoulder. The air warmed with the soft woody scent.

"Talk to me about what you saw tonight." She took a sip of her beer then set it on the table. "You look like you need to get it off your chest."

He took a hard pull off the Hefeweizen, set it down, and then folded his arms across his stomach. His eyes narrowed as he stared down at his feet, looking a little lost and a little sick.

"Found her in a dumpster near Adam's Elementary. Leaned up against the back with her chin on her chest." He shifted his hands into his lap and leaned toward his beer again. He gripped it with both hands, turning it slowly as he stared at the label. "All she had on was a short pink skirt. No shirt." He took another drink then swallowed hard. "Her arms were propped in her lap like she'd been holding a book or something."

The muscles in his jaw tightened, his gaze tracking off toward the dining table by the window. An old steel and white Formica set from the sixties that came with the place. Always looked like the top was covered with crumbs. His hazel eyes turned watery as he gritted his teeth.

He hit the arm of the couch with his fist.

"Her hair and skirt were soaked in blood. Bastard gagged her then cut her throat. Sat there while she bled to death then put her in the dumpster."

He ran his hand across his face, covering his eyes and Kip moved closer, still rubbing his shoulders.

"None of the others had been killed that way, but the posing, the type of victim matched—"

"It's the same guy," said Kip. "He's playing more games with you cops."

Bowker nodded. "Like leaving a body just blocks from the precinct?"

"Exactly. Each of those places means something to him. We've got to figure out what and why."

"What about the posing?" His mouth twisted into a grimace. "What the hell is that about?"

"Remorse."

"Bullshit!" Bowker glared at her. "This guy doesn't feel a thing."

Kip shook her head. "He does, Bowker. You know he gets off on the power trip, on controlling these women. But after he acts out his rage, he carefully arranges her body. Dresses her at least part way. Props her up like she's still alive. Like he feels bad about what happened to her. Get it?"

The anger faded off his face and he looked like he was a million miles away. He'd seen all five bodies. She wondered if he was going over the condition of each one in his mind.

"Like you'd pose a doll," he said in a quiet voice.

Kip nodded. "Bet he's got pictures of each one he posed, too."

"But how does that show remorse?" he asked, confusion creasing his forehead.

"I knew this guy once," said Kip. "Short fuse. Always pissed at someone. One night, he shows up at a party all teary-eyed and angry, drinking Jack Daniels like it was Coke, gulping down each swig like he was dying of thirst. When I asked him what was wrong, he stared at me with this gut-wrenching expression. 'I just had to kill my girlfriend,' he said and guzzled down more Jack. Shot her in the chest. Said he didn't want to do it, but she just wouldn't stop nagging him. With the tears still running down his face, he told me how he'd washed her face and hair, put her favorite barrette in her bangs. He draped a blanket across her and laid her on the couch. Turned himself in the next morning. He's serving twenty-three years in Walla Walla."

Bowker was nodding, taking it all in, his brain chewing on everything. He took another sip of his beer and was quiet for a long time.

"All the victims were found in such disparate places," he said finally.

"To us maybe. We've gotta figure out why these places mean something to this guy."

Before he discarded Sarah like the others.

"Two women were found near parks," said Bowker. "Three were found in alleys or dumpsters."

"That's really weird. Why dumpsters for some and parks for others?" Kip frowned and took a long drink from her beer. The cold liquid soothed her, softening the world's hard edges. "He liked some better than others," she said, turning toward her.

"That has to be it, but why? Carolee Eddleston, Amanda Pierson, and the woman tonight were found in or near dumpsters. What about these three is similar? I need more info on tonight's victim. The M.E.'s supposed to call me when they have a positive ID on her."

"Emee?" Kip asked.

"Medical Examiner. They're running the body against missing persons. Should have an ID by morning." He groaned. "I've gotta be in by 7:30 tomorrow."

Kip glanced at her watch. After one. It was already morning.

He ran his hand over his eyes again. "God, I just want to forget what I saw tonight, but it's right there." He held his palm up toward his face. "Staring at me when I close my eyes."

Kip moved closer, nodding. "Let me help you forget," she said and pressed her lips to his, tasting his mouth still wet with beer.

He pulled her into his arms, his mouth covering hers with hard, deep kisses. He was all bottle rockets and firecrackers, his hands pressing her down onto the couch, slipping under her T-shirt.

They shared the need to feel life tonight, the warm pulse of breath, the softness and heat of skin against skin.

She rolled his Henley up over his shoulders and pulled it over his head, tossing it to the floor. His chest was smooth, leanly muscled in all the right places as her hands explored.

She let him pull off her T-shirt and snake down her sweats as she kicked off her Converses. She was naked beneath him and the stroking of his fingers across her bare flesh drove her wild with need. She pressed her body hard against his, struggling to get his jeans off. He stood up, quickly pulling them off.

"Don't forget to serve and protect," said Kip, tugging on his arm.

He gave her a wry smile as he fumbled his wallet out of his jeans pocket, showing her a condom.

After a moment, he was naked and beside her on the couch, exploring her body as she explored his. Her mouth found his again and she sipped his lips, sprinkling urgent kisses down his neck. He cupped her breasts, kissing them, stroking until his hands slipped between her legs. She shuddered, pulling him tighter against her. Then he was inside her.

She gasped, moving with him, wanting the length of his body against hers, needing to feel his heart pound against hers, feel that pulse of life beat for all it was worth. It was raw, burning, and wild, his thrusts almost frantic and she moaned her pleasure against his ear. She hadn't been with anyone since Donny, but no one had ever overloaded all her senses like this rookie Seattle cop.

All this time, pretending not to need anything from anybody, she ached for the closeness of someone she trusted.

Someone like Tristan Bowker.

He gripped her hands, his fingers entwining hers, his rhythm deepening, quickening, building until she felt the rush of pleasure explode like firecrackers through her shuddering body.

She gasped for breath, throwing her arms around him, holding him as close as she could until she felt his release. He collapsed against her, breath huffing against her cheek, and she didn't want morning to take him or this moment away.

Nuzzling her neck, he stroked her breasts.

"You're so hot," he whispered against her ear.

She nibbled his mouth, brushing her lips across his, down his neck, against his earlobe.

"You're incredible," she replied.

She felt his grin against her face as he wrapped his fingers in her dark hair.

"I never want to move from this spot," said Tristan.

Kip wrapped her arms around him. "Stay with me 'til morning, huh? We could feed each other stale cornflakes in our underwear after more hot sex."

He laughed and already she felt his body's heaviness. He was exhausted and desperately needed to sleep.

"Okay, how about a warm bed and a caring body? Keep those nightmares at arm's length."

He rose up on his elbows, his hazel eyes burning with surprise and desperation. "How'd you know about the nightmares?"

Kip shrugged. "Any time you deal with this kind of bad stuff, you get nightmares. I guarantee you I'll have some about that morgue. Let me help you keep them away."

He stroked the hair out of her eyes. "I'd like that."

Sitting up, Kip took hold of his hand and led him toward the back of the room where her bed sat against a pale blue wall. She crawled in first, underneath the lavender and green comforter decorated with

Aspen leaves and swirls. Underneath was just a sheet. It'd been too hot for the threadbare quilt she normally kept on the bed. He slid in beside her as she picked up the clock.

"Set it for six thirty?" she asked.

Tristan nodded.

She set the alarm then snuggled into his arms. Until morning, she told herself. She wouldn't look any farther ahead than morning, but deep in the pit of her stomach, she felt an emotion she'd never known before.

It wasn't the ever-present remorse churning from her artificial conscience. No, this was something very different. Something that made her heart beat faster when she met his hazel-eyed gaze, her stomach warm at the sight of his smile, and her chest ache when his hand touched her skin.

These were dangerous sensations. As she laid her face against his chest, felt his lips gently kiss her hair, and then settle into that steady rhythm of sleep, she knew she couldn't turn away. It was a warmth her cold heart hadn't felt in years. For just a little while she wasn't alone in the world. She wasn't raging against it either.

No, in his arms, falling asleep, she felt safe and wanted. And it was intoxicating.

11

BEFORE SUNRISE, September 2nd

THE SCREAMS HAD DIED AWAY hours ago. The wooden box had gotten lighter inside.

That meant another day was approaching, another sunrise beyond the darkness. Another day Sarah still lived.

As long as she was still breathing, there was a chance to escape this horrible man. And the claustrophobic hell of this wooden coffin.

How many days had passed?

Still, the fear trembled through her, the cording so tight against her flesh. What happened to the screaming woman? Which box would he open next?

She knew there were others. Like her, they called out in the darkness, voices nearly drowned out by the sound of wind chimes. It sounded like hundreds of wind chimes, their voices like sharp discords against the chime's crystal notes. But those kindred voices made their way down the hollow lifeline connecting her to the living, connecting her to all of their suffering and crying in the darkness.

He hadn't touched her since he'd buried her, but in the night, when the box was nothing but blackness, she heard him dig up the others.

His grunts had echoed in the blackness and Sarah's chest twisted into a knot. Yet, she was so grateful that she lay forgotten under the soil, unnoticed. She never wanted to smell his rancid, whisky breath or feel him pressed against her again.

Her hands shook and went cold as she remembered the sounds of pleading, the desperate sobs, and the sudden deadly silence.

Who was the woman behind the screams? Had he killed her? How many days ago had that been? One? Two? She'd lost track of the days.

Tears funneled down her cheeks. Did Kelly even know she'd come out to Seattle as a surprise? Did Kelly have any idea she was even missing? Did she even care?

Sarah gritted her teeth, knowing there was only one answer to that question. An unconditional yes.

All the time that Kelly had been away in prison, Sarah had wanted to visit her, mend the rift of distance between them, the one her mother created by moving away. Kelly had always been good to her, never mean or nasty. She'd always been patient and careful. Maybe no one else saw Kelly's promise and potential, but Sarah did. She believed in her older sister and she prayed Kelly wouldn't let her down.

Above her, the drone of music echoed and the scratchy voice singing turned her to gooseflesh.

"Never lettin' go...forever mine to hold...sleep, baby, sleep... forever mine to keep..."

Her breath quickened at the rasp of shovel in earth.

Scritch, scritch, scritch. Dull thud of warm earth against grass.

Slurred mumbles, snippets of that horrible song. Her heart pounded against her rib cage.

"Time to play, Sarah, my sweet."

His voice echoed down the PVC pipe and Sarah wept, her body

trembling. The pleading words bubbled up from her dry throat, half-whispers as his shovel thunked the top of the box.

"Sleep baby sleep...forever mine to keep," his rough voice crooned as he pried open the box lid.

Why didn't he stop singing that horrible song?

"No, please," Sarah cried. "Please don't—"

The lid slid free of her face, revealing the pale night and moonless sky. Tree tops poked at the edge of her vision as his face swam into view. Traces of acne marred his cheeks, his dead-eyed gaze leering at her as he ran his hands across her torn blouse, stroking her skin.

"Let's play, Sarah."

His hands slid across her breasts, across her bare stomach to her panties.

"No! No, please!"

He gritted his teeth, slapping her across the face then grabbing her by the hair. "I said let's play." His hand snapped to her throat, his grip crushing.

Through her tears, Sarah struggled to breathe.

She nodded emphatically, whispering okay over and over until his grip on her throat fell away. He was leering at her again, almost cooing, singing that horrible song as he violated her all over again.

She shut everything down, staring up at the fading stars, grateful for the few moments of air and sky, and begged Kelly to save her.

When he'd finished with her, he grabbed her by the chin, forcing her gaze to meet his pale blue eyes.

"You'd better start being nicer to me, Sarah. I might get tired of your bitchy moods. Leave you for the cops to find some night. Like Terri. Terri got all bitchy, so I got rid of her. She's with the cops now." His grip lightened to stroking. "She was such a fake. Don't make me give you back, too, Sarah."

She nodded so hard and fast her neck cracked.

"Tell me you'll be a good girl, okay, Sarah?"

Her teeth began to chatter, the fear cold and wild inside her.

"Say it, Sarah," he said in a soft voice, running his hand down her throat. He took hold of her long blonde hair and pressed it to his face, closing his eyes a moment. "Tell me you'll be good."

"I'll—I'll be a good girl. Please...I'll be a good girl."

He patted her on the head then climbed out of the box.

The lightening sky vanished abruptly beneath a sheath of pine wood followed by the sharp blasts of the nail gun pounding nails into the lid. She was in the dark again, trembling and sobbing, but he'd left her alone and he'd left her alive.

A small bottle of Arrowhead water dropped down the PVC pipe and she snatched it up with her free hand. Next, two Twinkies fell through. Sarah grabbed them and tore open the cellophane with her teeth. She barely tasted the first cake as she devoured it in two bites. She hadn't eaten in days.

Only when the Twinkie was gone did she unscrew the cap on the bottle and guzzle the cold water. She left the other Twinkie unopened—for when she couldn't take the hunger any more.

As she drank, tears rushed down her face to salt her lips and she prayed Kelly would find her before this monster opened her box again.

12

6:48 A.M., September 2nd

"KELL, WAKE UP."

Lips pressed against hers, gentle kisses that stirred Kip awake. Her eyes rolled open.

He sat on the edge of the bed smiling, smelling of her almond shampoo and oatmeal soap. He wore last night's Henley and jeans and his short hair, still damp, was combed off his tanned forehead. And still, those hazel eyes smoldered. She wanted to roll him back under her covers for a few more hours.

"Hey," she said, reaching out to stroke his stubbled cheek. "Did I oversleep?"

He shrugged, gently smoothing the brown hair out of her eyes. "The first couple of hits on the snooze bar were my fault." He leaned down and kissed her on the lips again, deeper, and she pressed her mouth harder against his. Then he pulled back and she felt his reluctance.

"I've gotta take off, Kell. Gotta drive back to Ballard for work clothes and a shave."

Kell. She smiled. She liked that nickname.

Still groggy, she sat up, holding the comforter against her chest, and couldn't help but wonder if last night was an accident. A weak moment for both of them.

Was it just awkwardness for him now? Was he trying to get out of here as fast as he could?

She stared into his unblinking gaze, looking for anything that said he'd wanted last night to happen.

His smile and the gentle touch of his fingers against her chin reassured her. No, he had to get to work. She knew that. He had a killer to catch.

And she needed to keep digging for clues, see what she could shake loose at The Midnight Hour. After work was the perfect time to hit the club.

But first, before work, she needed to mail a package. With Northwest Parcel Pickup.

And find out which drivers delivered to the downtown area. Sarah was running out of time.

"Will I see you tonight?" he asked and his hopeful expression made her smile widen.

It killed her to shake her head no. "Can't tonight. Have plans after work."

His eyes narrowed and he studied her a moment. "What kind of plans?"

"Having drinks at The Midnight Hour," said Kip, leaning against the wall.

"Alone?"

When she nodded, he looked a little relieved and a little worried and that amused Kip. She'd never had anyone worrying over her before.

"We're still investigating that place, but of course, you already know that."

"Of course." She didn't look at him, instead playing with a long blue thread that coiled up from the comforter and wrapping it around her index finger.

He shook his head and she couldn't read his expression.

"This guy doesn't frighten you, does he?"

She wished he did frighten her, even a little. Then she'd feel more like everyone else. Almost human. All she felt for this predator was anger and a burning need to take him down. For what he did to Carolee. For what he may be doing to Sarah and the others he'd taken.

Despite having the artificial conscience for over a year, one emotion she rarely felt was fear.

She'd felt it a few times, but never that deep, bone-chilling fear that froze people like deer in headlights. That kind of fright came from a fear of dying, something she didn't have, but deep in her gut, she knew she wouldn't let her little sister down.

"No, he just pisses me off. And I *will* find him."

His eyes widened. Maybe he was surprised or maybe he just thought she was blowing around hot air?

"Is it the chip that keeps you from feeling fear?"

She drew her knees up to her chest, wondering how many people were walking around with one of these artificial consciences. Apparently, she was the first he'd encountered. Slept with. Maybe because he was new on Seattle's force or the treatment was too new? He seemed as confused as he was fascinated by the little device. And she was getting a little tired of explaining about it.

"It doesn't control me. It reminds me—like one of those little fitness watches, like an alarm going off. *I* choose to pay attention or ignore it. Besides, this isn't about the chip. It's about who *I* am." She poked her chest with her thumb. "Me. And I'm not afraid to die, Tristan. I never thought I'd live to be twenty-five, so anything beyond that's icing to me."

He seemed to understand about the chip (at least until the next time he asked about it), but then that familiar brooding look flowed over his face. Not all angry like his partner. Just kind of sad and sober, like he wanted to change something out of his control.

"A little fear's healthy, Kell. Keeps us from thinking we're superheroes."

"What's wrong with a little superhuman effort?" she asked.

He smiled. "Nothing, I guess. As long as we don't step in front of trains and try to jump over buildings."

Kip chuckled. "That's called stupidity."

Still deep in thought, he nodded, looking kind of troubled. Worried.

"What if I met you there? Later."

Still trying to play the hero. It was sweet, but it wouldn't help Sarah.

Kip shook her head then met his gaze. "And ruin my chance to get information? No, they'd know you were a cop and everyone would shut down on me."

At first, he looked annoyed, but then he sighed, bowing his head, finally nodding at her. Good. Not stubborn like his partner. God, his partner! What would St. James think if he knew Tristan had spent the night with her?

He'd think Tristan had jeopardized the whole case.

Maybe he didn't think she was still involved when he found out about Sarah, but Kip doubted he'd cut her any slack.

"I hate it, but you're right," said Tristan finally. He rubbed his forehead. "How about you meet me for breakfast afterward? Fill me in on what you found out?"

Kip smiled then leaned over and kissed him on the nose. "My place. Scrambled eggs and cheese. No partner."

Followed by a night under the covers.

He kissed her, his mouth tasting like coffee and her mint mouthwash, and she kissed back.

"Two A.M. and no partner," he said, his voice rising. "If you're not here by then, I'll be out looking for you."

"Have a good day, Detective and catch lots of bad guys," she said with a smile, sliding out of bed.

That had included her once. She held her head high. But never again.

His gaze shot down the length of her nude body and he grinned. "I will now," he said with another quick kiss, and then he hurried out the door.

Kip listened for the slam of car door and rumble of engine before she staggered into the shower, wishing she felt his caress along with the warm water against her skin. She closed her eyes, calling back the memory of him, the warm scent of his skin against hers.

Tonight, she told herself, not wanting to scrub away his scent, she'd be with him for breakfast.

BY 8 A.M., Kip was out the door with a newspaper-wrapped vase, headed for Second and Blaine. She cradled the teal green art vase Seph had given her (a birthday present) and hurried to the bus stop, black Converses slapping the damp pavement, and caught the Metro south. Toward Boeing field and Northwest Parcel Pickup's headquarters.

She wore cargo shorts and a long-sleeved blue T-shirt under a plain white T-shirt that hung out below the blue one. Tucking her hair behind her ears, she stared at the *Seattle Post-Intelligencer* masthead wrapped around the vase's gentle curves. Signed and hand numbered by Seattle glass artist, Annie Phelps. It was a nice piece of glass. Northwest Parcel better not break it.

She changed buses at Second and Pike, climbing into the back of the bus. Sucking on a mint to cover the nauseating stink of diesel, she ended up on the southern end of Alaskan Way, just below Elliott Bay and the shipyards. To her left, Rainier was out, filling the clear southern sky with its impressive white peak. Like the mountain's image had been super-imposed on the sky.

So beautiful and a little dangerous, she was always a welcome sight.

The heat had burned off the haze early, letting the mountain out in full view. Already, the air felt sticky. Another hot September day. She didn't know how Seph had caused the heat, but she'd met people with stranger stories (like people with chips in their heads). She knew the story about Persephone and Hades.

Maybe Seph *was* queen of the underworld?

It was certainly hot enough.

Kip walked inside Northwest Parcel Pickup's small, squat red brick building with its metal bars on the front windows, and carried the vase like a baby.

Inside, the room was wide and the ceiling was low, a faded brown counter stretching across the length of the room. The place smelled like wet newspaper and cardboard. Two clerks stood behind the counter, dressed in black pants and black polo shirts, that light blue evergreen tree on the left side.

"May I help you?" a short, thin woman asked, wearing a pale blue visor, her brown hair tied in a ponytail.

She had a square face and looked helpful enough.

"Need something shipped downtown by this evening," said Kip, setting the vase down like it might shatter right there in her arms. "It's very delicate and I want somebody local to carry it. A friend recommended you guys."

"We're happy to handle the packing and shipping, but I do want to make you aware that because we're a bonded courier service, our prices are higher than say, FedEx. But your item is guaranteed to arrive on the day you specify, at the time you specify. And we guarantee the condition of the item."

Kip frowned. "All I care about is my artwork arriving in one piece to the buyer. She needs it by 10 pm tonight. I don't trust it to anyone but locals."

The woman smiled and picked up a three-part invoice form. "We appreciate your confidence in us and we're happy to deliver your artwork."

This would cost her a fortune, she knew, but if it got the names of drivers, then it was worth it. Maybe Nick would let her work a few extra hours? Yeah, right. He'd already tried to fire her twice.

The woman asked for the address and Kip gave her Pacific Blue Tattoo's address and Seph's name as the recipient.

"And your name?" asked the woman.

Kip hesitated a moment. "Phelps," she said in a quick voice, settling into the part.

"Annie Phelps?" the woman asked, her face brightening as she looked up from the invoice.

Kip nodded. Might as well play it to the hilt. "That's me. I take my glasswork very seriously, so I'd appreciate some extra care with this piece."

"Of course! You do such amazing work. I own three of your pieces and can't wait to buy more. I love the dichroic wall sculptures you do."

"Thanks very much. Dichroic glass is hard to work with, but the result's spectacular."

Kip knew a glass artist once. Lived in Renton and totally obsessed about her pieces. Used to rent a space in Pike's Market. She worked with that dichroic glass like this vase. Wouldn't let anyone touch her work, including customers who wanted to buy it. Nearly killed her husband one night when he cracked a piece in progress. Despite the stitches, the guy stayed with her. She was probably still next to the wildflower vendors, fighting customers not to sell her work.

"I'm thrilled you've decided to try Northwest Parcel Pickup as your local courier."

Kip offered her a half-smile as the woman continued writing on the invoice.

"Please describe the item you're shipping."

"Here," said Kip, unwrapping it. The woman oohed and ahhed

over it. "It's an older piece. Called..." Kip ran through a few names in her head. "Puget Sound Underworld."

"It's lovely," said the woman in a quiet voice as she reached for the vase.

"Careful now," said Kip, sliding it out of her reach to cradle it. "It's very delicate."

"I'll be careful, I assure you," said the woman who slowly slid the vase out of Kip's hands. Tilting the vase very slightly at a few different angles, the woman described it on the invoice and Kip forced a look of nervous concern on her face.

"Value?"

Kip inhaled sharply. Not a clue, but she better make it expensive. "Fourteen hundred dollars."

The woman's eyes widened. "Really? Fourteen hundred?"

Kip pointed at traces of gold throughout the vase. "The gold's twenty-four karat. Took me eight tries to get this one right."

After that, the woman got all quiet as she finished the paperwork and figured the delivery cost. Sixty-eight bucks to have it delivered. Kip resisted the urge to flinch at the price, knowing UPS would only cost about a third of that.

"So, is uh—John still delivering downtown? My friend, Sadie told me to ask for John." Kip frowned. "I think it was John."

Still smiling politely, the woman picked up a clipboard near a black desk phone. She scanned the page. "No. No John on that route. Looks like it'll be either Ben or Steven. Ben's usually the regular on that route, but Steven does it part time."

"Does Ben also handle routes on and near Stewart Avenue? Near that new dance club."

"Dance club?" the woman asked, her face scrunching.

"The Midnight Hour. The owner commissioned two twenty-inch vases from me. In reds and oranges."

The woman turned toward a map taped to the counter and ran her index finger down a list of streets and then across the map. "Looks like that's still Ben and Steven. When the pieces are ready, just give us a call and we'll pick them up for you. We'll pack and deliver them on the date you specify."

Kip nodded as the woman glanced at a calendar.

"Well, I think we have everything we need, Ms. Phelps. Here's your receipt and we'll mail you a copy of the signed packing slip when the driver receives it. It will be delivered by ten tonight as you requested."

Kip's brow furrowed. "How late do you deliver?"

"Most delivery requests are between five A.M. and nine P.M., but we deliver seven days a week, twenty-four hours a day. Our drivers work in eight hour shifts and we assign them to regular routes."

"So, if I like Ben or Steven's work, can I request them for other deliveries?"

The woman smiled. "'Fraid not. We try to maintain routes so our drivers become familiar with their territories."

"How long have these drivers worked for you?"

"Ben's been with us since we opened in '87. Steven came aboard in '94." She laughed. "Really, there's no need to worry. Both are experienced drivers."

"Okay, that makes me feel more comfortable," said Kip, taking the invoice and folding it. "Thanks very much,"

"So—when's your next show?" the woman asked.

Kip looked up. "Show?"

"At the gallery," said the woman.

"Oh, uh—sometime before Christmas."

"I look forward to it." Another polite smile as the woman carried the vase over to a packing stand with rolls of bubble wrap and white tissue paper, folded white boxes, and a bin of those foam peanuts that sticked to everything. She set the vase in the center of the table.

"Me, too," Kip muttered.

"Thanks very much, Ms. Phelps."

Kip nodded and hurried outside toward the bus stop.

Two drivers to check out: Ben and Steven. She didn't have last names, but those should be easy to get. At least she hoped so. She'd take her break about delivery time and do a quick check inside the Northwest truck. Bound to be a name in there somewhere.

She glanced at her watch. Almost nine. Plenty of time to look up Freida Mason, Sheer Desire beauty consultant. Besides, it was a chance to get out of the heat.

KIP CALLED Freida the moment she got back to her apartment and found the business card from Carolee's smock pocket.

"Hello?"

"Freida?"

A pause. "Who is this, please?"

"I'm Kelly Thorpe, a friend of Carolee Eddleston's." Kip plowed on despite the woman's gasp. "A few months ago, she gave me your business card, said I should contact you if I wanted to be a Sheer Desire consultant."

"Oh! Yes! As a matter of fact, I am looking for a few new consultants. Have you ever used Sheer Desire before?"

"Yep, bought some from Carolee and liked it quite a bit. Especially that sparkly lip gloss."

"Terrible thing that happened to Carolee, wasn't it?"

Kip couldn't tell if she was sincere or not. "Yes, it was. She didn't deserve to die like that."

The woman sighed. "No, she was a sweet girl. Like my own daughter."

Kip rolled her eyes. Carolee probably barely knew the woman.

"Well, let me tell you a bit about Sheer Desire. It's the best product you'll ever use."

Kip held back a groan as Freida began her sales pitch. This woman was all saleswoman—too much for Kip's taste.

The word *phony* screamed from her lips as she chattered away about the benefits of this cosmetic and how different it was from every other cosmetic. *Blah, blah, blah.*

Kip pretended to be interested, agreeing about how unique it was and everything and how she couldn't wait to sell it to all her friends.

Freida offered to meet her at a nearby Starbucks and arrange to get Kip started. Kip agreed and ended the call. Scowling, she cast a glance toward the bathroom, knowing she'd have to putty herself up a bit before she met Freida. Make herself look like somebody who cared about clothes and makeup.

She headed into the small white bathroom with its white tub/shower combo parallel to the toilet. Kip kept a small bag of makeup on top of the toilet tank underneath the thick lavender towels hanging on the wall.

She'd used makeup only twice in the last few months.

She slapped on foundation and powder, running the dark grey eyeliner pencil around the upper and bottom half of her eyelids, making her pale blue eyes look larger. Brushed on an old Cover Girl blush that she'd bought in a weak moment at Wal-Mart once. Plum something or other.

Lying on the white pedestal sink was the unopened box of Sheer Desire Lip Gloss she'd taken from Carolee's closet. The sparkly stuff. She took out the slender tube and smoothed it over her lips. It felt sticky and Kip fought the urge to wipe it off and scrub the rest of the junk off her face. The powder and blush weren't so bad, but the liquid foundation was too much. She wore the eye pencil every day.

Changing into a light blue blouse and tan pants, Kip slipped her bare feet into Birkenstock knock offs and headed out to the Starbucks by Ivar's on the pier to meet Freida Mason.

THE HEAVYSET, nervous woman sipped a whipped cream topped Frappuccino by the windows that faced Elliot Bay. Her hair was that deep, fake auburn color and cut in a bob around her heart-shaped face. She smelled flower-sweet against the smell of fresh ground coffee. Two silver boxes of Sheer Desire makeup sat on table beside a small stack of napkins and a handful of papers. The place was warm with fresh brewed coffee, the rasp of steamed milk overpowering every other sound. But the air conditioning made the outside's stickiness disappear.

Kip bypassed the front counter (she'd spent all her money at the parcel place) and approached the woman.

"Freida?" she asked, leaning toward her.

"Yes. Kelly Thorpe?" the woman asked. She set her plastic cup on a napkin, wiped her hand, then held it out to Kip.

Kip shook her hand in a strong grip. Freida's was a wimpy shake, her hand cold and clammy from the iced drink she'd held.

"Nice to meet you, Kelly," she said, motioning Kip to sit.

Her makeup looked airbrushed. It was nicely done, Kip had to admit. Nothing over the top or puttied, no obnoxious bright eye shadows or fluorescent lipstick. She looked like an ad for nice cosmetics.

Freida talked nonstop about being a Sheer Desire beauty consultant, not even pausing when she handed Kip a small plastic bag of sample cosmetics and papers with pricing and available products. Kip feigned interest, waiting for the chance to interrupt with questions.

"How long was Carolee a consultant?" Kip asked.

"Not quite a year, but she was one of my best sellers. How did you know her?"

Kip's jaw tightened. "I went to beauty school with her."

"Terrific," said Freida, her dark eyes studying Kip. She frowned ever so slightly.

"I dropped out though," said Kip, glancing down at the papers. "Couldn't afford to keep going."

Freida leaned forward. "Carolee was paying her tuition through Sheer Desire. If you worked hard, you could, too, Kelly."

Kip set herself. Here it comes, the make big money pitch. She thought about Carolee being Marky's mule and suddenly it occurred to her that maybe she hadn't been his mule after all. Maybe he'd just been a buyer? Had she been Freida's mule?

"You have men's skin care products, right?"

Freida grinned, showing her square, over-white teeth. "Of course! An award-winning line of skin care and aftershave products." She winked. "Got someone in mind?"

Kip allowed herself a small smile. Tristan. She'd love to demonstrate a nice body lotion on him. Or shower gel. She nodded.

Reaching into a white and navy tote bag beside her, Freida pulled out three or four small charcoal grey tubes and spread them in front of Kip.

"Here," she said, patting Kip's hand. "Try these out on your man and see if these aren't the best products he's ever used."

Kip picked the tubes: chocolate merlot body lotion, forest glow shower gel, and spiced body scrub.

"Those were Carolee's favorites. Her top sellers for men."

Had her killer been a client?

"She have a lot of male customers?" Kip asked, studying the list of men's products. She saw the Arctic Nights body talc listed, the words *special order* in parentheses.

Freida's smile broadened. "Oh, yes! From the beauty school and at the club where she worked." She waved Kip off. "Mr. Weatherford, her boss, was one of her best customers. He'd sometimes order two hundred dollars of product at a time." She tapped the tube of chocolate merlot body lotion with a well-manicured coral fingernail. "This is his favorite," she said in a half-whisper. "If you sign on, I'll send him your card. He's needing a new consultant since…" Her face paled. "Well, you know."

Kip nodded. Too well. "Is there a startup fee?" Kip asked, studying Freida's face.

Freida nodded. "For eighty dollars, you get a basic consultation kit that contains samples, demo products, forms for customer orders and company product lists."

"Could I take a product list with me and think about it for a day or two?"

"Sure," said Freida, leaning back in her chair. She picked up her drink and took a long sip. Then she reached into her tote bag and grabbed a small plastic bag with Sheer Desire scrawled in script across the front. More samples.

"Take more of these samples with you and try out the products. Trust me. You won't be sorry."

Kip thanked her, gathered up her samples, and headed toward the door, but stopped. She moved back to the table.

"Freida? How do I receive my orders, if I become a consultant?"

She knew the answer before it slid out of Freida's mouth.

"I use a local courier for all the cosmetics deliveries. Northwest Parcel Pickup. They deliver the products wherever you specify."

"Thanks for the information," Kip said and stepped outside into the heat.

She checked her watch: almost twelve thirty. As she walked up the street to the metro stop, she played through the possible suspects in her head.

Rudy Weatherford, Midnight Hour club owner.

Ben and Steve, drivers for Northwest Parcel Pickup.

An unknown. Somebody working for Weatherford or somebody off the street.

She shuddered at the last possibility, knowing how real that might be.

Then she thought back to the bartender in the club. The woman remembered seeing a good-looking guy with a cardboard box with an old phone book inside. The guy's arm in a sling. What had he hidden in that sling? And how did the cocaine connect? Carolee had unknowingly muled drugs for someone, but that hadn't gotten her killed.

Sarah had nothing to do with drugs.

Her gut told her it wasn't Rudy Weatherford, but maybe someone he knew well. A good friend that maybe his wait staff didn't know? She needed to get close to Rudy Weatherford. Find out if he was a drug user or a killer. Or both.

Somebody connected to his drug running scheme was killing tattooed blondes. Maybe Weatherford knew?

Either way, she'd find out. Tonight.

IT WAS five 'til four when Kip got to work. She walked through the alley and in through the back door. In case Nick was up front trying to be chatty. Or trying to fire her again. She didn't have much to say to the guy, even if he was her boss.

She needed her job, but she didn't trust Nick anymore.

The moment Persephone saw her, she rose from her station, an eagle half-finished on some Goth chick's shoulder, the buzz of needles falling silent. She wore a pale pink lingerie top, short olive skirt, and fishnets in those black Prada boots she always wore. The place smelled hot with Speed Stick and that citrusy antiseptic smell she hated.

"Kip, we need to talk."

"Here I am. Talk."

Kip started to set her backpack behind the counter when the phone rang. Kip answered it with the familiar Pacific Blue Tattoo greeting while Seph tapped the toe of her Prada's against the maple wood floor.

Some guy asking about tattoo prices. She hooked him up with Ross who didn't have any customers.

Taku sat in the first station, working on some guy's thigh, but his gaze kept flicking to Seph as his needles buzzed orange across a rising sun, the outline of a samurai warrior already in place. Even Ross kept staring at the front. What was going on?

"Kip, listen to me!" Seph pressed her fists against her hips, a grimace on her face. "Detective St. James was in here looking for you."

At the mention of St. James' name, Kip stiffened, letting a glare scrunch across her face. "So."

Seph grabbed her by the shoulder and pulled her toward the back room. Her backpack slid off her shoulder and hit the floor. "It's worse than *so*, Kip. He had a warrant."

Her mouth fell open. "A warrant? For what?" She'd been in regular contact with her probation officer and hadn't so much as littered since she stepped out of prison. She was clean.

Seph shrugged. "From what I gathered as he talked to somebody on his cell, he had some piece of evidence that had your fingerprints on it."

Kip groaned, squeezing her eyes shut for a moment. The cardboard box. She'd touched it, looking inside, studying the label fragment. She mumbled a few choice words. What a stupid, amateur thing to do.

Guess St. James hadn't given up on her as a suspect after all.

"He's coming back to arrest you, Kip," Seph replied, shaking her by the shoulders. "Are you listening to me? If he returns, you're going back to prison."

Prison. The word ripped through her like a knife.

No, she wouldn't go back there. Sarah needed her help and she couldn't do anything from a cell.

"I'm your friend, Kip. Trust me. Tell me what's happening?" Her eyes were steel blue like Elliott Bay on a sunny afternoon. Seph usually let things roll off her. Kip wasn't used to seeing her riled up.

Kip sighed, hanging her head. "The killer left a cardboard box behind at the club. Like he's been daring the cops to find him all this time and stupid me touched it. Like it was a prop or something."

"Oh, Kip—that's got to be St. James' evidence. You know it's enough to hold you."

A person of interest. That phrase haunted her now.

She nodded at Seph as her heart squeezed into a knot when she thought of Tristan. What would he think of her now? She was just getting to know him. Would he think everything she'd said to him was a lie? She couldn't stand it if he stopped believing in her.

Her gut wrenched and she sagged for a moment, Seph catching her as she began to sink. Damned chip.

"What is it? You okay?" Her blue eyes were wide and Kip saw her genuine concern. At least Seph was still hanging with her.

"T—Tristan," was all she could stutter.

The corners of Seph's bow-shaped mouth lifted in a slight smile. "If he believes in you, he'll know better. You've got to trust that."

Seph was right. She had to trust him. She had no choice. She nodded, getting the strength back in her knees.

"I'm okay. It's just the chip."

Seph let her go and she wandered toward the massive spool table, her brain racing with places she could go, anywhere she could hide from St. James long enough to find Carolee's killer.

One thing was certain: she had to get out of here.

Nick had probably already fired her anyway when St. James walked in with the warrant. St. James had probably already staked out the front, watching for her. Was Tristan there, too?

Seph followed behind her, grabbing Kip's hand and pressing a key into her palm.

"Go to my place and wait for me there. Bayside on Elliott Avenue. Number 1201."

At first, that sounded like a good plan, but then Kip remembered the delivery tonight.

"Dammit, the vase! Look, Seph," she said, holding Seph by the shoulders. "I setup a delivery from that Northwest Parcel place tonight. Two drivers cover the downtown route and I'm almost certain one of them's connected to Sarah in some way. I need to see him, find out his name. One of them's either involved or saw something."

She let Seph go, pacing instead.

"You can't hang around here now!" Seph cried. "You know St.

James will have the place staked out, just waiting for you to return. I can keep you safe, but not here."

Kip held Seph's gaze. "You don't understand. I've got to see this guy. It's the eyes."

"The eyes?" Seph asked, squinting.

Kip pointed her index and middle fingers at her eyes as she tried to keep the desperation out of her voice, but it gushed out. She exhaled a quick breath, but didn't look away.

"If it's him, I'll see it in his eyes. I've known too many of them, Seph, seen the things they destroy, heard their excuses and bullshit. Besides...the box I touched? It had part of a Northwest Parcel label on it. I *know* one of their drivers is connected."

"Are you sure?"

Kip nodded so hard it hurt her neck. "Positive. Whoever's killing these women is hunting them on familiar ground. He travels for his job, so he knows every inch of these streets, like they were his backyard. He knows Ballard, too. And what better fit for that than a local courier with several years' experience."

"I'm sure the police are checking—"

"Nobody's checking out the couriers, Seph!" Kip thrust her hands in the air and began to pace again. "But my gut's leading me there! He probably has routes downtown and up in Ballard. Delivering at all hours would put him near dance clubs. To this guy, it's a candy store of beautiful women. He's somebody who feels inadequate around women, so he uses little tricks to lure them or drugs."

"Drugs? Like cocaine?" Seph frowned, her gaze flicking from Kip to the store room door. Maybe she expected St. James to shove it open at any moment? She was making Kip nervous.

Kip shook her head, turning to face her. "Most likely date rape stuff—roofies, GHB, that kind of thing. A bartender at The Midnight Hour recognized my sister's picture. Said she'd been in with some guy and left looking very sleepy. With his delivery truck parked outside, he could have shoved her inside and no one would have seen her. So, I've got to see this driver. Tonight."

Seph's face looked pale, her gaze traveling past Kip. She looked sad, taking it all in with a shake of her head.

"Your time is so short here and to see a life as so disposable, to be used for someone else's momentary pleasure...that's horrific. And there's something to be said for winter—when everything slumbers." A deep sigh escaped her lips as she turned back to Kip.

"They're predators, Seph. They hunt for the sheer pleasure of it. Get off on other people's fear and their ability to dominate them. And I'm close to him, Seph. St. James can't stop me from catching this guy." She stiffened, straightening to her full five-foot-seven height. "I won't let him."

"Okay, we'll figure something out," said Seph, taking hold of her arm and leading her to the back door. "For now, go to my place where you'll be safe." She grabbed Kip's backpack and held open the back delivery door. "Hurry," she said, thrusting the pack into her hands. "Before St. James sees you."

Feeling defeated, Kip knew she had no choice. For the moment. She reached out and squeezed Seph's arm, taking her backpack. Then she slipped through the service door into the alley again. Her chest tightened as she ran down the narrow space, past a blue trash bin, around puddles of water, and matted, damp newspapers.

In six years, she'd run full circle—into a Seattle alley, running from the cops.

Her sandals scuffed pavement as she ran, listening for footsteps behind her, the rustle of a jacket, a careless whisper.

The alley buzzed with the passing of cars, but no cops met her when she emerged on the sidewalk.

A quick scan.

Three women with white capris and fanny packs. A guy in a blue polo and khakis, phone in his hand. Two kids with skateboards.

A midnight blue Charger parked three blocks up the hill.

Cursing under her breath, Kip turned right.

She rushed past the women and ducked around the corner, heading away from the waterfront.

Her sandals slapped pavement as she caught the tail end of the walk sign and crossed 1st Avenue at Virginia, veering left. Onto Pike Place.

Heading north.

Two grizzled old people walking with canes and sweating in windbreakers, hobbled past.

A high school girl with her book bag, two guys in shorts and tank tops, t-shirts tied around their waists.

She weaved around the girl and the guys, rushing past two men in charcoal suits and yellow spotted ties, turning down Bell Street.

The air smelled like diesel and hot asphalt, the occasional cool breeze coming off the bay carried a whiff of freshly popped corn and a trace of fried fish from the piers.

Ahead, a midnight blue Charger. Parked. Windows too dark to see inside.

Kip's heart beat up into her throat and she backed away. Back east toward I-5.

Another corner. Two. Western Avenue.

Elliott Bay sparkled between tall buildings as Kip broke into a run, turning left then right again.

Ahead, Elliott Avenue and the tall, silver rise of Bayside Condos near the piers.

She pounded the pavement, her backpack slapping against her shoulders, soles of her feet burning as she rushed up the walkway and surged into the cool, almost refrigerated lobby.

Ahead were the two elevators and she walked casually toward them, keeping her gaze off a desk near the door. A black sign pointed arrows toward laundry, poolside, Bayside beauty salon.

Kip hurried past.

The elevator dinged when she pressed the up button and in moments, the doors slid open.

She rushed inside and pressed the button for the twelfth floor, but saw the key hole beside the number. She inserted Seph's key, turned it and the number twelve button lit up.

The building's top floor.

Doors closed and her stomach rose with the elevator as it climbed into the sky. It dinged as it stopped, the doors swishing open.

Into a penthouse apartment.

Kip whistled out a breath as she walked across the marble floors, a warm sandy color. The room was all curves, shaped kind of like a kidney bean. And it was all windows, too, all of them filled with Elliott Bay. The Bainbridge Island ferry glittered green and white as it glided away from Pier 52 and into the bay.

Her big purple couch was all curvy and modern-looking, the walls filled with almost tropical paintings. No beaches or palm trees. Kind of a European feel. Like Italy or someplace. Stacks of rounded white buildings above a deep blue, nearly purple sea.

Crusty old vases propped in wire stands or on half-height pillars were all over the room. Like someone had just dug them out of the sand.

And her pale gold curtains were like silk scarves that pooled on the marble floor and hung in folds above the wall of windows. Baskets of fake fruit sat on the glass coffee table and another glass end table. Weird looking fruits in purples and golds that Kip didn't recognize. The whole place smelled like lemons and grass and something a little exotic that Kip couldn't quite place.

It looked staged, like someplace out of a house decorating magazine and with an elevator that opened into the place, it reeked of money. Not the kind a tattoo artist brought home. Even an award-winning artist like Seph.

Kip sat down in an overstuffed gold chair that flanked the coffee table and stared at the colorful books spread across it. *Greece* in crisp blue letters across a thick white border, those white buildings next to a sparkling blue sea. Like her paintings—those places were of Greece.

Archaeology of the Aegean splashed across a book cover that was all black except for a terra cotta vase like the ones in Seph's living room. *Ruins of Pompeii*, the cover read. It had a superimposed picture of an erupting volcano over the Pompeii ruins. *Modern Mythology* was open and the text was all marked up with red lines and corrections.

Kip raised an eyebrow. Corrections?

The names Hecate and Hades were circled and underlined a bazillion times, followed by paragraphs of—Kip squinted—Greek letters. Seph was fluent in Greek? A cold shiver rushed down her arms.

Maybe there was something to Seph's stories after all?

A telephone rang, startling Kip.

She whirled around, staring at an old black telephone perched on the edge of the kitchen counter—a pale, creamy granite. The high-pitched ring echoed through the room three times before an old school answering machine kicked on.

"I know you want me," said Seph in a sultry voice. "But I can't answer right now. Leave me a message. And if it's a really good one, I might just call you back. Adío!"

The answering machine beeped.

"Persephone, I'm tired of talking to this infernal machine." An exotic-sounding man's voice, with a buttery kind of tone, patient regardless of what he said. "I want you to come home. Please —stop all this foolishness and just come home. Do you hate me so much that you prefer the company of mortals to mine?" He sighed, the sound deep and soul-rattling. "You're my sunlight and the summer has been so grey. Every day, I look for you beyond the gate, listening for Cerberus' excited barks. But it's all dark and grey. Come home, Persephone. Please."

The machine beeped and the room was silent again.

Stunned, Kip stared at the red, flashing light. Seph's husband.

It was obvious the guy was crazy about her. For a moment, she imagined how that might sound on her answering machine. But it was just her imagination. There'd never been someone like that in her life.

For a short while, she thought maybe it would be Tristan, but she'd already blown that. All because of a stupid cardboard box. No doubt St. James had already convinced him that she was involved. That she was trash.

Her chest ached at the thought and she turned away from the answering machine beside the phone, staring at the flyers and junk mail perched on the edge of Seph's counter.

One flyer stood out from the rest: *Bayside Beauty. Hair Lightening Sale! Highlights and colors twenty percent off. Stop in today!*

Blonde hair.

She stared at a lock of her own medium brown hair, a dangerous thought pushing its way to the surface.

What would she look like as a blonde? An older version of Sarah?

Nobody'd recognize her as a blonde.

And if she put on the right clothes—hired her favorite tattoo artist—maybe, just maybe it'd be enough to attract a killer?

13

4:26 P.M., September 2nd

"I DON'T CARE what you found, Keith—you're wrong!"

Tristan paced around his blue RAV4, the bile strong in the back of his throat. The hot, humid air clung to his pale grey, short-sleeved shirt, and charcoal dress pants. He felt bathed in sweat as he glared at St. James standing there smug and so pleased with himself. His short-sleeved white shirt and black pants clung to his body.

He wanted to bury his fist in his partner's mouth. He didn't give a damn that they were right outside the precinct either. Kell was innocent and he'd do everything in his power to protect her.

St. James thrust the report at him again and Tristan slapped it away.

"You can deny it all you want to, Tris, but it's right there. The facts." He snapped the back of his hand against the page. "Isn't that what you're always shouting about, Mr. By-the-Book? Getting all the facts?"

"Facts? Let's talk about facts, partner." He grabbed the papers out of St. James' hand. "All you've got is circumstantial. It places Kell at the club, nothing more. All this is based on your biased opinion that Kelly Thorpe is involved. Besides, you wouldn't have even been at that club asking those questions, if Kell hadn't led us there."

"You're high!" St. James shouted, waving him off. "The fourth victim worked there! We've been all over that place for days."

"And got nothing until this morning."

St. James stabbed at his chest with his thumb. "But at least I got it! And your little felon was the subject not the source. Let's get that straight right now."

Tristan wadded up St. James' papers and threw them onto the pavement. His partner's face reddened.

"Pay attention to the profilers, Keith! We're looking for a middle-aged white male."

St. James gritted his teeth, getting in Tristan's face. "And some white males have girlfriends! Like Kelly Thorpe. Someone who'd cover for them. Someone who'd cover up murders and abductions."

"Her own sister?" He pushed St. James out of his face, tapping all his Midwest manners not to punch the guy.

"Hey, why not? Maybe she hated her sister?" St. James pulled the warrant out of his jacket pocket and shook it at Bowker. "The judge agreed with me. Now, do your job, Bowker, and let's bring her in."

Not in this lifetime. Kell didn't deserve this.

He thought about those intense pale eyes and her hard-edged look that had melted away in that first kiss. How they seemed to be lit from the inside afterward as she lay beside him, playfully teasing him with smiles and kisses. He'd thought of nothing else since he'd left her apartment.

God, his chest had actually ached when he found himself alone in his own place, smelling her warm vanilla scent on his clothes. He'd never felt that way about a woman before. And her darkness fascinated him as much as her light and sometimes brutal honesty.

Tristan smirked as he leaned against his vehicle, crossing his arms. "You bring her in. It's your warrant."

"Dammit, you're my partner! You're supposed to back me up."

"I'm right behind you, buddy. The tattoo place is six blocks away, so I'll be right here backing you up."

St. James glared at him, his face turning red. "What's with you? Was sex with her that good, Bowker? Good enough to get you written up?"

"You bastard!"

He snapped up from his slouch and lunged at St. James, shoving him backward. St. James nearly fell.

He staggered backward, catching himself then rushed at Tristan, slamming him against the SUV door.

St. James let go, his chest heaving as he wiped perspiration off his forehead, sweat ringing his white sleeves. His dark hair was in damp ringlets at his neck and around his face. His grin was dark.

"That's the Bowker I've wanted—to meet for a while." He struggled to catch his breath. "You really think—she's innocent, don't you?"

Glaring, Tristan jerked open the SUV's door. "Arrest her yourself," he huffed. "I'm—I'm going home."

With careful movements, St. James closed the SUV door. Then he went quiet as he stared at Tristan, finally moving closer, his brow pressed into a tight frown, his gaze scrutinizing.

"Oh, shit," said St. James in a soft voice. "It's worse than that. Much worse than that." He shook his head. "You've fallen for the little psychopath."

Tristan reached out and grabbed St. James' shirt. "Don't you ever call her that again. She's got a name. It's Kelly Thorpe and she's paid for her mistake. She's been combing these streets night and day since her sister disappeared, doing our job for us. This morning, she told me she was going to that club." He took a deep breath and raked his hand across his forehead, wiping away the sheen of sweat. "Probably found the box before you got to it."

He tried to hold onto his anger, to shove it right back in St. James' face, but he couldn't. The pain and unfairness of this whole mess crept up, tightening his features, and he let go of St. James' shirt.

She had nothing to do with the murders and he'd make sure everybody knew it. If he had to go before the judge and dispute St. James' evidence, he'd do it. They could write him up any way they chose. He wouldn't back down. Kell was too important to him.

"If you showed the club Kelly's picture," he said, gesturing at the rumpled papers in St. James' sweaty hand. "I bet you'd get enough evidence to discount her prints on that box."

Sullen, St. James rubbed his chest where Tristan's hand had been.

"You're wrong," said St. James, shaking his head. "You're a good guy and you care about the law, but you're wrong on this one. She's got you fooled, partner. I just hope it doesn't get you knocked down to meter duty."

Tristan stared into St. James' annoyed, tired gaze. "Then prove me wrong. Come back to the club with me and let me show them her picture. See what they can tell us. Then if you're still not convinced, I'll...I'll handle the warrant." He pointed a finger at his partner. "But it'll be my way, Keith. She's been through enough and I want it as painless as possible."

St. James shrugged. "I've already got plainclothes watching the place, keeping tabs." He shook his head. "Damn, Tris. I never figured you to fall for a chick like that." He kicked at the pavement with his black loafers, hands in his pants pockets, silent for several moments.

Tristan's eyes narrowed. "How would you know? You don't know a damn thing about her." The edge left his voice again. "Once you get past her mask, she's sunny and charming and amazing. She's the most brutally honest person I've ever met and she makes no bones about what she did. She's accepted responsibility for it."

"All right," St. James said, holding up his hand. "I see how much this means to you. You're a good cop, Bowker—one I trust with my life. I'll give you a shot at it." He squinted, pointing a finger at

Tristan. "But if I'm not convinced, or have even the slightest doubts, we're back to take her in. Agreed?"

Sighing, Tristan nodded at him. He didn't have any choice. He just had to trust that he knew Kell better than any of these people. In his heart, he knew she had nothing to do with the killer, but somehow, he had to prove it to St. James.

"Okay. I agree."

He and St. James went quiet, each one staring at the ground or their hands. Finally, St. James gave him a quick pat on the back and Tristan returned it.

As they stood out in the sweltering heat, Tristan broke the awkward silence.

"Did the ME get an ID on our Jane Doe yet?" Tristan asked, changing the subject.

St. James nodded. "Name's Terri Hayden. Twenty-one. From Kirkland. Worked downtown at a boutique. Hung out at clubs after close. She'd been with two friends then left them to walk back to the store. She never made it back to her car."

Tristan's heart twisted. "When did she disappear?"

"Mid-July, I think," said St. James with a shrug. I'll have to check the case notes."

Tristan gazed at the tangle of uniforms dispersing at the back door, other people walking away from the precinct's hallway windows. Show was over.

He stared down at the pavement, smelling its oily scent and his own sweat.

"He kept her a long time. Longer than the others." He turned his puzzled gaze to St. James. "Why is that? He only kept Carolee Eddleston eight days. He kept this one six weeks. Why?"

St. James shook his head, raking his right foot across the pavement. "I wish I knew."

One woman worked at a boutique, the other was a hair stylist. Kell's sister was a sophomore in college. He thought back through the other victims: Kara Bishop was a barista, Amanda Pierson a receptionist, and Grace Wells a tech support specialist.

Of the five women murdered, three had been found in or near dumpsters: Pierson, Hayden, and Eddleston. Why? Why not all five?

It meant something to the killer, but what?

The killer hadn't liked these women as much as the others, that's what Kell said. A receptionist, a hair stylist, and a sales clerk.

What did these three women have in common?

He needed to find out more on these three women. And he needed to talk to Kell, get her opinion, compare it with the profilers from out East. But if he knew Kell, she'd already noticed St. James' stakeout and would be hard to find now.

He'd talk to Persephone.

St. James motioned Tristan toward the midnight blue Charger across the lot and started walking. "C'mon. Let's head over to The Midnight Hour and see what they've got to say. You got a picture of Thorpe?"

Tristan smiled as he slid his phone out of his back pocket. A shot he'd taken of her the night they brought her in on the murders. She had her arms folded against the table, looking away for just a moment. Those full lips just beginning to purse, her brow just starting to furrow. Those blue eyes intense. She looked deep in thought, halfway between dark and light.

And to him, devastatingly gorgeous.

St. James rolled his eyes and waved him off. "I had to ask. Come on, I'll drive. You man the AC." His breath whistled out as he opened the car door and heat roiled out. "Damn, it's so hot. I'm not used to this."

Tristan climbed into the passenger side and flicked the AC on high after St. James started the car. He angled two of the vents at his face and closed his eyes, letting the air hit him. He thought about the three women again as he snapped the seatbelt across his body.

"What kind of boutique did Hayden work in?" Tristan asked,

casting a sideways glance at St. James as he pulled out of the parking lot.

"Something about the moon." His face scrunched in concentration as he turned the corner. Radio squawked. Air conditioner hissed. "Eclipse. Yeah, that's the name."

"What kind of clothes?"

"Skimpy from what I could tell. Lots of see-through fabrics and short, short skirts. My kinda shop." The stoplight turned and the Charger lurched to a stop. "Not cheap. The shorter the skirt, the more expensive. Go figure."

Tristan squinted as the light changed and the Charger rolled forward.

"Party clothes," Tristan muttered. "The kind of stuff women liked to wear to clubs." Clubs. His eyes widened. "Hey, do you know if Wells or Pierson hung out at downtown clubs?"

"Don't know about Pierson. Wells was a homebody. Her hobbies were reading and online chats."

"What kind of online chats?"

St. James shrugged. "The singles kind. She was young and single, according to her landlord. Didn't really bring many people home with her, but her friends said she spent all her time on the computer. We've already interviewed the people she talked to over the course of the week and examined the subpoenaed chat logs. No mention of her going out to any clubs. She went out for coffee and never came back."

"Where?" Tristan asked as the light turned red and the Charger rolled to a stop.

The radio murmured about suspects and shots fired, two units on the scene. No call out to them.

St. James flicked his gaze to the radio then back to the road, tapping his fingers on the steering wheel.

"Downtown. You'll have to check the case notes for the specifics, Tris. All I remember is downtown and it wasn't a place I'd heard of."

Tristan was still learning to appreciate fine coffee. He'd been thrilled when the first Starbucks had rolled into his sleepy

Midwestern town and he'd tasted a latte for the first time. But when he moved out to Seattle, he learned Starbucks was just the beginning.

He quickly learned about organic coffee, Sumatran, Kona, Costa Rican—even Jamaican Blue, but sometimes, he just wanted a plain old cup of coffee without all the fuss. The super tall, soy milk, double shot, extra foam—well, it just made his head swim. Latte. That's as complicated as he got. And even that drove St. James nuts.

After a few more turns and a few more stoplights, St. James pulled up across the street from The Midnight Hour. Looked more like a warehouse than a club. But that was the idea. He was never much of a clubgoer, could dance if he drank enough, but most of the time, he didn't like all the loud, throbbing music.

The door was a big, red metal door and a very tattooed young guy with pierced eyebrows glanced up at them through a wall of bangs.

St. James flashed his badge. "Need to speak to some of your wait staff."

With a shrug, his expression of boredom unchanged, the young man opened the door. The place wasn't quite open yet, no music pulsed across the dance floor. The bartenders, dressed in dark clothes, leaned against the bar to the left, chattering and laughing as they arranged glasses and bottles. The wait staff, dressed in black leather, sat in booths on the opposite side of the room, counting out money, stacking cardboard coasters, and white cocktail napkins that read, *The Midnight Hour* in deep red. Cigarette smoke burned the air and Tristan felt his eyes start to water.

"Over there." St. James nodded toward a thin woman smoking a cigarette. "That's the woman I talked to."

Dark hair and tanned skin, she bent over the table, arm crooked and cigarette pointing at the ceiling. Smoke coiled up toward the exposed pipe ceiling as her gaze focused on a pile of coins she separated as she counted.

Tristan pulled out his phone and held out Kell's picture as he followed St. James to the table.

"Good afternoon," he said with a warm smile and showed his

badge again. "I'm Detective St. James. I spoke to you this morning regarding an investigation we're conducting."

She nodded and motioned with her cigarette for them to sit down. "You have more questions?"

"Yes, we do," said Tristan, sliding quickly into the booth. "It concerns the box that we examined this morning." He extended his hand. "Detective Bowker. And you are?"

St. James stood beside the booth, taking the place in before he sat down. He gave the room one more thorough scan before he sat down and put his back to it.

The woman smiled at Bowker. "Denise Archer."

"Well, go ahead, Bowker," said St. James, poking him in the side. "Show her your photograph."

Tristan cast an annoyed look at his partner as he slid his phone with Kell's photo across the table. The woman named Denise crushed out her cigarette in the nearby ashtray and picked up the phone. She blew out a thin stream of smoke before she drew the image closer.

"Oh, God," said the woman, a horrified look on her face. "Not her, too!"

"No, it's okay," he said, waving a hand at Kell's picture. "She's not a victim."

Denise slumped back in the booth, her chest rising and falling sharply. "Don't do that!" she cried, a hand on her low-cut tank top.

"I'm sorry," said Tristan in a soft voice. "She's very much alive. I just wanted to know if you recognized her, could tell us anything about her—anything you observed or heard."

St. James rolled his eyes and propped his elbows on the table, steepling his fingers as he tapped his foot against the table's base.

"Sure," said Denise, nodding. "She was in a night or two ago, showing a picture of her little sister who's missing. She was real upset about Carolee Eddleston's murder, but it was her sister she was most concerned about. I was here the night the girl was in—"

Tristan shot forward. "Wait a minute, you saw Sarah Thorpe?"

Even St. James sat up when she nodded.

Tristan grabbed his phone and pulled up the missing person's photo of Sarah Thorpe. He smiled. A younger, blonde version of Kelly. He held it out to the bartender.

"That's her. Greg waited on her and the guy she was with. She ordered Diet Coke. He ordered Jim Beam on the rocks. I remember thinking how young she was and how she was definitely not twenty-one. Another screw-up at the door."

"And that's why no one bothered to tell law enforcement that Sarah Thorpe had been seen in here," Tristan said, knowing the club wouldn't have willingly volunteered this information unless pressed.

"Excise fines—you know." Denise slid a cigarette out of the Marlboro Lights pack beside the ashtray and flicked on the lighter, leaning in to light the cigarette she rolled between thumb and forefinger. She took a long pull and exhaled the smoke through her teeth.

Tristan nodded for her to continue. "What else do you remember?"

"The guy kept trying to get her to order a drink, but she insisted on Diet Coke. She looked kinda nervous, kinda scared, but mostly she looked really sleepy. The woman in first photo thought maybe she'd been drugged."

Date rape drugs. Rohypnol, GHB, ecstasy. Tristan made a note to recheck the blood chemistries on the five bodies. He didn't remember the Medical Examiner finding any of these drugs, but he'd better double check.

"The guy," said St. James. "Was there anything special about him? Anything you remember?"

Nodding, Denise took another drag off her cigarette and propped it in the ashtray.

"He had on a sling. His left arm. Had this bulky cardboard box with him. Half sealed with tape and all. The girl carried it for him. Left it behind when he led her out of the club." She gestured at Kell's photograph. "When I mentioned the box to this woman, she asked to see it, so I brought it out. She and I looked inside the flaps. All that was inside was an old, heavy phone book, like it had been ripped out of an old phone booth. Remember those?"

He nodded. Only as a kid, but he'd seen them in enough old movies.

"The young woman told me that if the police came by, make sure they knew about the box. So, I handed it over to you first thing, Detective."

Tristan couldn't stop the smug, *I-told-you-so* grin spill across his face. He stared long and hard at St. James who just glowered at him, looking away. He crossed his arms across his chest and Tristan heard him curse under his breath.

Denise picked up her cigarette again. "What else can I tell you guys?"

"You've been an enormous help, Denise," he said, casting a smirk at St. James who jumped up from the booth. He reached into his shirt pocket and slipped out his business card. "If you remember anything else about the guy that Sarah Thorpe was with, please call me right away."

"I hope she doesn't end up like the others. She looks like she's just a sweet kid."

"We hope so, too," said Tristan, sliding out of the booth.

Denise rose with him. "He was really good looking, you know? Except for the acne scars, he'd have been a good underwear model. Hard, tight body—like he worked out. Nice blue eyes. They were a little too intense for me though. Like he was trying to devour you with his eyes. He looked at her like that. But at a casual glance though, he was hot."

Tristan made note of the blue eyes and acne scars. "How old would you say? Height? Weight? Hair color?" He pulled a small pad of paper out of his shirt pocket and clicked his pen.

Denise stared at a wall for a moment then her gaze flicked back to him. "His hair was a medium to dark brown, I think. He was probably six feet. Not heavy, not a bean pole. A little acne scarring.

But his face was chiseled, strong jaw. Had on khakis and a denim shirt, white T-shirt underneath. Like business casual."

"You saw quite a lot, Denise," said Tristan, writing furiously to capture all the details.

"Hey, when you tend bar, you size people up quickly. The tippers, the penny pinchers, the jerks, the nice guys—and the dangerous ones." She sighed. "Too bad Carolee never tended bar."

Tristan nodded. She probably never saw him coming until it was too late.

"If I called one of our sketch artists, do you think you could work with them on a depiction? A picture of this guy would really help."

"Of course. Have them stop by any time tonight. I'm here 'til close."

"Terrific! If you remember anything else, call me."

She smiled at him, holding up his card. "I will. I pegged you as a nice guy the moment you sat down." Her gaze moved to St. James. "And you...you're kind of a bad boy, aren't you?"

Tristan snickered.

St. James managed a smile then pointed at Tristan. "Bowker can't help it though. Those Midwest boys have that polite gene bred into them."

Denise smiled. "I'm from Wisconsin."

"Illinois," he answered. "Thanks again, Denise."

She handed him his phone back. He slid it back into his pocket and followed St. James outside. The heat slapped against him like a brick wall, almost taking his breath. He moved slowly down the sidewalk toward the car.

"You gonna call off the goon squad now, Keith?" he asked as St. James unlocked the car and slid inside.

When the passenger door clicked open, Tristan hefted himself inside and snapped on his seatbelt.

"Dammit, I hate when you're right," he said in a quiet voice and reached for the radio. He contacted the plainclothes on stakeout and called them back to the station. "There. Satisfied?"

He nodded. "Thanks."

"Don't mention it," St. James said and slammed the Charger into drive, pulling away from the club.

Tristan held in a laugh as he flicked on his cell phone and called the precinct. When he got the switchboard, he asked for the sketch artist on call and left a message for them to contact Denise at The Midnight Hour about creating a composite. Then he settled back in the seat, letting the air conditioner drench him in cold air and wondering where he'd find Kell after St. James' stupid warrant trick.

Seph would know. One way or another, he'd track Kell down. Tonight.

His thoughts drifted back to the three women who'd been found near dumpsters and he started making lists in his mind: check victims' blood chemistries, gather more information on occupations, contact the sketch artist about the composite, find Kell and apologize —again—for his idiot partner.

He gripped the bridge of his nose with thumb and forefinger, trying to understand this predator—just long enough to catch him.

Sometimes they were never caught. He knew that scenario well.

For over twenty years, the unsolved murder of his own father had haunted him. Hours of playing catch in the backyard, cookouts on the patio, trips to the water park where his dad had followed him right down that big, scary slide—all lost that morning his mother told him the news. He remembered the broken look in her eyes, the devastation and grief that had stared back at him through her tears.

And the heavy absence of him. The house so big and empty. And quiet. So very quiet.

He'd looked for him everywhere that day, so sure he'd bounce out of his office, laughing and smacking the pocket of a baseball mitt with a grass-stained baseball as he called for Tristan and his older brother, Eric.

The world was never safe again after that. Just a lonely walk with only fuzzy memories, some home videos, and old photos to remember Francis David Bowker. He and Mom and Eric made a pact never to forget him. They still celebrated his birthday together every March. The father that Tristan idolized had been with him such a short time, taken from him for no reason. No motive, no suspect—just senselessness.

He'd always believed that justice would find its way to such faceless killers, but after twenty-plus years, he knew justice needed a little help. So, he'd joined the police academy after college. Eric became a prosecutor and then a judge in Maryland. Mom remarried just last year after so many lonely years of missing him.

Dad's death had forever changed all of them.

Solving cases didn't bring him back, but for a few moments, Tristan felt like he was bringing a little justice to his father's memory. God knew he and Eric had tried to solve their father's murder.

Years of pounding pavement, tracking down suspects, re-examining the crime scene—over and over. That's why Tristan came out here, to get away from the pain of dead ends and dried up leads, not even a trace of DNA left to re-examine.

"Keith," he said in a low voice. "What if we never find this guy? What if he goes on killing for years, like the Green River killer or that BTK guy?"

Tristan stared out at crowds of people—so many of them tourists —clogging the sidewalks. What a great place to hide in plain sight.

St. James sighed, rubbing his forehead. He turned into the precinct parking lot. "We can't think like that. We have to believe we're gonna catch this guy. Those two killers were eventually caught."

"Yeah, twenty years later. They still have Green River women in the morgue, even some of Bundy's victims. I don't want to see that happen again."

"But we have an eyewitness, Bowker," said his partner, flashing him a quick grin as he parked the car and turned off the motor. "And maybe we'll soon have his picture?" He patted Tristan on the sleeve. "Look, I know you've gotta be thinking about your dad's murder about now. I've seen you poking around the databases in your off hours. But we're gonna get this guy, Tris. I promise you."

"I hope it's a promise we can keep."

St. James nodded grimly then opened the car door. Heat roiled as Tristan stepped out and moved toward his RAV4.

"I'm heading down to Pacific Blue Tattoo."

Stopping at the hood of Tristan's Toyota, St. James cast an almost remorseful look his way. "If you see Thorpe...tell her I said thanks. And sorry."

"I will. Thanks, Keith."

He poked the front tire with his loafers then moved toward the building. Tristan climbed into his SUV and squealed out of the parking lot as he headed toward Pike.

14

6:17 P.M., September 2nd

TRISTAN WALKED into Pacific Blue Tattoo. The place smelled clean and cool, the AC running full force. After sitting outside in a hot car, he wanted to fall into that coolness, but right now, he only had Kell on his mind.

A ceiling fan beat the air in silence, the room noisy with buzzing. Two guys in torn t-shirts and shorts sat in chairs up front, reading *Wired* and some tattoo magazine. All he cared about right now was protecting her, making sure she was safe, but he knew Kell well enough to know how impossible that might be.

Seeing the receptionist's chair empty made his heart clench. He wondered if her boss had fired her, creating a mess out of Kell's already hard life. He wanted to put his arms around her and hold back the world, make her feel safe and wanted. He knew that would make her howling mad, too, but it didn't stop him from feeling that need. He also wanted to take her back to his place for some quality time between the sheets, but all of it was on her terms.

He sighed. If she ever spoke to him again after St. James' screw up.

He'd tried calling her cell phone several times, but she didn't answer.

Persephone saw him and waved. She wore her trademark skimpy blouse (this one pale pink) and those tall, black stiletto boots. Very attractive as always. She never failed to boost his heart rate.

But he had another woman on his mind—warm brown hair, pale blue eyes, and all attitude. A woman he thought about constantly, one he couldn't wait to wrap his arms around.

He stepped closer to Persephone's chair where she worked on a tattoo of an eagle taking flight. Her subject was a black-haired white female, lying on her left side in a barber-like chair. Persephone sat on a wheeled stool, hunching over the girl's arm, her needles buzzing against the shoulder.

The girl looked barely nineteen and wore black men's pants and a black t-shirt, black Doc Martens. Her skin was white pale except for her shoulder that blushed red underneath the eagle's spread wings. And the greasy black rings of makeup raccooning her eyes.

She seemed unaffected by the constant motion of the needle against her shoulder. The sight of that needle made Tristan fight not to cringe.

"Be right with you, Detective," said Persephone in a distant, almost accusing voice.

His jaw tightened. She was pissed at him, too. Dammit, Keith!

The girl in the chair turned her hard gaze toward him. If she could have spat at him while lying down, she might have tried, judging by the disgust on her face. He met her angry stare and held it. She may not respect him or his profession, but dammit, he did his best to keep these streets safe.

He met her gaze with an unwavering stare. Finally, she looked away.

Tristan nodded at Persephone and wandered back toward the receptionist's desk. He glanced down at the office in the back where a guy with a Van Dyke beard sat doing paperwork. He wore a dark blue Modest Mouse T-shirt and jeans torn at the knees, revealing intricate colorful tattoos. The guy was Nick, he soon realized. Tristan remembered him from Kell's comments. Her boss.

He was tempted to go in and hassle Nick, like her boss had done to Kell over the past few months, but decided against it. That would just make things worse for Kell, but man, was he tempted.

Instead, he leaned against the reception desk, noticing the other artists glancing up at him. The entire place seemed like it was hating on cops.

Again, he cursed St. James under his breath for creating such a hostile environment. Especially for Kell.

He'd get little cooperation from these people now.

With all the cops swarming the downtown streets for the past two hours, he didn't blame them for being angry. He'd be angry, too if someone staked out his place, driving away customers and bringing down an air of suspicion on the whole business.

St. James had a talent for pissing people off and Tristan was really tired of trying to unruffle feathers and smooth over his bravado displays of authority.

Persephone spent another fifteen minutes with the girl in black until finally, she led the girl up front and stepped behind the desk. Without saying a word to him, glancing at him or even nudging him out of the way. The girl slid a hundred-dollar bill across the counter, still glaring at Tristan, and Persephone penciled in another appointment in the appointment book. The girl, awkwardly skinny, turned away toward the waiting room. The two guys tossed down the magazines and walked out with her into the heat.

"What can I do for you, Detective?" Persephone asked in a chilly tone, her voice sounding tired. She looked a little annoyed and a little sad as she turned to him, all business.

"I need to find Kell."

She laughed. "You and half the police force. Who've been

dogging us since four o'clock. Get it through your heads—she's not here. Better polish up your investigative skills, Detective."

Tristan felt his hackles raise. The room went suddenly quiet.

"Look, I'm not happy or proud about what went down here today. My partner was out of line—and just plain wrong. He went off on his own to get that warrant on Kell. But I just cleared Kell of any involvement, so she can come out of hiding. The warrant's been cancelled—I saw to it personally."

Couldn't she see how much he cared about Kell? That he'd have never done something like this to her.

Persephone's eyes widened. "There's no warrant now?"

"No warrant," said Tristan. "I found a witness who cleared Kell of any involvement. So, no more warrant."

"Thank the gods," said Persephone, sinking into the desk chair. Her hand moved to the phone, then she stopped, staring at him a moment.

Tristan held out his hands. "Would you give me a little credit here? Haven't I earned even a little of your trust by now?" Her expression didn't change. He slapped his hands against his side, turning away from the desk, but his anger made him turn back. "Look, I'm being straight with you. Kell means a lot to me and I'd never do anything to intentionally hurt her." He laid his hands on top of the desk. "You've got to know that much about me by now."

Her playful blue eyes were deadly serious as she gave him the once-over.

"She trusts you," she said finally. "I will, too." Persephone picked up the phone, her fingers flicking across the numbers. She held the receiver against her ear and waited. "Kip? You there? It's Seph." She waited another moment. "Look, your man's here. He says everything's okay and you're clear. And he's dying to see you." Her gaze fell onto him and she smiled. "He doesn't think I can see that in his eyes, but I do. If you hear this message, come by the shop. And yes, you'll still have a job. I'll make sure Nick knows everything. See you tonight. Adío."

"Thanks, Persephone," said Tristan, extending his hand to her. "Can't tell you how much I appreciated that."

She laughed, but shook his hand anyway, like she thought it was a cute gesture on his part. Would he ever figure out these women? He doubted it, but it might be fun trying.

"You're sweet," she said and patted him on the cheek. Then she leaned very close to him, her lips brushing his ear. She smelled like oranges and spice. "Twelve oh one Bayside Condos," she whispered. "On Elliott. She's there now."

"Your place?" he asked, stepping back.

Persephone nodded. "She'll be back here in a couple of hours though, so you'd better hurry."

He couldn't stop the grin from spilling across his face. He reached up to his chin, running his fingers across the day's shadow, checking for scratchiness. Needed a shave, but not too awful. She'd have to forgive him.

"Now, if you'll excuse me, I've gotta talk to the boss." She nodded toward the office. "Make sure he hasn't stupidly decided to fire Kip again."

Her boots clacked against the maple floors as she sauntered toward Nick in the office. The other tattoo artists had stopped staring at him, returning instead to their customers sitting impatiently. The steady buzz resumed, hurting his head. He hurried outside to climb into his SUV and find this condo.

IT WAS a ten-minute drive with traffic to the building. He pulled up to the door and left his vehicle on the circle, flashers winking orange. A rent-a-cop approached, a little short and a little chunky, curly brown hair. No academy calisthenics for him.

"Sir, you can't park there—" He stopped in mid-sentence when Tristan held out his badge.

"Detective Bowker, West Precinct," said Tristan. "I need access to unit 1201 as part of a missing persons investigation."

The rent-a-cop smiled. "I assure you, sir, Ms. Hadis is not missing. I saw her leave only a few hours ago."

Tristan shook his head. "She has information that has bearing on my case. I just spoke to her at her place of work and she gave me permission to enter her condo. Call her."

Nodding, the rent-a-cop waddled back toward the building's front door. "I'll call her and verify that, sir. I'll also need to record your badge number and confirm it with West Precinct."

Sweat beaded across Tristan's brow from the heat, feeling more like a mask. It was making his temper very short. Would this guy just get on with it? He nodded and leaned against his RAV4.

"Fine," he said in a short tone. "I'll wait."

The chunky rent-a-cop took his time calling Persephone and then West Precinct, but he came back soon after, nodding at Tristan.

"Ms. Hadis has cleared your entry, sir. And West Precinct did indeed confirm you're a detective there."

Hmmm, imagine that? He fought not to roll his eyes and moved away from his SUV, following the rent-a-cop to the front doors.

"Glad to hear they still claim me."

The man laughed like it was his job to laugh at everything and led Tristan inside and across the expensive marble lobby that smelled like too much potpourri. At the end of the pale grey marble was an elevator. When the doors whispered open, the rent-a-cop stepped inside, thrust a key on a lanyard into the key hole beside the number twelve. Tristan stepped onto the elevator as the rent-a-cop turned the key and stepped out of the elevator.

"Thanks," he replied as the doors closed in front of the guard, his hands on his hips, looking smug and proud.

With a gentle nudge, the elevator began its climb up to the twelfth floor. Persephone made damned good money to afford this place—whether or not she made it at Pacific Blue Tattoo, he wasn't sure. She had some money behind her, at any rate. From what or who, he didn't know and didn't really care as long as it was legal. Probably the daughter of some millionaire.

He let out a whistle when the doors parted on a panoramic view of Elliott Bay. And the expensive furniture. From the burled woods, silk fabrics, and unusually shaped (make that, custom designed) furniture, this place was furnished with only top of the line pieces. It smelled like lemon oil and herbs. Rosemary? Sage? He wasn't sure.

"Kell!" he called, stepping out of the elevator. "It's Tristan. Everything's okay now. I got it all straightened out."

He wandered closer to the windows, studying the paintings of Greece that hung on the walls. Whitewashed buildings and deep blue sea, the Greece he remembered from a college backpacking trip across Italy and Greece. That's what he remembered best—pure white and a deep, true blue.

When he saw the phone on the kitchen counter, he moved toward it, looking for an answering machine. It was flashing a number three. Had Kell even heard Persephone's message? Was she even here?

"Kell? Answer me!"

He walked past the kitchen toward a narrow hallway that led to two bedrooms. From the bedroom on the right, the sound of running water echoed. He pushed the door open. A queen size bed with an iridescent green and blue comforter. The walls were a pearly, metallic blue. A beaded chandelier hung over a bed that was covered in throw pillows.

Why women piled all those damned pillows on a bed, he'd never know.

He picked one up, a neck roll pillow in some soft, silky jade fabric with fringe. He frowned. Fringe?

All those pillows got in the way of everything and making the bed up every morning was such a pain. His last girlfriend piled those things up in mountains. Nearly smothered him whenever they'd had sex. He tossed the pillow onto the bed and moved toward the bathroom.

Steam filtered out from the slightly ajar door, a woman's voice singing. He stepped closer. A Sarah McLachlan song. Something about angels. He smiled. Kell's voice, a buttery alto, was sultry against the rush of the shower. She had a nice voice, pleasing to the ear. Smooth like merlot. He'd never heard her sing before.

"Kell?" he called, loud enough to carry over the singing and the water.

She stopped singing abruptly. Something thumped against the floor.

"Tristan?" she called out. "That you?"

He moved against the door. Ten minutes ago, the thought of a hot shower was appalling, but imagining that steamy water rushing over her hips and thighs, across her small, firm breasts... it burned through him. He was desperate to feel his hands against her skin, press his lips against her warm, drenched mouth.

"It's me," he answered, the steam billowing around him as he stepped into the bathroom.

"If it's you, you'd better be alone."

Her lush silhouette danced behind a thin, ivory shower curtain and his pulse raced. She stuck her head out, a smile on her face, but his mouth fell open and he stared at her in shocked surprise.

Gone was the rich brown hair, replaced by the palest blonde. Even wet and pasted against her scalp, the lightness of her hair was obvious. His heart pounded into his throat.

"Like it?" she asked.

He stumbled backward a step. "Why, Kell?" he demanded when his voice came back to him.

She shrugged and slipped back behind the curtain. "Just needed a change, that's all."

"Change, hell!" he shouted and grabbed hold of the curtain.

He pulled it open to get another look at her shock of blonde hair. The sight of it chilled him to the bone. He winced, remembering Terri Hayden's pale hair pooled in the bottom of a body bag. Carolee

Eddleston staring past him, skin milk white, posed like a Barbie doll in the alley.

It made him shake.

He could see Kell motionless, posed. Lying in damp leaves, her hair pooling around her. Flash of the medical examiner's camera in the half-dark alley. Her eyes empty and staring past him.

But Kell's unblinking, pale blue gaze held his and he stared into her fiery eyes, trying to understand why.

For that moment, he had full connection to her, understood the darkness and the light that shined bright from her gaze. And in those shadows, he saw a desperate sister willing do anything, try anything.

And if that meant, bleaching her hair blonde to lure out a killer, then she'd do it—had done it—in a heartbeat. No reservations. No regrets. No concern for her own safety.

He sighed. And that included him, too. She'd risk everything to make things right.

He saw shades of himself in her, he realized, knowing he'd probably do the same thing for his family. In those sad blue eyes, he saw her affection for him. And something more—something long term that scared him as much as it must have scared her.

Something, he realized now, that could never be.

Feeling sick, he turned away, leaning his palms on the vanity as he stared into the fogged mirror. It hid his face and hers, obscured the pure emotions he'd seen in her eyes.

"Tristan, don't."

The spray of water fell silent, followed by the rustle of a towel and wet feet padding across tile. Her hands were against his arms now, stroking, caressing—holding on. She leaned against him, the dampness seeping into his clothes.

"Don't what?" he asked, unable to keep the weariness, the edge out of his voice. "You've already decided on this sacrifice. What else is there to say?"

He felt her wet cheek press against his shoulder and by God, Kelly Thorpe was trembling.

"There's no choice, Tristan. If I don't do something drastic, she'll wind up in the next alley, in the next dumpster." Her breath caught and she stiffened, but she kept her cheek against his shoulder.

"Oh, great—so you *and* your sister wind up dead in an alley somewhere. That'll break this case wide open."

A swell of anger rose in him and he punched the wall, the thick cotton towels on the rack absorbing the blow. She was standing in front of him now, that awful blonde hair dripping, beads of water clinging to her cheeks and eyelashes. No emotion on her face as she stared at him.

"I'm not afraid to—"

"To die, so I've heard," he snapped, turning toward her. "Was there ever anything but sex between us, Kell?" He pinched the air with thumb and forefinger. "Some tiny little something that made you think about a future with me—just for a moment?"

"Future?" Her eyes widened and he saw the fear wash over them. "My God, Tristan—you barely know me."

He shook his head. "I thought I did. I thought I felt something between us, some burning hope that you'd still be here after this case is solved."

He smashed his eyes closed, images of milk-white skin, dead eyes staring at the sky, posed just so, the stink of dried blood and garbage surrounding him. The horrible, heavy silence that always surrounded corpses, the occasional click of the ME's camera, the rustle of plastic bags.

He rubbed his eyes, trying to erase those images—Kell in that white nylon bag—and the cold fear balling in the pit of his stomach.

But worst of all, he knew he couldn't stop it. None of it.

Soft as a kiss, her hand was against his arm. Then his face, cupping his chin.

"You barely know me, but what I see in your eyes..." She hesitated, drawing in a quick breath. "Tristan, is what I see in your eyes—"

"Love?" he asked, his voice flat.

He hadn't realized it until now, now when she might get herself killed with this crazy stunt. The thought of losing her ached through him.

Her hand went to her mouth. She was still shaking.

"Don't mess with me, Tristan," she said, her voice hard. "That's not a word I'm used to hearing."

"I know," he said, his voice barely above a whisper. "It's not a word I'm used to saying." He straightened up. "But I'm saying it now. I love you, Kelly Thorpe, and if you get yourself killed, I'm going to be so damned pissed."

He hadn't expected the grin that lit her face or the arms thrown around his neck. She pressed her body against him, burying her face against his shoulder and he was lost.

"I don't do this to hurt you, Tristan," she said against his ear. "I've done nothing else but think about you since I saw you on the street interviewing bystanders." She nuzzled his neck. Forehead. Mouth. "And it's just gotten worse from there. But I can't let my sister die."

He couldn't help himself. He folded his arms around her. "And I can't let you die either." This was crazy. It was too dangerous, but he felt powerless to stop it.

"See, I've figured out something," she said, her voice louder this time. "Of the two bodies I saw, both were found in or near dumpsters, right?"

He nodded.

"When I had my hair bleached today, I saw a woman in there getting her hair retouched."

Tristan frowned, stroking the damp hair off her face.

"That's when they only bleach the dark roots that are showing. So, you don't look like a skunk or something? So, what did you figure out?"

"See, Carolee and the woman at Harborview both had dark roots showing. I'd bet money that the third victim found in a dumpster had dark roots showing, too."

"But what does that mean?"

"I'm not sure, but my guess is this. This guy wants them perfect somehow. When he takes a blonde and her roots start to show, he finds out she's not a natural blonde. So, he gets rid of her." Kell swallowed hard, going quiet for a moment. Finally, she found her voice. "Sarah colored her hair. Depending on how fast her hair grows, he's gonna see her roots soon. Then he'll get rid of her."

Tristan felt his stomach twist as he thought back to Amanda Pierson, posed and found near a dumpster. But she'd been placed in a suggestive pose, her legs spread, hands on her thighs. She only had on a tank top, torn open at one breast. She'd been a pale blonde and thinking back, he remembered seeing her dark roots. At the time, it hadn't meant anything.

"And the other two victims? The ones found near parks. They were natural blondes. I'd bet money, Tristan."

"I'll check that out first thing tomorrow," he replied, his brain shooting through reams of case notes and reports, trying to recall as much as he could.

"One other thing. I'd bet money that this guy's mother was a hair stylist. And he's trying to find the perfect mother he never had."

Tristan pulled away, holding her at arm's length as the observation flooded over him. He flashed back to the victims. One was a receptionist—at a hair salon. A place not eight blocks from The Midnight Hour. One was a hair stylist. Both women were left by dumpsters.

"My God, Kell—I think you're right. It fits!"

Kell nodded. "His mom was probably a bleach blonde. Probably controlling and not too concerned about who she slept with. Probably hung out in clubs and brought home lots of strange men. Abusive to him. He was probably molested by some of these men. He loved and hated her at the same time."

His brain was churning through the details now and he sank down on the nearby toilet.

"Loved and hated her...he may have imagined himself in competition with the men she brought home."

Kell leaned against the wall. "Exactly. So, this guy is collecting women who look like his mother, a woman he finds cheap and sleazy, even though he loved her. He's trying to find the perfect match, but the fakes—the nightclub goers…"

"To him, they're the whores who hang out in chat rooms or buy skimpy clothes. The ones that bleach their hair and get tattoos are the fakes. The ones that deserve to die, right?"

He shook his head. None of those women deserved to die. They were just looking for the same things everyone wanted: someone nice to be with, someone to love them.

She nodded at him. "So, he kills the fakes, tapping all that anger against his mother. But the care he takes with the bodies afterward—dressing them, posing them—is him feeling sorry for his victims."

Tristan sighed, his gaze meeting hers again. God, she looked so different with the blonde hair. It was beautiful on her, but he was terrified it would get her killed.

"One of the women hung out in a singles chatroom," said Tristan. "Another worked in a boutique—short skirts, see-through blouses."

"Then it fits."

He nodded. "I've got the bartender at The Midnight Hour working with a sketch artist. We should have a sketch of the guy who left with your sister later tonight."

Kell grabbed his sleeve, her eyes turning intense. "What are you going to do with the sketch?"

He shrugged. "Release it to law enforcement officers, compare it to mug shots."

"What about giving it to the press? Make a big deal about it in a huge press conference with lots of official uniforms and important people."

"This guy's all about the publicity, isn't he?" Tristan scowled. Probably loved to watch the six o'clock news to see his handiwork.

"He craves it," said Kell. "I'm sure he drives past the places he left the bodies as often as possible. Gives him a sense of power. Plus, he gets off on it. Makes him feel important. Include the bit about his mom being a blonde-haired stylist. Somewhere out there, there's somebody who'll recognize this guy."

"I'll get it the papers tomorrow. St. James will be all over it. He loves the spotlight." He smiled at her, reaching out to caress her face. "You're brilliant, Kelly Thorpe." Then he pulled her close. "And the hottest woman I know."

She leaned her body against him then removed her towel. Her wet, sinewy body rubbed against his and he wanted his bare skin against hers. Now.

"Prove it," she whispered in his ear, nibbling his earlobe then sliding kisses down his neck until he was pulling off his shirt and pants.

"You asked for it," he said in a low, feral voice, easing her down on the bath mat.

At last, he felt her wet, naked flesh pulsing against his bare skin. And he was just getting started.

15

7:48 P.M., September 2nd

PERSEPHONE CHECKED her voicemail from the shop and the sound of Hades' smooth voice rolled through the phone. Trembling, struggling for breath, she rushed into the back room so no one saw her distress. The air smelled cool, spicy with hints of her Opium perfume.

The weariness and longing in her lover's voice hurt more than she'd ever imagined. But it was a resigned message, accepting of whatever she decided to do.

Gone was the bold, lovesick man who had carried her off on his chariot (in quieter days). She'd hated him then, taken from her mother so young, still dreaming of her first kiss and wildflowers. Taken to the brooding depths of spirits and darkness.

He never laid a hand on her, but she felt his passion burn, lighting the underworld's dim halls with a glow that eventually warmed her.

Seph wrapped her arms around her middle and her skin prickled with gooseflesh. She envied Kip and Tristan. She felt that glow between them, remembering when it had been hers once. Remembering Hades' tenderness, his gentle wooing, his dark hair growing lighter in her presence. (She liked his sandy hair best.)

When she willingly pledged herself to him, loving him and never wanting to be away from him, she'd swallowed the pomegranate seeds. As the centuries rushed past, his glow dimmed until it disappeared beneath his winter broods.

Never so bright as Kip and Tristan's fire.

A goddess envying mortals? Wouldn't Hera laugh in her shrill, catty voice? Of course, she couldn't blame the woman for her neuroses. Gods knew what she'd gone through with her unfaithful husband, Zeus.

Why hadn't he come after her? Why hadn't he shown her he cared?

Just once, she'd wanted Hades to court her, treat her as his beloved—like he had that first spring when brought her to the meadow, returning her to her tearful mother. His eyes looked wet, his knees weak as he turned and walked away, a little unsure that she'd return to him in the fall.

Later, on her return, the winter months brought out his brooding and eventually, his silence. And no matter how hard she tried, he remained so until she left him in the spring, relieved to be out of that darkness, thankful she had six months in the light.

But the mortal world had lost some of its light, too.

The latest psychopathic mortal was loose in another city, but this time, she was so close to the mortals affected. This time, it had unsettled her more than she'd ever expected. She exhaled sharply, pacing the room. She wanted an end to the slaughter as much as she wanted an end to Hades' brooding silences. No matter where she went, she couldn't escape the shadows.

She needed Hecate's advice. Helios' bright face. And she needed them now. Tonight, there would be an ebony moon, Hecate's favorite time. She'd be easy to call.

Seph rushed out of the back room, walked to her station, and grabbed her purse.

"Nick, I'm going out for an hour," she called toward his office and hurried toward the door. "Be back before ten."

"Bye Seph," Taku called from the front desk where he'd written down an appointment.

She waved at Taku, not waiting for Nick's response as she rushed out into the sultry night air.

This heat was her fault, it was true, but she couldn't go back the underworld. Not yet. There were irreconcilable issues between her and Hades. Besides, Kip needed her help. As an immortal, she really couldn't interfere, but whatever grey help she could provide to Kip, she'd give.

For as long as she could.

Hurrying to the nearest bus stop, Seph climbed aboard a bus headed for the piers and in a few minutes, she stepped off near Pier 52. Where the ferries ran. Only between land and sea where it was all one ocean, could she summon the crossroads to the underworld. And consult with Hecate.

The ferry terminal smelled of popcorn and coffee as she purchased her ticket and walked to the back of the station, waiting to board the ferry. She checked the wall clock: 8:03 P.M.

The ferry, sleek white and green, floated at the dock, ready to be boarded, ready to whisk her across the glittering bay waters. Only a handful of people waited, dressed in shorts and capris, carrying books and tablet computers for the thirty-minute crossing to Bainbridge Island. But she'd be getting off sooner than that.

Right on schedule, she boarded the ferry.

The air was sultry against her face as she stood alone on the ferry's bow, waiting for it to slip gently across the bay. And the air to cool. She'd taken this journey so many times over the years. On boats, ships, yachts, and triremes. In every body of water in the world. Maybe this time, it should be her last?

The ferry gave a long, mournful call and glided into the bay.

Seattle's skyline slid into the distance, fading into that ubiquitous grey haze over Seattle. Not even the extreme heat could burn it all off. The emerald city glittered like a smoky jewel.

She turned her gaze back toward Bainbridge Island when two porpoises leaped in front of the ferry's bow. Smiling, she leaned against the railing, watching the sleek black and white porpoises riding the wake. Beside them, Nereids played. She watched their glittering seafoam bodies surge through the wake beside the porpoises. They giggled and chattered at her.

"Persephone! We've missed you!" they called in child-like voices. "Come and play with us."

Whenever she'd made this journey before, the Nereids' presence had always made her sad. Now, they made her laugh. Still, she envied their child-like innocence. Something she'd lost long ago to the underworld, something she'd hoped to reclaim among the mortals. But with a butcher loose, that innocence seemed lifetimes away.

"Next trip," she whispered into the wind. The wind swirled past the Nereids, carrying her words to them.

"Do you promise?" one of them asked, her seaweed hair flowing around her cherubic face and slender shoulders.

Persephone nodded. She looked forward to it.

Waving, the Nereids plunged beneath the surface and sped away with the porpoises.

Persephone turned her face into the wind. "My dear friend, Hecate, I call for the crossroads." Taking a deep breath, she reached out her hands to the air.

Shadowy fingers reached out and grasped her hands, pulling her from the ferry's deck.

A rush of shadows. Rise of sea waters. When the world cleared, she stood in the middle of a crossroad. Three footpaths, worn smooth, stretched into a tangle of trees and brush. Woods surrounded her on all sides, cedar trees towering above the smooth, ruddy trunks of madrona trees. The air smelled of sea salt and fresh rain.

"Hecate!" she called, turning to look in all directions.

She waited, but no one answered.

"Hecate, please!"

At last, Hecate appeared on the center path and walked toward her. Her eyes were polished ebony in her flat, squared face. She wore a long, thin dress—shimmery charcoal—that clung to her slim body. Her hair flowed thick and wavy around her shoulders, tamed only by a heavy silver barrette at her nape. Always an attractive, stylish woman.

"Persephone," she said, her voice low and gravelly. "You know the arrangement. The season has passed. Hades has been so worried."

She looked Seph up and down with her wise, discerning gaze, noting this year's fashion, Seph knew. But she didn't say a word. She clapped her bony hands together.

"You should see the improvements he's made to the castle in your absence." Hecate turned and started down the path that led toward a shadow looming ahead.

Persephone sighed, following with reticent steps. This would hurt him deeply. She had no wish to hurt him, but pleasing him was destroying her. Hecate had saved her from a lifetime of shades and shadows, negotiating six months of light every year. She looked out for Hades, too, Seph knew. Hades took his duties seriously and of all the gods, he had the most responsibility. They took advantage of his sense of duty until Hecate had set her watchful eye on him.

"I'll follow you to the gates, but no farther. Please ask Hades to meet me there."

"What? But why the gates?" she turned and scrutinized Persephone again. "Has something happened?"

Yes, she'd finally grown up.

She wasn't that foolish young immortal picking flowers near Eleusis or the headstrong young woman trying to ignore her mistakes and their consequences. She was the daughter of a goddess. She wouldn't return to the underworld's gloom and darkness. Even if the gods took her god-essence, she would not stay.

"Please ask him to come to me."

Hecate's thin face shadowed with concern as she turned away, rushing ahead, and fading into the shadows. With slow steps, Persephone followed until she felt the shadows engulf her.

For a moment, she was falling.

She closed her eyes until the ground felt solid against her Prada's. A long corridor stretched ahead toward dim light and shadows. The air smelled cold and stale—gritty. She shivered, feeling the cold of shades as they passed around her, heading toward the gates. They had already crossed over on Charon's ferry and would spend the rest of their days here until they were allowed to cross over to the Elysian Fields.

And into the sunlight, Persephone thought with a sigh and folded her arms against her torso. Were any of them Kip's mortals, the ones murdered? The one who died in the alley that night?

Ahead, the massive black gate rose, casting a long, dark shadow along the path. More shadows stealing the sun.

Cerberus crouched beside the gate, a low growl crackling in the silence. She moved toward the massive, shaggy black, three-headed dog.

"Cerberus?"

When the three-headed dog saw her, his serpent tail thumped against the ground. He whimpered and scrambled toward her. His three canine tongues licked her hands as he pranced around her.

Smiling, she knelt beside him and stroked the nape of one of his necks

"He's missed you."

She froze at the sound of Hades' velvet voice.

Inhaling slowly, she rose from the ground, afraid to look into his eyes. He lifted her chin. A smile lit his pale complexion, his brown eyes bright. Such a warm brown for the ruler of the underworld. His blond hair had darkened a little.

"Have you, at last, missed me? Tired of your mortals? Is that why you've finally returned home?" His strong hands cupped her face, warming against her skin. "I was so tired of talking to that machine of yours, the one that stole your voice."

She slipped away from his touch and the smile fled from his face.

"No," she answered, looking away. "I've come to tell you that —" She sighed. "This is difficult."

His hands were at her shoulders and she felt his kiss against her neck. She wanted to cringe but couldn't. He was making this so hard.

"What is it, my love?" he asked, his voice soft and distracted.

She turned, holding him at arm's length. "I've come to tell you—that I won't be coming back here. At least not to live."

He laughed for a moment, but his voice quickly faded, the shock at last dulling his features. "You're serious, aren't you?"

She nodded. "I am so weary of living two lives, Hades." She bit her lip and slid her hand into his. Gently, she brought his hand to her face and pressed his fingers to her lips, kissing them. "My soul is dying in this empty place. Once, you were the only brightness in this realm, but even you have faded from me."

"You're bound by the arrangement made by your mother, Demeter —by the pomegranate seeds you willingly swallowed. If you ignore that...the gods will take your god-essence." His voice was a half-whisper.

"I—I don't know what will happen, but I'll risk it if it'll end this constant migration."

Sadness touched every feature of his face, his brown eyes growing watery as he pulled his hand away. Guilt stabbed her chest.

"Do I still mean nothing to you? After all this time?"

She closed her eyes. He meant so much to her, but he never showed her the same sense of preciousness. He only loved her under his terms. She'd sacrificed everything for him, yet his love only lasted six months of the year. She felt like a wild flower, brittle from frost, dying slowly with the sun's rise.

"I ask the same of you, Hades. I don't think you've ever known me at all."

Anger sharpened his features. "You'll return," he snapped. "You won't risk your immortal soul, your godhood—not for this. Not for mortals."

"Sometimes, they need our help and for centuries, we've turned our backs on them."

"They're beyond our help," he said, his voice filled with bitterness.

He cast a hurt, longing gaze at her and then turned away, trudging toward the gates. Already, his form was greying in the dim light.

She waited until he had disappeared into the shadows before she turned and walked away from the gates, back toward the crossroads.

As she stepped through, Hecate's hounds appeared briefly. Then, everything darkened until she felt the solid deck of the Bainbridge ferry beneath her feet, the one bound for Pier 52. The inbound one that had crossed paths with her outbound ferry.

Evening had finally fluttered its silver fingers across the city and it glittered against dark waters. She huddled against the railing, feeling weak, and watched the lights until the ferry reached the dock.

She checked her watch: nine nineteen. Time enough to pick up a mocha and wait for Kip's delivery guy.

As she walked toward the nearest coffee house, her stomach clenched. What would happen to her when she failed to return to the underworld? For choosing mortals over her immortal husband? What price would she pay next for swallowing six pomegranate seeds?

16

9:29 P.M., September 2nd

KIP STEPPED out of Tristan's RAV4, a block down from Pacific Blue Tattoo. He rolled down the window, leaning his smiling face toward her. She shifted the shopping bag she carried into her left hand and pressed her lips to his in a long, satisfying kiss.

"I'm going to grab a coke and keep watch for this delivery guy," he said then sighed. "But I've gotta call St. James in on this one. Get him going on the press conference."

Kip didn't even flinch. She knew bad cop would be around some time. Just hadn't expected it tonight. She'd deal.

"Figured he'd show up."

Tristan shrugged. "For what it's worth, he asked me to tell you thanks and sorry."

"Thanks for what?" she asked with a frown. Sorry, she understood and it was about damned time.

"The box," said Tristan. "It was the first real lead we've had in the case."

She quirked a thin smile, but didn't say anything. Maybe bad cop would come around after all? Jury was still out, she decided and stepped back from Tristan.

She pointed a finger at him. "Don't crowd, okay?"

He held up his hands like she'd turned a gun on him. "You'll never know I'm here," he replied.

Nodding, Kip cast a warm look at him then turned toward the sidewalk, hurrying up the block toward Pacific Blue Tattoo. The moment she stepped inside, old building smell tickled her nose, quickly covered by citrus and germicide. Seph sat in the receptionist's chair, twirling a thick black lock of her hair around her index finger. When Seph looked up, her mouth fell open.

"Gods!" She jumped up from the chair, rushing around the desk to touch Kip's hair. "What'd you do?" She shook her head, her face kind of scrunching up a little, like she was pissed or scared or something. Her hands snapped to her hips. "What did you do?"

"Bleached it," Kip said, turning. "Like it?"

Taku and Ross walked up front, neither of them having customers at the moment. Ross whistled at her.

"Nice, Kip," said Taku, smiling.

Both artists shrank back when they saw Seph's face. They quickly decided to go back to their stations. Her eyes were all dark and stormy now. Kind of like Tristan's had been when he'd first seen it, too.

"You can play coy all you want to," Seph shouted, pointing a finger at her. "But I know what you're doing. And let me tell you, it's crazy." She slapped her hands against the desk. "Just crazy!"

Kip shrugged. It was the best way she knew to trap this guy. She'd play the bait if it got her near enough to Sarah.

This guy had no idea what he'd get into if he grabbed her. He had no idea that he was the hunted one now. She was every bit the predator when she needed to be. She pressed her thumb to her right temple. The chip in her head proved that.

Sarah didn't have much time and neither did the other women that this guy had taken.

"Not so crazy," Kip said. She pulled Seph back behind the desk, out of Taku and Ross' earshot. "You need to understand just what I am, Seph." She gestured toward the picture window, at the hard-edged streets beyond it. "I'm not like those other women. Hell, I'm not like any women. I've got what it takes to face this guy one-on-one if I have to."

Seph rolled her eyes as she crossed her arms, stepping backward, her mouth all thin and pressed together. Seph thought she was all talk, that she was crazy or some other thing that discounted what she was.

But Kip knew. She knew the monster better than anyone. But for once, she needed that monster. Tonight, it was useful.

Only that part of her could face this demon.

"You're going to get yourself killed, Kip." Seph's voice was low and scary, like she knew the future. "This isn't a game. Why do you mortals play with your lives like hot coals?"

Kip felt the anger burn through her. "You think I'm playing? You think it's fun to have your sister in the hands of some twisted creep doing violent things to her? Maybe killing her at this very moment!"

Seph sighed, the frustration rising in her voice. "No, of course not! That's not what I meant."

She pressed her fingers against her forehead, closing her eyes a moment. Maybe she had a headache or maybe she knew she was wrong? Finally, Seph looked up, putting her hands on Kip's arms like she really gave a shit.

"This stuff is for keeps. And there isn't a lot of sunshine on the other side until you've earned it."

"Nobody knows that better than I do," said Kip. "So, either help me or get out of the way."

A lot of what Seph said didn't make a lot of sense, but Kip knew that wherever it came from, it came from the heart. She always knew where Seph stood. That's what she liked best about her.

Shaking her head, Seph squeezed Kip's arms then let go. "Tell me what you want me to do."

Kip let a tight smile touch her face as she thrust the bag at Seph. "These are your clothes, but I need to borrow them. Can you help me dress hot—like you?"

Her laugh brightened the place and the mood as she took the bag, sifting through its contents.

"Chanel, Versace, Vera Wang—you've got good taste," said Seph.

Kip shrugged. It had all been chance and a little help from Tristan. He didn't know it at the time.

She motioned Kip toward the back room. "Let's get something on you."

Following her back, Kip unbuttoned her blouse, tossing it onto the spool table. She shimmied out of her tan pants as Seph handed her a short, very sheer skirt. Pink. Kip hated pink, but Tristan liked it.

Anything for the Detective, she thought with a smile.

She sucked it up and slid on the skirt. It hung loose and straight halfway down, falling into silky, flared layers. Next, Seph handed her high-heeled shoes. They were tan and all straps. Lots of straps, all of them covered in glass jewels.

She pulled out a tight-fitting light grey blouse in some shiny fabric. Holding it up to Kip's shoulder, she gazed at it a moment then shook her head no.

Sorting through the other clothes, she came up with a sage colored camisole that she handed to Kip without a look. Kip pulled on the body-hugging material. It clung to her breasts and stomach. Seph's mouth fell open when she saw a blue dolphin on Kip's right shoulder.

"You got a tattoo? And you didn't let me do it?"

Kip rolled her eyes. "Relax, it's a temporary. If I like it, I'll call you."

Chuckling, Seph stepped back and studied Kip. Feeling self-conscious, Kip reached up and ran her fingers through her shoulder length hair, still smelling chemically despite Seph's watermelon shampoo.

"I pronounce you hot," she replied.

Kip took a few steps in the sandals and frowned. "These will destroy my feet before the night's over."

"I hope that's all," said Seph, just loud enough for Kip to hear it.

Ignoring her comments, Kip reached into the shopping bag and pulled out a thin, silver Sheer Desire box. She slid out the tube of sparkly lip gloss and wanded it across her lips, blotting them against each other. She was ready.

With Seph beside her, Kip returned to the reception desk and sat in the chair, barely able to cross her legs. The blue dolphin tattoo was bright on her shoulder. The phone rang almost immediately and Kip answered, giving out pricing info and requirements to some guy asking a bazillion questions about tattoos. When she finally hung up, she felt eyes staring at her. Glancing around the room, she caught Taku and Ross staring.

"What are you looking at?" she called to them.

Ross offered a crooked smile and returned to some design he was finalizing. Taku winked at her then buried his face in something on his phone. Dorks. Hadn't they seen a skirt before? The best look was from Nick who couldn't stop staring at her.

"You should dress up more often, Kip," he finally said as he walked past the desk to return a copy of *Wired* to the table. "You look beautiful."

Kip tried to hold back her smile, but couldn't. She'd never felt pretty before. And seeing that reflected back from the guys was kinda nice.

At ten 'til ten, one of Taku's usual clients walked in. A gruff looking guy with a beard and beady brown eyes, five minutes late as usual. The guy mumbled something about a bus and the heat, but stopped at the desk, looking Kip over. Taku was up at the desk with lightning speed and steered his client back to his station in the corner. Kip didn't like the guy's almost leering stare at her. Made her want to stomp around the desk and gut punch him. But Nick didn't like her assaulting the customers, so she just gave him a cold look and returned her gaze to the appointment book.

The Northwest Parcel guy would be here soon. She wondered if it would be Steve or Ben. She thought back to that night at the club when she'd run into that Parcel delivery guy. Seemed nice enough, smooth skin, nice eyes, and hint of a smile. Okay, he was definitely one to look at, someone to get sweaty with, but he wasn't Tristan.

Somehow, none of them compared to Tristan. Hell, they paled by comparison.

The bell on the front door chimed as it opened. Seph's ten o'clock —ten minutes early. The Goth chick, back to have the eagle finished. Her hair was bunched in a ponytail holder on top of her head, a small barbell through her left eyebrow and a silver ring in her nose. She slouched into a chair, her heavy shoes clumping against the wood floor. She wore a white blouse over a black camisole, sleeves rolled up, and black pants.

"Seph'll be right with you," said Kip.

She reached under the desk and flicked switch one on the rigged-up box by the phone. Nick had slopped together client lights at each artist's station. When the light turned on, they had a client waiting. It looked like Frankenstein, but it worked pretty well, she had to admit. For ancient, outdated tech. Why didn't he just use an app?

Seph clacked up to the desk, smiling as she motioned to the Goth chick.

"Rita? Come on back."

The Goth chick unfolded herself from the chair and stepped toward Seph who was already moving back to her station.

The front door bell clanked again as a tall guy walked in, carrying a big white cardboard box. Pale blue evergreen on a white label.

Kip's breath caught in her throat.

Another guy walked in behind him. Kip glanced up, excitement pounding in her throat. She licked her lip, her tongue tasting like petroleum jelly.

Both men wore the black uniforms of Northwest Parcel Post. One of them was tall. The other average height. The taller one had hard eyes, dark blue. He was attractive in a Tom Cruise kind of way, except for the faint acne scars on both cheeks, giving him a slightly rougher look than the other delivery guy. The other guy's face was smooth, his green eyes dull with boredom.

The taller guy paused at the desk, leaning on it with his clipboard. "Are you Persephone Hadis?" he asked Kip, smiling.

She looked him square in the face, deep into the stormy blue eyes. A hint of cruelty clung to his thin-lipped mouth, something rough and dark behind his eyes. He kept smiling at her, but it never reached his eyes that seemed more bored than anything. But he trained his gaze on hers, a deep lingering stare and Kip didn't look away. Like he was sizing her up somehow. She maintained her stare with steady strength as the monster awakened inside her.

"No. Are you Ben?"

He shook his head. "No." He pointed toward the shorter guy holding the cardboard box. "That's Ben. I'm just learning his route, before he goes on vacation next month."

A lie. She saw it in the widening of his pupils, heard it in the tone of his voice.

Kip nodded, pressing her sparkly lips together as she watched the driver called Ben handing Seph the package, having her sign for it and all. Kip's gaze flicked to the clipboard, trying to see the driver's name. An S taunted her, but she couldn't see anything else. He kept glancing at her, a polite enough smile on his face, but there was something else behind it, something murky and unknown.

Something dark, she realized. A monster, she speculated, one much worse than her own. One he was expert at hiding.

"You work here long?" he asked, his voice like warm butter.

"Almost a year," said Kip.

She tossed her blonde hair back deliberately.

"I'm Steven," he said, offering his hand.

Kip hesitated then shook his hand. Strong grip, thick hands almost deliberately overpowering. Killing soft.

"Steven, huh? Not Steve." Had these hands touched her sister? Strangled Carolee? Cut Terri Hayden's throat?

He frowned, shaking his head. "Steven."

"Nice to meet you, Steven," she said, watching Seph sign Ben's clipboard and set the white cardboard box down on a cabinet at her station.

"Everybody's got a name," he said, smiling seductively at Kip. "What's yours?"

Carolee. Grace. Sarah. She fought the urge to grit her teeth.

"Kim," she said, staring defiantly at him. He wouldn't have her real name, nothing personal, not even a nickname.

Her stare was piercing, unblinking until he finally glanced down at the counter, his hands fisting around his clipboard. He didn't like her strength. When he looked up, the anger had evaporated into all charm and poise. Something every serial killer needed to gain his victim's trust.

"Seeya around, Kim," he said and turned toward the other delivery guy as he walked toward the door.

His clipboard slid out of his hands and hit the maple floor. A test, Kip realized. She played the helpful woman, the victim of societal manners (things that sometimes, got women killed), and jumped up from her chair to pick up the clipboard. She fought hard not to glare at him, instead painting on an *I'm so helpful, please reward me for being so helpful* expression.

She struggled to put on that searching look, the one that needed his approval. She'd seen it on her mother's face for years.

"Here you go," she said in a soft voice, trying her best to sound meek and controllable.

"Thanks darlin'," he said, his hand brushing hers as he took the clipboard. "You're a sweetheart." His gaze fell to her cleavage, devouring her with his eyes as he inspected her like a New York strip at the meat counter. Kip wanted to punch his face.

"Any time," she answered, smiling at him, a little flirty.

He winked at her and followed the other driver out the door. She watched him walk outside, wondering what corner Tristan watched from and what he saw when a monster walked out the door.

Did he see it? Did he even feel it?

Kip recognized it in the microseconds of vacant stares and angry contemplations as the emotions played across his face. Saw it in the cruel gaze that changed to charming in an instant. Almost disturbing, but fascinating to her in a strange way. Looking at another monster was looking into her own face.

And she began to calculate how he would come for her.

17

10:03 P.M., September 2nd

TRISTAN SLOUCHED against the seat of his RAV4, watching Pacific Blue Tattoo's picture window where Kell sat like a siren to bait a predator. His pulse raced, his mouth dry. He kept a close watch, a careful eye on the scene.

He couldn't miss anything. Not now. Kell's life might depend on it.

He cursed himself for not standing up to her and ordering her not to do this. But he knew he had no control over her. Kell did as she pleased and she'd have sooner told him to go to hell if he'd even tried to force her. He picked up his Coke can and took a long drink, his gaze locked on Kell.

A late model black van drove up. Dodge Caravan. Washington Plates 935-GTU.

"Showtime, Keith," said Tristan, poking his partner who sat with eyes closed beside him.

St. James groaned and sat up. "Delivery drivers?"

Tristan nodded. "Two of them. That's strange."

"One in training maybe?" St. James offered as he laid a small pair of binoculars against his eyes.

"Maybe. Confirm the plate, will you?"

St. James read it off and it matched what Tristan had sighted in the growing darkness. The heat wasn't quite as oppressive at night, but it still clung to parked cars and streets. He tugged at his collar, wiping the beads of sweat off his upper lip as he watched one of the drivers lean against the reception desk where Kell sat.

"Something's going on at the desk," Tristan muttered.

"Relax, Bowker," said St. James, panning the building with his binocs. "He's just talking to her."

"He may be a killer."

"I know, but for now, chill—they're just talking."

Tristan exhaled through his nose, tapping his fingers against the armrest as he watched Kell and the delivery guy by the desk. St. James was right, of course, but he'd seen first-hand what this bastard had done to five women. He didn't want another woman—especially his woman—to be the sixth.

St. James popped open the passenger door.

"Where you going?" Tristan asked.

"A little sightseeing," he said and slipped across the street.

Under the cover of twilight, St. James crept up to the van, but Tristan couldn't watch him. He had to focus on Kell and the tattoo shop, had to catch any clues that surfaced, make sure she was safe. It was his job.

No, it was more than that. So much more than that.

Kell suddenly rose from her chair and hurried around the desk. She bent over in those skimpy clothes and he watched the bastard grope her with his eyes.

His fingers curled into fists.

When she straightened, she held something in her hand. A clipboard, he realized when she extended it to the delivery driver.

The driver moved in really close to her, a full half minute going by before he let go of her and stepped away.

Shit, they were leaving!

He scanned the street, the parked van for a sign of St. James, but when the drivers climbed into their van, St. James was nowhere to be found. Tristan sighed in relief, picking up his Coke again, a quick sip as the vehicle drove off. Seconds later, the passenger side door of his RAV4 popped open.

He jumped, startled.

"That was close," Tristan replied, casting a quick gaze at Kell who still sat behind the desk and then at his partner.

"No shit," he said with a huff. He took a moment to catch his breath.

"Find anything?"

St. James smirked as he laid his binoculars on the dashboard. "Just a couple of last names. Ben Lambert and..." He scrunched his eyes closed a moment. "Steven...Steven D. Platt."

Tristan slapped him on the shoulder. "Good work."

"Yeah, it was, wasn't it?" St. James snickered as he pulled out his phone. "Detective St. James. Yeah, need some names run. Need 'em in a hurry. One is Ben Lambert the other is Steven with a v as in Victor. Middle initial Delta. Last name Platt, no e. Yeah. Call me when you've got home addresses. Thanks. What? Bowker? He's right here with me. Yeah. One sec."

St. James handed him the phone. "The ME's been trying to get a message to you."

Tristan took the phone, pressing it hard against his ear. "Bowker."

"Detective, the Medical Examiner asked me to get this information to you ASAP," said a woman he recognized as Chelsea from Records.

"Go ahead," he answered.

"The substance, Rohypnol was found in one of the victim's bloodstreams."

"Which one?" Tristan asked, frowning.

"Grace Wells."

That didn't bode well for Sarah Thorpe. With a witness speculating on whether the girl was drugged, it was very likely that she'd been slipped something in her drink.

"Anything else?" he asked.

"One thing," the woman named Chelsea replied. "Something you'd asked about before...white petals found in one of the victim's hair?"

Tristan sat up straight, his fingers turning cold. "What'd they find?"

"The examiner didn't recognize the petals, so he consulted a local specialist on Seattle flora and fauna."

"And?"

"The ME said you had good eyes, Detective. The local specialist indicated that those petals were from a very rare tree in the Seattle area."

His heart beat faster. "How rare?"

"Very," Chelsea replied. "There's only one known tree left in the area, according to the specialists. He called it a—a double flowered catalpa."

He felt his heart beat up into his throat. "Where? Where does it grow?"

"In Ballard. Near Addams School."

Ballard. It was a brick against his temple. Terri Hayden had been found near the old Addams School, but no petals. Only the Eddleston woman had petals in her hair. What connection did the killer have with the school? It didn't make sense. First thing tomorrow, he'd check out the old Addams School again.

"Thanks, Chelsea."

"Have a good night, Bowker," Chelsea said and hung up.

He handed the phone back to St. James.

"What was all that about petals and trees?" St. James asked.

"Not sure," said Tristan, his brain already chewing on the data.

"There were white flower petals in the Eddleston woman's hair. Apparently, those petals come from only one tree in the area."

"Where?" his partner asked.

"In Ballard. Near where the Hayden woman was found." He sighed, pinching the bridge of his nose. "Was it coincidence or is the bastard still toying with us?"

St. James pulled out a folded piece of paper from his back pocket. He spread it out on the armrest as Tristan flipped on an overhead light. A map of Seattle, from southside to Shoreline. Five stars dotted the map like bread crumbs marking a trail. A trail that started near Pacific Blue Tattoo and ended in a hook below the Ballard locks.

Tristan felt the hot anger burn through him. What did it mean?

"What's close to Pacific Blue Tattoo?"

St. James gave him a funny look. "The Midnight Hour."

"What's close to Addams School?"

"Lots of stuff, Tris," said St. James with a groan. "It'd take us weeks to cover an area that size."

Tristan stared at the map. Two of the victims had been found near parks. Parks. He ran his index finger across the map, searching for green splotches that indicated parks.

The Locks to the south, Woodland Park to the east, and Discovery Park farther south. None of them more than ten minutes from the school. One of the bodies had been found near Woodland Park.

There was a piece missing here and he had to find it.

His thoughts moved to Kell and his heart beat into his throat. He had to find it fast. He opened the door to his SUV and stepped out, the air warm and heavy. He was sweating already. St. James climbed out behind him and together, they walked into Pacific Blue Tattoo.

18

10:18 P.M., September 2nd

KIP FELT ALL FUNNY INSIDE, excited when Tristan appeared at the door, but the feeling turned to revulsion when his partner followed behind him. Her mood turned instantly dark. Tristan walked up to the desk, a smile tugging at the corners of his mouth.

What was he smiling about?

He leaned over the desk and she lightly kissed him on the lips. He smelled like cedar and warm car, the sugary taste of Coke on his lips.

"Everything all right in here?" he asked in a quiet voice, his gaze only on her.

She nodded, casting a sideways glance at St. James. "One of the delivery drivers—I think you should look closer at him."

St. James slid up next to Tristan and Kip stiffened, but the arrogant sneer wasn't there. Surprised, she let herself relax, watching him, waiting for his next move.

"I got their names," St. James said almost under his breath. "Which one you want us to check out?"

Kip squinted at him, feeling a little off guard. The helpful St. James? He hadn't seen this side of Tristan's partner. "Steven," she said, watching his expression.

"Platt, no e," said St. James. He looked her right in the eye when he said it. Like she was a real person. She was impressed. "Look, Thorpe—you've been a big help and I appreciate it." He motioned at her hair. "And I gotta say you're the bravest chick I've ever met. Just don't get dead for Bowker, okay? See, he's got this thing for you and I'd hate to see it get messed up."

He almost smiled, but looked away before it could touch his face.

What an ego, Kip thought with a smile. She knew he had a reputation to maintain. Still, he was being nice for once, not even threatening her with jail this time.

"Thanks, St. James. That means a lot from you."

He chuckled, leaning his elbows on the desk. "You got that right, Lady."

When she glanced at Tristan, his expression had turned dark and he seemed a million miles away. In a moment, though, he looked at her with those patient hazel eyes, but tonight, she saw the embers burning beneath them. He was deeply troubled and she hated thinking she was partly to blame. She laid her hand on his sleeve, caressing his forearm.

"You okay?" she asked.

He forced a laugh (fake—he sucked as an actor) then nodded. "So, what happens next?"

Is this the part where you get yourself killed?

She could almost hear him saying it, frowning, his stomach in knots. She sighed. She wasn't used to guys who actually felt things.

"You can't stay here," she said. "I know he'll be watching the place soon."

Watching me, she wanted to say, but didn't.

Learning her routine, finding out where she went after work.

That was half his fun. Planning the capture. She was prey now; she'd seen it in his eyes. He loved the hunt. She'd make that part easy on him because she wanted him to take her to the others.

He'd be damned sorry when he did though. That was a promise.

Tristan turned around, glancing out the picture window, at the occasional car or bus that passed by. People on the street who slipped past. He was nervous and it showed. He licked his lips. His eyes flicked back and forth. With a thumb pressed to his temple, he rubbed his forehead with his fingers.

She moved around the desk and slid her arms around him, holding him against her. She felt the slamming of his heart that jarred his chest with every beat.

"I don't want you to do this," he said in a soft voice, barely above a whisper.

St. James had wandered over to Seph's station and was talking to her while she worked. The Goth chick seemed annoyed, but kept quiet.

"I'm sorry. I have to."

"What if you're overpowered? What if we can't find you in time? What if you're—"

His voice choked off in his throat and he couldn't finish the sentence. He looked away, toward the window, his eyes narrowing.

Then it hit her and she felt even more guilty, a gnawing pain rising in her stomach. His father had been murdered and now, she was putting him in this horrible position again. Somehow, she had to give him peace of mind.

"What about one of those anklets that track your movements? Like I had to wear for a year."

She watched the idea blast through his thoughts, his whole demeanor changing. The life came back into him. "A GPS anklet! Maybe that would give us the edge?" He kissed her hard on the lips and she felt some of his tension ebb.

"I've gotta get back to work," she whispered in his ear. "Nick's just dying to fire me."

He let go of her and motioned at St. James who trotted back over. He pointed at Kip. "Two A.M. Scrambled eggs and cheese. Your place. I'll bring the jewelry."

She smiled. "I'll be there."

Suddenly, he got all serious again. "What if you're not?" he asked in a quiet almost pained voice.

The question stabbed at her stomach. What if she wasn't? It was a good question.

Kip let out a hard breath, a hand on her hip. "If I'm not, then you damn well better find me. Before I get to him, because I guarantee you there won't be much left of the guy when I'm done."

With a determined nod, he stepped out into the night and Kip felt a little queasy seeing him go.

19

10:32 P.M., September 2nd

THE COUNTDOWN to eleven o'clock began.

Taku and Ross had a stream of clients tonight. Persephone worked steadily on two college girls: a brunette and a redhead, each one getting a watercolor tattoo on their forearms.

Kip heard them whispering about the downtown murders, acting all excited like it was so cool to get a tattoo because of it. Like they were living on the edge or something. Idiots. She wondered why these two hadn't already been thinned from the herd.

No dumber than she was, she realized. Dying her hair and slapping on a temporary tattoo as bait. It was fun to live on the edge as long as you weren't in any danger of falling off (or getting your throat cut).

But at least, she knew what was down there. At the bottom.

Her mother called around 10:45 P.M., asking for any news. She sounded exhausted and Kip felt a pang of regret, knowing exactly what the woman was going through.

She gave her a little information about a lead, someone who saw Sarah. That seemed to brighten up her voice a bit. She even thanked Kip, hanging up a little less agitated. She rarely watched anything but the local news and Kip hoped that she hadn't hear about the situation in Seattle.

As the days wore on, Kip knew she was bound to find out. Not from her though, she decided.

At five 'til eleven, the two girls paid for their tattoos and left the store, climbing into a silver Sebring convertible and speeding off into the night. Kip hoped they'd make it home.

Seph walked up and leaned on Kip's arm. "Got a minute?" she asked, waving at Taku then Ross as they left for the night. Nick sat in his office with the door open, radio blaring.

"Sure, what's up?"

"I need you to come with me somewhere."

Kip frowned. "Where? What do you mean?"

Seph exhaled hard. "It's a place—kind of between places."

Between places? What was that about? Kip shook her head. "I don't get it. What's between places?"

She flapped her arms against her sides, looking kind of flustered. That wasn't like Seph. She wasn't the kind of chick that got flustered.

"Don't judge, okay?" Her voice had a knife edge. "Just trust me and come out to the alley." She turned on her Prada's and flounced into the back room.

Kip groaned as she went to the windows and let down the wheat grass shades. She turned out the neon blue "open" sign and locked the door.

"Nick!" she called. He looked up from his paperwork, turning down the radio blaring Soundgarden's Black Hole Sun. "We're going out the back."

"Careful out there, Kip," he replied, pointing at his hair.

For Nick, that was actually nice.

She waved and hurried out the back with her backpack on her

shoulder. She'd stuffed her clothes inside along with those Sheer Desire samples she wanted to try on Tristan tonight.

Seph stood out in the alley waiting on her.

"Okay, where's this place you're talking about," Kip replied.

"No matter what happens, you follow me, okay? You'll know when."

Kip crossed her arms, the strap of her backpack sliding down as Seph began to singsong in some language Kip didn't recognize. Then her words shifted to recognizable ones.

"Dear Hecate, we stand beneath an ebony moon." She waved her arm in the air. "Show us the crossroads."

Ebony moon? Kip squinted at the sky. There was no moon. At first, a light breeze rustled through the sweltering alley and it felt good on Kip's face. She turned into the coolness and would have sworn she heard voices.

When she looked ahead, three pathways appeared: one gravel, one dirt, and one asphalt. In the middle of them stood a tall, thin woman with wavy black hair tied at her neck and a shimmery dress, all silver and kind of like smoke. Two big dogs lay at her feet, their fur short and silky. Dogs that looked like that famous William Wegman poster of the dog in roller skates. She smiled, cupping her hand in the air a moment, then she turned her gaze to Seph and motioned at her.

Seph started toward the woman, but stopped and clamped her hand on Kip's wrist.

"Hey!"

Without a word, Seph lurched forward, dragging Kip down the asphalt path to the center where tall grass grew. With a yawn, the dogs stretched out in the grass, ignoring them. When Kip glanced behind her, the alley—the city—was gone.

"He won't see you, Persephone," said the woman, arms folded against her stomach. "He's furious at you staying behind."

Seph's jaw tightened. "Mr. Persistence himself has given up? Then he really has lost all feeling for me."

The woman clicked her teeth. "What do you expect, Persephone? He's respecting your decision."

"Hades?" She blurted out. "As if. I remember a man blind with passion, kidnapping me under my own mother's nose. He never gives anything up unless it suits him."

Kip frowned. "The guy kidnapped you?"

Seph ignored her comment. "If he loved me, Hecate, he'd have come after me and told me as much."

"You've hurt him," the woman called Hecate replied. "He's not left his room since you came to the gate."

"Fine," said Seph, turning around. "We'll leave then." She grabbed Kip's arm again and started down the asphalt path.

Kip nearly fell twice in Seph's high-heeled Chanel's. God, she missed her Converse's about now.

"Persephone, wait—I'll talk to him."

Seph grinned behind her back. "I knew he wouldn't let me go without seeing me," she said in a whisper.

"Who's he?"

"Hades," she replied. "My husband."

"Hades? You mean like Hell? Look, Seph, I'm not into devil worship or anything."

Seph laughed, moving back up the asphalt. "No, no—he's not a demon. He's a god. He looks after the dead, shepherding them to penance or rest. Hades is a caretaker, nothing more." She snorted. "Demon. I wish he had that much fire in him, but he seems more ambivalent than hot. Or cold."

Kip shrugged. None of this made any sense to her. Not that all of Seattle suddenly disappearing made any sense either.

"Didn't you read your mythology in high school?"

"I was rarely in class," Kip said with a shrug. "Mostly in detention, so I didn't do much homework."

"You don't remember Zeus and Hera? Apollo and Athena?" She fluffed up her hair a bit. "Me? Persephone?"

Kip rolled her eyes. "I vaguely remember stuff about Greek gods."

She cocked a hand on her hip. "And I'm not buying that you're some kind of god, Seph, so knock it off."

"Goddess," Seph corrected her with a click of her tongue.

"Whatever."

"Take the dirt path," said a voice, a smooth-sounding guy's voice, but Kip didn't see anyone.

"He speaks," said Seph, staring up at the sky.

There was sky now. Kip blinked and glanced above her head at the brilliant blue with white puffy clouds skimming past. Like time was racing by. Everything smelled clean, like it had just rained.

"It's kind of spooky here," said Kip. Wherever here was.

"This way," Seph replied, motioning her past the woman with the dogs.

Kip snickered, picturing them in roller skates, and followed Seph.

The farther down the path they walked, the darker the sky became. Shadows crept closer as they walked across a meadow of wildflowers. They smelled like baby powder as Seph bent down and picked a white lily. She pressed it to her nose, inhaling deeply.

"Eleusis," Seph said out loud. "You *are* a romantic."

And suddenly it was night, a full moon overhead, burning cold on the greying grasses that were bald in some spots, volcanic rock poking up as everything sloped downward. Into some rocks. And a cave. But there hadn't been a moon tonight.

"We're going in there, aren't we?" Kip replied, scrunching her face into a frown.

"Duh. He is the god of the underworld. That's why it starts with *under*."

"I'm cool with you going to see your man and all, but remind me about the part that actually involves me."

Kip side-stepped a crevice, the heel of one shoe pinching between two rocks for a moment. She stumbled a few steps forward then got her balance back. These heels sucked, no matter how much they cost.

"Because of your connection to her and the recentness of her death…well, I thought maybe you could talk to Carolee."

Kip stopped in mid-stride. "Talk to Carolee? Are you high? She's dead. I can't just go talk to her somewhere!"

Seph shook her head. "You can with the queen of the underworld at your side. Look, it'll only be for a few moments, before she moves on to her rest. You won't be able to ask much, so think before you speak."

Sure, no problem. She was used to interviewing dead people. She was so not telling Tristan about this.

Ahead, a humongous chain lay on a path that wound toward a dark gate, slightly ajar. Kip wondered what was at the end of that chain and the harness that attached to it. What kind of huge-ass dog had that thing held?

A tall, wiry guy with sandy-colored hair like Tristan's stood on the path. He wore a white button-down and brown pants. He had bright brown eyes, a chiseled nose, and full lips. Not at all bad to look at. He carried himself like he was someone important, like royalty, but there was gentleness and some distance about him. Like he was either sullen or just didn't care. His pupils dilated when he saw Persephone and he drew in a quick breath.

"You asked that I come to the gate a second time and once again, I can't deny you."

"If only that were true," said Seph, her eyes kind of watery.

She was gone for the guy. It burned in her face. This guy was no idiot. He had to see it.

His gaze fell to Kip and all she could do was stare at him. "I put Cerberus inside to sleep. To protect your friend."

Kip swallowed hard. Had to be much worse than dogs on roller skates.

"Thank you," said Seph. She was quiet a moment then spoke up. "As you no doubt, already know, my friend here needs your help."

He raised his eyebrows at her. "The living need *my* help? How can I help you?"

"Hades, a friend of hers was murdered and the beast is still loose."

He shook his head, a sad look making his brown eyes all droopy looking. "I have no hold over the living." His eyes darkened quickly. "But I've seen many of those predators in my halls and I've sent them down accordingly."

"What she needs is information," Seph continued. "If you could allow her friend a moment with Kip, it might help find the killer. Before he kills any other mortals."

His gaze drifted to Seph and he seemed deep in thought.

"Why, Persephone?" he said finally. "You break my heart and then ask favors of me? Why shouldn't I just walk away?"

Seph moved toward him, taking his hands in hers. His eyes snapped closed and he seemed lost in her touch for a moment.

"Because you love me."

He shook his head, a pained expression on his face.

"Because you know I love you."

His mouth fell open a little as he opened his eyes to stare at her.

"Win me back, Hades. Make me want to return to you." She nodded at Kip behind her. "Start by helping her."

His eyes narrowed a moment, the thoughts racing across his face.

"If I help her, will you return home?"

"No," Seph said with a groan. "Don't turn it into a bargain. Don't force me to return and ruin what little hope we have left. Together, we're as cold as this cavern. I want the warmth back—the heat. Not the indifference."

"What do you leave me?" He thrust out his hands. "A dim hope that maybe—someday you might come home to me. No, it's got to be more." He reached out and cupped her chin in his hand. "I'm asking you as a lover, come home to me. I will help your friend, but please...I don't want an eternity without you."

Seph bit her lip, her eyes so watery they might drop tears at any moment. But she sucked it up. Held it all in, nodding at him.

"Roses wouldn't hurt," Kip said to him with a wink. "Riding in on a white horse wouldn't suck either."

To her surprise, he smiled, his eyes brightening a bit. He stepped toward her, laying a hand gently on her shoulder. Kind of a paternal touch that was nice.

"I'll bring her here to speak with you. These few days have been difficult for her because of the way she passed from the earth. I've comforted her as much as I can, but perhaps a few moments with a familiar face might help?" He pointed at the ground. "Wait here. I won't be long."

Kip hobbled around the damp, rocky passage in Seph's Chanel's, the thin material of her skirt and camisole letting the cavern's cold dampness seep into her bones. It was nearly a hundred degrees in Seattle and here she was freezing.

"He's a good man," said Seph to break the silence.

"Then why won't you go back to him?" Kip asked.

Seph glared at her, making Kip grin.

A faint glow emanated from the black gates ahead as Hades stepped through the opening, a woman in pale blue walking beside him, arms hugging her body, her blue eyes intense against her pale skin.

Carolee.

Kip felt the gnawing begin in the pit of her stomach. Carolee wore some kind of blue top and pants and Kip wondered if that was the last thing she'd been wearing when she died. She seemed shell-shocked and Kip felt like her heart had been smashed, knowing she'd been through some kind of hell. Hades kept an arm around her shoulders, kind of cradling and protecting her at the same time.

"Carolee?" Kip called and ran toward her, turning her ankle only once.

She reached out and touched Carolee's hand and saw the teal and purple drama mask on her arm. It was the last image of Carolee she remembered. Maybe that's why she still saw the tattoo?

"Kip?" Her haunted gaze turned toward Kip as Hades stepped back from her.

Kip couldn't stand it any longer. She threw her arms around Carolee.

"You feel so warm," Carolee muttered. "I'd forgotten what warm skin felt like."

"I'm so sorry," Kip choked out, feeling tears ringing her eyes and clinging to her eyelashes. "I'm so sorry for what happened."

"The warmth, it feels so good." She held Kip out at arm's length. "I miss the warmth, you know?"

Hades reached out and touched her shoulder. "You'll feel it again soon. You went through a terrible thing, but when you're ready to reach for the warmth, it'll be there. His promise."

She smiled, but the paleness remained. Of course, she was pale, Kip reminded herself. She was dead.

"Carolee, the guy who did this to you...please, I need to find him. He has others. Help me stop him."

She shook her head, the smile fleeing. "I—I didn't know him. His face." She shuddered and Kip slid her arm around Carolee's waist.

"Scars? Did he have scars?"

"He'd had acne once," she replied, staring past Kip. "I saw the scars."

"Good! That helps! Names—did he say any names? Mention any places? Where you were kept—anything?"

Carolee shook her head slowly, her gaze tracking off toward Hades. She was in deep shock, even in death.

"It was so dark." She held out a hand. "Like this place."

"Underground?" Kip asked.

Carolee nodded. "Couldn't move around. So dark. It was always so quiet, except for the birds, the wind chimes—and his digging. And singing." She pressed her hands to her ears. "Digging and singing until I thought I'd go crazy!"

Dark. Underground. Digging? Wind chimes? Where could that have been? She felt her pulse pounding. Was it Seattle's underground? Seattle was such a huge city though—it could be anywhere. "Singing what? What was the song?" Kip cast an uncertain look at Persephone.

"I ate twinkies," she replied.

"The song, Carolee—do you remember it? Any of it?"

"Sleep baby sleep. Forever mine to keep." She looked at Kip, no emotion on her face. "That's what he kept singing."

"Where did he take you, Carolee? Did he drug you?"

Carolee shook her head. "I don't remember. She was there first. I heard her screams. It's all grown so fuzzy. I want it to disappear—all of it."

She stepped back from Kip and moved back to Hades.

"Please let it fade," she begged Hades. "I'm tired of the pain. I want to sleep now."

He smiled at her, laying a hand against her blonde hair. "She's ready to go on, now."

Not yet. She was the only witness. Why couldn't she tell her more? "My sister, Carolee!" she blurted out. "He has my sister."

Carolee's eyes widened and she turned around. For several agonizing moments, Carolee stared at her.

"He buried us in the ground until he wanted to touch us," she said, her voice achingly sober. "Not far from Seattle. The drive wasn't long. At times, no one seemed to be around for miles. But when I heard voices nearby, the wind chimes hid our screams. There were others...I heard them. Felt them nearby, but the wind chimes. Hundreds of wind chimes. Blocked out everything."

"The Sheer Desire," said Kip, knowing she was running out of time. "There was cocaine in the boxes."

She nodded. "Rudy's. Arctic Nights—special order. I found out too late," she said and turned toward the gate, walking away. Hades followed, a comforting, guiding hand around her shoulders.

Time to pay Rudy Weatherford another visit. But Carolee's words nagged at her.

Wind chimes. Hundreds of wind chimes.

Where in Seattle was there a place with hundreds of wind chimes? And a place where no one was around for miles? A place where women were buried under the ground. She sucked in a bitter breath. Including her sister.

20

11:11 P.M., September 2nd

KIP SUDDENLY FOUND herself outside the back door to Pacific Blue Tattoo, no moon overhead, and the heat softer in the alley. Had that all been a dream, she wondered?

When she looked up, Seph's VW bug was parked on the cross street and Seph leaned against it, waiting. It was a pale mint green.

Kip hurried toward it. "Seph, why isn't your car ever the color I remember?" She climbed in the passenger seat.

"Because I change it whenever it bores me," she said with a shrug, her bracelets clanking as she climbed into the driver's seat. Her spicy perfume filled the car, making Kip want to play Led Zeppelin's *Kashmir*.

"You can drop me at The Midnight Hour," Kip muttered, leaning back in the seat, grateful not to be feeling the burn in the balls of her feet from Seph's expensive heels.

Seph shook her head. "Drop you nothing. I'm coming, too."

"You can't!" Kip felt the anger churn up.

Seph would ruin everything.

"Relax," Seph said, turning left practically on two wheels. "I'm not coming in with you. I'll just be in there, okay? How can you object to someone watching your back?"

Kip smiled. She couldn't.

"Thanks, Seph. I owe you."

She shook her head. "Nah, mortals are a blast. Thanks for the ride."

Seph pulled up two blocks before the club.

"Seeya inside," she replied and slipped out of the bug and walked down the street, away from the banged up red door.

Kip sat there for a moment or two, then opened her purse. Inside was the drink safe test card she'd picked up earlier. A couple of drops on the colored circles would tell her if her drink was spiked. Like the bastard had spiked Sarah's Diet Coke. The drink test was all she'd need.

With a deep breath, she stepped out of the VW and hurried up the street. More like hobbled, but she got there faster than she'd expected. She straightened up, shaking out her skirt and approached the bouncer with his tattooed sleeves and pierced eyebrows.

His gaze widened when he saw Kip and when he saw the tattoo on her shoulder, he smiled.

"Nice tat."

Kip smiled. "Thanks."

"Acropolis do it?"

"No, Pacific Blue."

He nodded his approval. "Good shop. You know Ross? He did this grizzly." The guy pointed to a grizzly bear, paw raised, on his right forearm. Ross was a master at wildlife. The bear looked like it might stand up and walk away.

"Yeah, he's great."

The guy was all smiles now as he opened the creaky red door and ushered her into the club with its throbbing bass, flashing lights, and thumping dance floor. It vibrated through her, taming a bloom of nerves as she sauntered into the club. The floor felt movie theatre sticky, the smell of spilled beer and sweet alcohol hung in the air.

Instantly, eyes were on her as she strutted her way to the bar. It almost felt nice to be noticed, but she remembered that Tristan had noticed her without the expensive clothes and blonde hair.

The guy at the bar was Greg. She remembered him from the night when that other bartender told her about the guy with Sarah. She slid onto an empty oil drum chair, some Lady Gaga remix pounding through the place.

"Hello," said Greg with a big sloppy smile. He stared, no—leered at her.

Dude, get a cocktail napkin to sop up the drool.

"What'll ya have, sweet thing?"

Sweet thing? He'd think sweet thing when she drilled her right Chanel heel into his nuts.

"Tanqueray and tonic," she said in a neutral voice.

"You got it," he said, practically licking her hand. He'd be licking a fist next.

Slowly, she turned around on the oil drum stool, scanning the room. On the dance floor, a tall, coal-haired woman danced with a dark-haired tanned guy. Even though she'd changed her clothes to a simple black dress, blending in a little, Seph still stood out anywhere.

Kip's mouth fell open when she recognized the guy and a slow burn started down her arms. Keith St. James. Dressed in jeans and blue button-down shirt. That meant Tristan was nearby somewhere. They'd all planned this behind her back.

If she hadn't been so impressed, she'd have been really mad.

She glanced around the room, searching the crowds, the edges of the dance floor. Wanting to catch a glimpse of Tristan.

She wanted much more than that, but it would have to wait 'til later.

"That'll be fifteen bucks."

She turned back to the smarmy bartender, barely hiding her

anger as she dug a twenty out of the purse at her waist. He handed her five one-dollar bills and she two, waving off the rest.

"Thanks, sweetheart."

Sweetheart? Kip ground her teeth together and cursed as she picked up her glass and took a sip of the dry drink. It had kind of a pine scent to it, one she'd developed a taste for over the last year or so.

Across the room, where the booths and tables hugged the wall, Rudy Weatherford with his weasel face and expensive tan suit sat laughing with two women, one with brassy blonde hair and over-tanned mahogany skin. Her face had already begun to wrinkle and sag from too much sun and her pink eye shadow practically glowed in the dark.

The other woman, thin and dressed in white capris and a red blouse, her dishwater blonde hair cut short like a boy's, laughed like a hyena. But the woman that drew her attention walked out of the shadows to throw her arms around Weatherford's neck.

Heart-shaped face. Heavy set. Faux auburn hair bobbed around her chin.

Kip felt cold dread hit the pit of her stomach and she took another sip of Tanqueray.

Freida Mason. What did *that* mean? She'd acted like she hadn't even known Weatherford. Maybe she was Weatherford's mule, but ol' Freida had a little herd of her own.

Several of the little silver Sheer Desire boxes lay on the table. In front of Weatherford and she couldn't help but wonder if one or two of those were Arctic Nights body talc. Er, cocaine.

Kip picked up her drink and carried it away from the bar, toward the other side of the room. Some dance song with French words rumbled through the place as she weaved her way through a group of people hanging on the edge of the dance floor. One guy bumped her, grinning, and asked her to dance, but she politely waved him off.

Brown eyes. No acne scars. Not tonight. She thought of Tristan. Not ever.

She sat down at a table beside Weatherford and his entourage, listening to their conversation which consisted of a lot of sexual jokes and come-ons. She smelled his heavy, almost perfumy cologne and wanted to gag.

Weatherford leaned back in his chair, hands clasped behind his back, grinning like a gargoyle as the women chattered like sparrows. But when he saw Kip walk past, he folded himself back into his chair, watching her with a wolfish look. The other woman suddenly looked all pissed off and cast glares at Kip who just smiled and sipped her Tanqueray.

"That's quite a tattoo you've got there, young lady," he called to her, motioning toward her shoulder.

She smiled her sweetest smile, hiding the *go to hell* look deep inside.

"Thanks, it's kinda new," she answered.

Nothing but dagger looks from the wrinkle queen. Hyena woman looked disgusted and stared into her martini, flicking the olive around in quick, angry strokes. But not Freida. Freida sat down at Weatherford's table and looked directly at her. Kip faced her square on.

If she was going to recognize Kip, it would be now.

Not a flicker of recognition in her eyes. Freida didn't recognize her as the woman she'd just pitched a Sheer Desire sales job to at a Starbucks.

Kip let out a quick breath, relieved.

"This your first time in the Midnight Hour?" Weatherford asked, licking his lips. He had to be in his fifties, had a weekend boat tan, and thinning hair.

She nodded oh so sweetly, staring shyly at him over her drink. "All my friends come here."

"Glad to hear that," he said, still grinning at her. "Tell 'em to keeping coming in. We take good care of our patrons."

Like you took good care of Sarah? Sending her out in the night, drugged, and on the arm of a serial killer.

Kip felt the anger tremble in her fingers and she gripped the edge of her chair to hold it back.

Ol' Freida looked downright vicious, nearly baring her teeth. She reached up to her bobbed hair, twisting it around her finger, her other hand tapping against the table.

Weatherford grabbed one of the silver boxes and tossed it onto Kip's table.

"What's this?" she asked, setting down her drink.

She picked up the slender box. Glitter glow lip gloss was written in tiny white letters on the end flap, the oh, too familiar Sheer Desire script on the side of the silver box.

"A new beauty product my wife sells," he replied, gesturing at Freida.

Kip had to work hard to hold in her surprise. Freida and Weatherford were married?

"First one's free," he said with a wink, still all smiles.

Freida was digging her nails into the table's edge, a forced, angry smile pasted there. Jealous as hell. He pointed at the box in Kip's hand as she opened it. "That's her new glitter gloss. Try it out. Show it to your friends. Freida's name's on the box to order more."

Kip opened the gloss and seductively swiped the wand across her bottom lip and then both sides of her upper lip, her gaze not leaving Weatherford's face. His leering smile widened. She licked her lips then smiled at Weatherford, nearly launching ol' Freida across the room.

"How's it look?" she asked, pouting for him.

"Damned hot, honey," he said, staring at her just a little too long. "Hell, if I wasn't married—"

Freida cleared her throat, her mouth pressed into a tight, thin line, her eyes dark and angry. Kip just smiled sweetly at her.

"I think I've used this product before," said Kip, her gaze flitting from Weatherford to Freida. "From my friend, Carolee, God rest her soul," Kip said, her gaze flicking upward. "I bought some from her. We went to high school together."

Freida's anger fled, quickly replaced by a sad almost frightened expression. Almost fake, but Kip wasn't sure.

"Terrible thing that happened to her," said Weatherford, shaking his head. He looked kind of sick about it, not guilty or scared, disgusted. Not the look she'd expected.

Kip nodded. "She told me about this lip gloss." She stared at the tube in her hand. "But I didn't get a chance to order it from her. I tried some of the other products though." Her gaze flicked to Freida. Wait for it. "My favorite was the Arctic Nights talc."

Freida's mouth drooped, bobbed open a little as Weatherford straightened up in his chair.

Kip took another drink of her Tanqueray as she watched Freida exchange a worried look with Weatherford. He kind of snapped a quick nod at her, motioning toward the bar and she gave the faintest nod, slipping away from the table.

"So, you bought Sheer Desire from Carolee?" Weatherford asked, laughing nervously.

"All the time," said Kip, pressing her lips together.

She glanced toward the dance floor. There was Seph still dancing with St. James, who wasn't a bad dancer. He kept up with the music's furious beats as well as Seph's moves and it was obvious he had the hots for her. But Seph was still in love with her man. She was friendly to St. James, but kept her distance.

By the time she'd answered a bunch of questions from Weatherford about the beauty products, she'd finished her drink. She excused herself, thanking Weatherford again for the lovely lip gloss and returned to the bar for a Sprite.

Greg was oh, so happy to wait on her, but still managed to charge her the price of a twelve-pack for one lousy Sprite. She paid, tipping him well, then nursed the Sprite along as she watched the room, looking for anything out of place, anything or anyone watching her.

Then he walked in.

Ben Lambert. Dressed in the black pants and black polo with Northwest Parcel Pickup evergreen on the pocket. Package in his hand. But the moment he stepped into the room, Freida Mason grabbed his arm, stroking it a little and then pulled him onto the dance floor. She chattered away at him and he not so discreetly glanced her way once or twice.

Looked like ol' Freida had a regular delivery schedule with the Northwest boys, apparently handling lots of Arctic Nights, Kip imagined. And something else.

Just for a moment, she caught sight of Tristan near the DJ spinning tunes in the back. Like, St. James, he wore jeans. His jaw was stubbled with the first traces of beard, his hair kind of messy. He wore a black Nirvana t-shirt and Kip smiled, remembering making love to him on the couch underneath her Nirvana poster. She wished they were there right now.

A hand touched her shoulder. She turned.

A blond guy with a pony tail and baggy jeans. "Nice tattoo," he replied, smiling at her. "You wanna dance?"

Kip nodded, setting down her Sprite. Why not. It was a good way to watch Freida and Lambert, maybe even catch a sentence or two of what they were squabbling about.

The ponytail guy held out his slender hand and she took it, letting him lead her out onto the floor. They danced to an old song, *Dirrty*, the heavy beat throbbing in her ears. It was too loud to hear Lambert and Freida. In a moment or two, they hurried off the dance floor, disappearing into the crowd surrounding the bar. Ponytail boy was a good dancer, turning and moving with the beat. He smelled like leather and sage. Kip had good rhythm too and played off him well, her body feeling fluid against the steady drumbeats.

She danced to another song that she didn't know and then thanked the guy for the dances. She returned to the oil drum stool where she'd left her Sprite. She picked it up and tipped it to her lips, but stopped.

Damn. She'd left her drink unattended.

She tilted the glass just enough to spill it. Sticky Sprite coated the glass and dribbled onto the concrete floor, including her fingers, as she opened her purse.

Grabbing the drink test card.

With a few drops clinging to her fingertips, she touched the green test spot, then the yellow one, smearing the green spot again. Quickly, she pulled out a tissue and pretended to blot a spot on her skirt. A quick look at the card showed blue and pink spots.

She felt a little cold. And angry. Her drink had been drugged.

Anger flushed her face as she glanced around the room, at the sea of faces, most of them innocent bystanders.

Had Greg the bartender dropped something in it? Maybe one of ponytail boy's friends? Or even Freida.

No sign of Miss Sheer Desire or Lambert.

Did Freida have something going on under the covers with Lambert, she wondered. It could have been anybody.

She picked up her drink again and pretended to drink it. Seph and St. James were still on the dance floor, the growing crowd swallowing them up. She looked around for Tristan again, but he'd faded back into the crowd.

For a moment, surrounded by all these people, she felt incredibly alone.

With a sigh, she pretended another sip of her drink and tipped it under the bar when no one was looking to dump part of it out. She waited five minutes then ten, ordering another Sprite. Her mouth felt dry, so she guzzled this one, leaning heavily on the bar. She laid her head in her hands, pretending to be a little dazed, wondering if someone had noticed. Finally, she laid her head against the bar.

"Hey, you okay?" Greg the bartender.

"I'm fine. Just a little dizzy."

"Let me get you some water," he said and quickly set a cold glass of water in front of her.

God, she was thirsty. She pressed the glass to her lips and drank it down, the cool water feeling so good against her hot throat.

Had she gotten some of that crap in her system? She cursed and continued to drink.

"Looks like you could use some air," said someone beside her.

"I'm fine," Kip snapped.

"No, really, your face is all flushed."

She looked up, expecting Ponytail Boy with his baggy jeans and thin hands, but Steven Platt sat beside her on another oil drum. The acne scars were as visible as the shark-like expression in his dead, hungry eyes.

She started to reach for his face, wanting to tear it off, but something sharp gouged her thigh. Her gaze fell.

He grinned at her, a hypodermic needle wedged between his fingers.

"No..." she mumbled through thick lips. "No!"

"Should have drunk your Sprite like a good girl," he said, stroking her hair, running a hand down her left arm.

"No...stp."

The words wouldn't come, no matter hard she tried.

"But good girls don't get tattoos, do they?"

He gritted his teeth, anger glinting in his blue eyes. His lips were against her ear and she smelled the sweet stink of Jim Beam on his breath, sweating from his body. "Good girls don't bleach their hair and pick up guys in bars either."

Her limbs were heavy, unresponsive. She cursed at him, but her lips wouldn't form the words.

He was against her now, smelling like fresh earth and musk. Sweet, gagging musk. He took her cell phone and laid it on the bar.

She wretched as he pulled her off the oil drum and led her past the dance floor.

She struggled against sluggish muscles, but nothing responded. Nothing moved as he led her out the red metal door. He mumbled to the bouncer about how she'd had too much to drink.

"No...stp. Ki-r."

"Sleep baby sleep," he cooed, stroking her hair as he led her to a black van. "Forever mine to keep."

The song! Carolee said he'd sung some song.

"Yr...ded," she struggled, slurring badly.

She couldn't control it, but the words rang through her thoughts like a mantra.

You're dead, she muttered over and over. Before this was over, she'd see him dead. At her hands.

Kip dragged her feet, struggling against the drug, against his hold, against the big mistake she'd made. She hadn't expected the needle.

But nothing responded except her heart hammering against her rib cage, in time to the song echoing behind her with its fierce drum beat. Then the words hissed above the bass, *sleep, baby sleep*. More drums and bass. *Forever mine to keep*.

Kip cringed. It was a stupid club song!

The Northwest Parcel Pickup logo disappeared as the van door slid open. He laid her on the floor like an insured package. Twine cut across her body, crisscrossing, gouging, the sandals falling away from her feet.

Cardboard boxes stacked around her and the faint flutter of a wind chime echoed through the dark van as the door closed. He climbed into the front seat, singing, and the van chugged off.

Driving and driving.

Fighting against the twine and the drug, she pulled herself up against the boxes to look out a window.

He didn't see her prop herself against the box, enough to see outside.

He didn't see her watch him turn onto Emerson then later onto Government Way. She fought hard to know.

To remember. To fight.

As she slumped back against the boxes, wanting to crush his windpipe and stop him from singing that stupid song, she saw the sign for Discovery Park.

Then she understood.

Only in a 500-acre park could someone bury women alive and hide them from the world.

A dark twinge of fear rushed over her as her eyes began to close. Even if Tristan and St. James figured out it was Discovery Park, it could take months to find her and the others. And who knew how many he had buried out here. She swallowed hard.

Where he was about to bury her.

She was on her own. Just her against this tattoo killer.

As the van turned the corner, a streetlight glinted in the window, catching the edge of a box cutter lying beside her legs.

Kip twisted around, nearly unconscious, until her wrists were against the sharp blade.

She rubbed her entwined wrists across it until she felt some of the twine give.

She felt the painless slice of the blade against the sides of her hands, knowing she was at least spilling DNA evidence all over the place.

He turned a sharp corner and the van tilted, tumbling boxes to the other side.

Kip slid across the back, away from the box cutter, and cursed. She'd needed that weapon!

She tried to sit up, to crawl back and reach for the door handle, but it was so dark and she was falling into a well. A deep dark well.

21

12:29 A.M., September 3rd

"KELL!" Tristan shouted, running across the dance floor. "Stop! Stop that guy!"

He pounded the concrete floor, his heart hammering in his ears, his hands cold with terror.

He screamed her name again, but his voice was swallowed up by the thundering music and motion of bodies on the dance floor. He watched helplessly, moving through mud, as Platt led a calm, obedient Kell toward the exit.

He shoved a couple of dancers out of his way, ducking past a gyrating female nearly flashing her tits with every turn, but he couldn't get to Platt in time.

The couple he'd shoved rushed at him, but he yanked his badge out of his back pocket, stopping them in their tracks.

The whole dance floor parted, but it was too late.

Tristan banged open the metal door and sprinted down the street toward the black van pulling away from the curb.

He veered left, toward his RAV4 parked against the opposite curb and threw himself into the driver's seat.

Slamming the SUV in drive, he cut the wheel hard to the right, squealing the tires as he brought the vehicle about.

And nearly ran over his partner!

St. James threw out his arms.

Tristan slammed the brakes as St. James shuffled around the side of the car and jerked open the door. His heart dropped when he saw the phone in his hand. It was Kell's.

St. James scrambled into the seat as Persephone reached the SUV. She flung open the back passenger door.

"Dammit, this is police business!" he shouted. "Get out of the car!"

"Shut up and drive, Bowker," she shouted, slamming the door closed.

That's exactly what Kell would have said, he thought and punched the accelerator.

The SUV lurched forward, swerving around an oncoming car, and screaming down the street in search of the black van.

His heart wrenched in his chest and he slammed his hands against the steering wheel, frantically watching for Platt's van. Dammit, he'd just watched the bastard lead her out like a little kid!

He'd just stood there with all his police training and years of street experience and let the bastard have her. Dammit! He hated himself.

St. James dropped a comforting hand on his shoulder and squeezed.

"Not your fault, buddy. It all happened so fast, but we'll get him."

"Fuck! The anklet!"

His heart turned to ice, his stomach torn to pieces. There it sat, wrapped around the floor shift where he'd left it, planning to give it to her at the apartment. Why hadn't he just taken a moment to hand it to her?

Would have taken only a minute.

St. James stared at the nylon anklet with its tracking device and shook his head, a sick look on his face.

"You didn't know it'd go down tonight."

"But I should have!" He bared his teeth, swerving around a corner until he squealed onto Western. "I should have, Keith. I'm a cop, for Christ's sake! And I can't even track her with her phone." He nodded at the phone in St. James' hand.

Tristan passed a car, then another, running a red light as St. James snagged the radio and called in the black van, the abduction, and their pursuit.

He swallowed hard, his hands aching from his death grip on the steering wheel.

Every time, he blinked, the dead women stared back at him with their unnatural poses and milk-white skin. Dead eyes staring past him.

He smashed his eyes closed and they burned with the image of Kell's dead gaze and the white body bag zipping across her face. No!

He willed his eyes open, rubbing a hand across his face as headlights bobbed in front of him.

Swerving at the last minute, he threw the SUV back across the double yellow before the median appeared.

"There!" Persephone shouted, pointing between him and St. James. "Up ahead—a black van!"

His heart hammered up into his throat as he zipped around a slow-moving truck and slid between two cars to grab a spot in the left lane. The light turned red, the van already through it.

"Tris, don't! This intersection's—"

He slammed the accelerator, shooting through the intersection, missing the stream of oncoming cars by pure dumb luck.

Horns blared, tires squealed, but he kept his foot on the accelerator as St. James gave their position over the radio and requested intercepts.

It seemed like only moments before the dispatcher radioed them, telling St. James the van had been apprehended and searched.

A grandmother and her two grandsons.

Tristan was on Alaskan Way now while St. James had every available unit looking for a black van in the vicinity.

There were dozens! And none of them had Kell inside.

His heart sank into his stomach. He should have stuck closer, shadowed her like a good cop would have done.

He should have stayed in Illinois.

St. James also put in the call for an APB on Platt, sending black and whites to his address. An apartment complex up north, just east of I-5 near UDub. It was all they could do.

But he had to do more. He had to.

He drove around for nearly an hour, St. James manning the radio and Persephone deathly quiet in the back seat. She seemed as shell-shocked as he was. Only a few hours ago, Platt had been a person of interest, but Kell seemed convinced he was the killer.

Why hadn't he paid more attention? Dammit, why hadn't he listened?

Tristan pressed a hand to his forehead, rubbing at the headache that had worked its way down his face to his temples.

He tried to call back Kell's descriptions, of how this guy operated, what he'd do first.

God, he had to get into this guy's head and figure out how to stop him! Somehow, he had to get to Kell before it was too late.

"That line of bodies, Keith—they ended below Ballard, right?"

"Yep, Ballard."

"From downtown to Ballard," Tristan muttered, his brain puzzling on those details, of Kell saying how the guy hunted on familiar ground.

That's where he had the most power, she'd said. *There was power in the places where we grew up*, Tristan thought.

Kell was a genius.

"Why the distance?" Persephone asked, leaning forward as Tristan sped up through a yellow light.

From downtown to someplace south of Ballard. From work to

home, he realized. "It's not his delivery route," Tristan said, casting an excited glance at St. James. "Keith, it's his way home!"

"But he doesn't live in Ballard," said St. James, frowning.

Tristan smiled. "Not anymore. I'd bet money he grew up in Ballard. Or near it." He pulled in a breath. "Kell's been trying to tell me that all along, but I didn't get it until now. Keith—get former addresses on Platt. One of those is going to be in Ballard."

Persephone slid her hand down his arm, patting his shoulder. "We're going to find her, don't you worry."

He reached over and laid his hand against hers. Persephone really cared about Kell. Like him, she wasn't about to let her down either.

He put his hand back on the wheel, stopping at a light he couldn't run without causing an accident. St. James was on the radio again, getting priors on Platt.

His stomach twisted into knots and he balled his hands into fists, thinking about what that bastard might be doing to her right now.

Every second counted.

22

1:56 A.M., September 3rd

NO MOON GLEAMED OVERHEAD, the forest dark and silent. Twine cut into her skin, grass cold against her bare feet as he dragged her deeper into the woods.

She shivered at the sudden cold, eyes opening to slits, arms sluggish, legs dead weights.

Her blouse was torn open, skirt ripped in two places, the ground hard and bumping against her. She felt a gag against her mouth and bit into it hard, trying to tear it away with her teeth. Or swallow it whole.

Anything to get at this bastard. Anything.

"Never lettin' go...forever mine to hold," he sang into the blackness of trees and brush.

The stink of alcohol hung sweet and musty in the air.

"Sleep, baby sleep, forever mine to keep."

Kip felt anger hot on her tongue.

God, she wanted to smash this guy's face in, shut him up, show him who was in control.

The distant flutter of wind chimes hung in the air, soft against the breeze. The delicate, crystalline sound grew closer.

His hands slid across her breasts.

Kip's anger burned hotter, bringing a little feeling back into her legs. A controlled twitch of her knee, a planned turn of her ankle. Things were starting to work again.

He threw her to the ground beside a shovel.

Kip swiveled her head around, staring into the shallow hole and at a wooden coffin setting beside it.

Still singing, he picked up the shovel and dug in the dirt, scooping out shovelfuls. Dropping them into a nearby wheel barrow.

All around her, tall evergreens and cedars hugged the starry night sky.

She craned her neck, past the coffin toward clumps of purple and red petunias every few feet from the hole.

Like headstones, she realized.

Something white poked up from the center of each bunch of flowers and she noticed long rolls of fresh sod covering the ground.

How many boxes did this sonofabitch have under that sod?

She flexed her fingers, able to bend them now with some control. The drug was wearing off.

She glanced at Platt happily digging up soil, not paying her much attention. He thought she was too groggy to understand what was happening. He expected that she'd be good for a while yet.

Mistake one, asshole.

Faint cries—muffled—mixed with those damned wind chimes.

She glanced around the clearing, at the chimes hanging like grapes from branches and brush: big ones, small ones, wooden ones, chimes with shells—even silverware. Her eyes narrowed.

With hundreds of wind chimes, you could drown out anything. And he had.

In a few minutes, he'd finished digging his little grave and tossed the shovel down beside her.

He grinned now, oh so sure of himself as he leaned down to stroke her face, running his dirty hands across her breasts and under her skirt.

Kip stiffened as he took hold of her underwear. With a snap, he rolled it off her hips and down her legs.

She gritted her teeth. *Mistake two, asshole.*

Closing her eyes, she tried to block it out, concentrating on moving her hands. Anger pulsed white hot through her, the grogginess fading.

She felt the boxcutter's slashes across the twine and the dried blood as she pressed her weight against it.

Dammit, they had to give!

"You're the prettiest one yet," he said, laying on top of her and trying to press his mouth against hers.

She turned her head to keep him from it.

"One definitely has to go now. Maybe that slut, Jenna?" He leered at Kip, fumbling to unzip his pants. "Or that bitch, Sarah. She's as fake as the others."

Sarah! She was still alive! There was still a chance.

He grabbed Kip by her hair and smashed her face against his.

"You're all sluts, no matter how pretty you are." He gripped her hair. "My mother was a slut. I'd watch her bleach her hair—even the roots—covering up that ugly dark hair to go off to those clubs. She'd bring a different one home every night. After she'd passed out, they'd come to my room."

Kip struggled against the twine, twisting ,and pulling.

Snap! One strand broke.

She grabbed hold of the dangling strand, working it off her right wrist. Some of the twine fell away.

Platt ran his hands over her shoulder and the blue dolphin there, stroking it like it was a kitten or something. "She had butterflies all over her back." He grabbed at her shirt. "And between her breasts.

Showed 'em off to my friends when she thought I wasn't looking. She liked things rough."

Kip jerked her hands apart, but the twine held fast.

Swallowing a curse, she rocked her wrists back and forth, loosening more twine that encircled her wrists.

"I'm not your mother," Kip said with a growl, baring her teeth at him. "I'm your worst nightmare."

His eyes sparked at her words and it seemed to excite him.

"Fight me," he said, holding her by the shoulders. "Go ahead. It's more fun when you struggle." His grin was big and toothy. "The rest never fought me."

Kip smiled at him. "You like it rough, huh?"

He gritted his teeth, his blue eyes haunted, burning with lust. And he was ready to pop.

"Yeah, baby—" His grip tightened on her shoulders. "I like it rough."

She pumped her knee up hard, slamming it into his nuts.

Intense pain flooded his face and he rolled off her, balling up in the grass with a whimper.

She laughed, enjoying the sensations rolling across his pale face. She inch-wormed away from him, still fighting against the twine wound hard and tight around her wrists and feet.

Another few strands popped, more falling away.

She could move her hands a little within the string, but not enough to slide them free. She glanced back, her stomach sinking, and cursed.

He was getting up.

23

2:28 A.M., September 3rd

"THIS IS SAM281. What'dya got for us, Dispatch? Over?"

Tristan white-knuckled the steering wheel, his stomach in knots as he waited for Dispatch to rattle off addresses.

Current one. No good. One from five years ago—still in the University District.

"What else? There's got to be more!"

He could be killing her right now!

He fought down the urge to punch the steering wheel as he drove north toward Ballard, using the back roads he'd managed to learn over the past year. Roads he didn't have to think about while he drove.

Roads he prayed would lead him to Kell before that bastard killed her.

Why had he let her use herself as bait like that? As a cop—no, as her lover—he should have said no, should have convinced her it wasn't worth risking her life.

Not a chance, he realized with a sigh.

With her little sister already in this guy's hands, there was nothing he could have said or done to stop her.

And he'd have done the same thing.

"Dude, you gotta go way back on this one," St. James said into the radio. "I'm talking high school records here. Juvey. Waaay back. Over."

In five or six minutes, he'd be near the old Addams School. And she was still lost out here in that psychopath's hands.

Some of my best friends were psychopaths, he remembered her saying once. Once that would have made him laugh, but it hadn't been funny for a long time. Especially now.

"Dispatch, Sam281. Over."

"Go ahead, Dispatch," St. James answered.

"Right on the mark, St. James. Platt had a few juvy priors. Ballard High School. Destruction of school property, setting fires, breaking windows, beating up kids after school—two counts of animal cruelty. Another prior in Discovery Park—more fires. Over."

Starting fires, beating up kids, hurting animals—the history was there. Tristan saw it now.

The making of a serial killer.

"What about addresses? Over?"

"Looks like this guy bounced around a lot. An address in Kirkland, staying with a grandmother—his guardian for a year. An address with an aunt on West Cramer...near Sunset Hills, back home to his mother in Ballard. Over."

"Wait a minute," Tristan snapped. "His mother lived in Ballard?"

St. James shrugged. "Looks like it."

"Any photos of Mrs. Platt?" Tristan asked, his voice loud enough to be heard over the radio.

"Why?" Persephone asked.

"Kip said she'd be blonde. Working as a hair stylist."

"Dispatch, did you get that?" St. James replied. "Need vitals and an occ on Mrs. Platt. Over."

"Looking it up now, Sam281. Over."

Tristan cast an uneasy glance at St. James. "West Cramer... Sunset Hills. Where's that?"

St. James opened a map on his phone as Tristan continued driving north. "On the north side of Discovery Park. Across the locks from Ballard."

Discovery Park...why was everything coming back to Discovery Park?

A cold chill raked his spine. At over 500 acres, it was the largest park in Seattle. With beach access and dozens of trails, it was a popular spot. A place people could feel alone in the wilderness just fifteen minutes from downtown.

He stiffened. A place to hide a few bodies.

"Keith, ask Dispatch the name of the aunt."

The radio squawked as he called Dispatch. "Sam281 to Dispatch. Need name and vitals on the aunt. Over."

Scratchy air crackled through the SUV, the minutes ticking by until finally, the dispatcher's voice filled the silence.

"Sam281, Aunt's name is Mason. Freida Mason. Over."

Persephone lurched forward and grabbed Tristan's arm.

"That's the name on the business card we found in Carolee's pocket," she replied. "Kip and I found it in her smock pocket, the one she left at her mother's house. We also found some cocaine hidden in the makeup boxes."

Tristan slammed his foot on the brake and nearly launched Persephone over the back seat.

"Cocaine? Holy shit, Seph! Why didn't you tell us you found cocaine back there?"

Dammit, Kell! He winced. Why hadn't she told him that! Why?

All this time, another angle, some evidence the investigators missed. He hit the steering wheel with both hands.

Seph shrugged. "Guess Kip didn't want to put a stain on Carolee's name until she knew where the coke came from."

That almost made him smile. It was so like Kell to protect the weak.

"Kip thought it was coming from the makeup consultant on that card. Freida Mason. Or the delivery service. She thought Rudy Weatherford was involved with the coke, too."

A cold chill ripped through him. "The Mason woman—Platt's aunt?"

Seph nodded and the chill turned into a sharp jab in his chest. Platt's Aunt.

Platt, a delivery driver for a private courier—it made sense. But how did the cocaine connect to the killings? He'd worry about that later. After he found Kell.

Right now, his gut told him to check out the Mason woman's residence.

"What's the address for Mason? The one on West Cramer. And fastest route to the scene."

St. James jotted down the numbers, mumbling street names, and Tristan floored the accelerator, passing cars—yellow line or not—making his way west toward Discovery Park.

"ETA, Keith?" Tristan asked, turning onto Nickerson, headed for Emerson."

"About ten minutes—but much faster with you driving. Dispatch, Sam281 en route to suspect's house. Code one. Request backup and support."

"Sam281, I used to live in Sunset Hills," said Dispatch.

Maggie Burton, he remembered her. Late forties, two kids and a police officer husband on disability.

"What can you tell us about it?" Tristan replied.

"Isn't that the house with all the wind chimes? Over?"

Seph grabbed hold of Tristan's shoulder and squeezed.

"Seph? What is it?"

"Wind chimes ...that's the place! Go—hurry!"

"How do you know that?" Tristan asked, casting a quick glance at her, his stomach in knots.

"Don't ask, Bowker—just drive." Seph.

A grim smile touched his lips as he punched the accelerator. *Hang on, Kell. I'm almost there.*

It wasn't too late. He couldn't be too late.

24

"YOU, BITCH!" Platt shouted, staggering up from the ground.

Still struggling against the twine, Kip managed to drag herself into the weeds when a big hunk of the string gave way.

Her right hand was free!

His shoes pounded the ground, the sound dull, muffled.

Good, he was still on the sod. He hadn't seen her in the dark yet.

"Where are you?" he shouted.

Wind chimes rattled through the clearing like a choir of soprano voices. Hiding the scritch of weeds and rasp of string as Kip fought to free her left hand.

Hearing the chimes made her grin. This time, they'd worked against ol' Steven Platt.

He couldn't hear a damn thing for all those beautiful chimes.

Frantically, she tore at the network of knots until the largest one came loose under her thumbnail.

Brush crashed about ten feet to her left.

Kip froze, smell of dry grass and the gentle night breeze washing away Steven Platt's stink. The sickeningly sweet stench of musk and alcohol.

"Kim-mee," he cooed, beating at the weeds as he walked through them. "Come out, come out. No one's gonna find you in the middle of nowhere."

MIDDLE OF NOWHERE. Kip rolled her eyes, struggling to untie her feet. *Nice try, asshole,* but she knew exactly where she was.

As a kid, she'd hopped as many buses and hitched as many rides as it took to get out to Discovery Park. Every chance she got.

She'd loved the huge dogwood and that seventy-foot apple tree, hollowed out by woodpeckers or something. Both were gone now, but life went on.

Like this wonderful old park, she'd survive, too.

Two knots gave, the twine falling away from her feet. She lurched up from the brush.

Right into Platt.

"Gotcha!" he shouted, laughing as his arms swept around her neck, squeezing. "You're going to pay for that. All night. That, I promise."

The box cutter rose in his left hand, shifting toward her throat.

Kip stomped her bare foot into his knee cap, her elbow aimed at his side as she rammed the heel of her hand against his nose.

The box cutter shot out of his hand and onto the sod.

He clutched his nose, cursing, shouting.

She grabbed him by his hair and shoulder, dragging him onto the sod, toward his wooden coffin.

"Now, it's my turn to play," she said to him in a sweet voice. "You picked the wrong chick to fuck with tonight. I promise you that. Bad move, picking a chick with no conscience."

Kip straddled him, pinning him against the sod. She leaned over him, grinning, laughing as she brushed her blonde hair across his face.

"I did five years in Walla Walla for armed robbery and manslaughter. Key word being slaughter. And I'm just getting started." She grinned at him. "Sleep, Steven sleep. And kiss your ass goodbye."

The hungry expression on his face and that dead look in his eyes began to change, his pupils widening, nostrils flaring.

She smashed her fingers around his neck, squeezing.

"Taste it, Steven. That's good old-fashioned fear. How's it taste? Like sweet, sweet karma."

He screamed, throwing Kip off.

Kip lunged at him, her fist slamming into his side. A kidney punch, right on the mark.

She dropped him to one knee and landed a hard kick at the knee holding him up.

"Who are you?" he demanded, struggling to his feet.

"I already told you," Kip said with a snarl. "Your worst nightmare."

A handful of dirt hit her in the eyes and she staggered backward, falling. Nearly blinded, she clawed at her eyes as he blindsided her, slamming her against the ground.

Everything shifted violently for a moment then tilted back again, his hands closing around her throat.

Squeezing. Crushing.

She couldn't breathe!

Kip grabbed hold of his face, clawing at his eyes, pulling harder until his grip loosened.

With a sharp jab of her elbow, she broke his hold and stumbled into the brush, her eyes burning and tearing, her chest heaving air.

Her vision cleared just as the boxcutter slashed toward her face.

She leaned backward enough to prevent the bone-cutting swipe, but not enough to avoid the slash down the side of her face.

Warm blood dripped down her cheek, falling onto her torn up olive blouse as she staggered out of the way of the next blow.

Circle around, her brain screamed. *Get the shovel!*

She stumbled backward, away from the next slice of the blade.

Kicked him hard in the chest, knocking him off balance.

Kip ran deeper into the brush.

Again, the wind chimes hid her movements. She winced. And his, too.

She ran past flashes of red and purple petunias.

Run faster, she chanted, rounding the last patch of flowers. Running toward the shallow grave.

And the shovel that lay in the grass.

Something dark flashed on her left, something else on her right.

She tripped over a small roll of sod.

Picking herself up, heart pulsing in her ears, face throbbing, she ran toward the edge of the hole—where she'd first broken free of him.

There he stood, leering, box cutter raised.

Freeze frame.

In slow motion, the blade flashed toward her and she couldn't stop it.

Her legs were granite slabs, her reflexes blown, the blade sinking toward her chest.

"Forgive me, Sarah," she heard herself say. "Sorry Tristan."

And he was there, in front of her, the blade at his breastbone. Slicing. Plunging with bloody results.

Tristan!

A scream tore out of her as Tristan sank into her arms, eyes wide with shock. He dropped like a rag doll onto the sod, his blood spilling across his Nirvana T-shirt, his face so deathly pale.

Rage exploded through her with white-hot fury. She turned, facing Steven Platt.

Tristan had been the one thing through all of this nightmare that had been real. Safe. Pure.

Lunging, she launched herself at Platt, fists knocking the boxcutter to the ground.

She beat his face and body hard enough to topple him and her into the hole. Blind rage propelled her forward.

She grabbed the shovel that lay beside the hole. Gripped it like a baseball bat.

Glaring, teeth bared, gaze unblinking.

He hesitated, a flicker of fear rising in his eyes.

"First, my sister and now, the man I love."

She cocked the shovel over her shoulder.

"Mistake three, asshole!"

With all her strength behind it, Kip slammed the shovel against Platt's head.

Once. Twice. Three times.

Until he lay still, face down in the blood-stained hole. Where he belonged.

"Tristan!" she shouted, panic bleeding through the anger as she threw down the shovel and rushed to Tristan's side.

Persephone was by him, St. James on the other side.

Sirens rose in the night above the tinkling of wind chimes.

Kip's bottom lip quivered, the warm metallic stench of Tristan's blood in the air as she bent toward her beautiful rookie detective.

"What were you doing?" she cried, a hitch in her voice as she laid her hand against his face, stroking. She gripped his hand and squeezed, making sure he knew she was there.

"Saving—you," he said in a soft, pained voice.

Images of the guy in that long-ago alley haunted her now, blood spreading across his shirt just like that night. She understood how his family felt now—and she hated what she'd done to them. The people that had loved him and had ached so terribly when he never came home again.

Now, all she could see was Tristan Bowker lying there. Beautiful, good, loving—she'd never deserved this man. And now, he was dying because of her.

Tears rushed down her face and she could barely breathe, barely talk.

Seph's hand pressed against the chest wound, trying to stop the bleeding. St. James's expression was grim as he laid his hand against Tristan's sandy hair.

"Hang in there, partner. Ambulance's on the way," said St. James, stepping backward.

"The girls," Tristan said in a half-whisper. "Sarah?"

Her chest felt like exploding. She had to find Sarah under the ground, but if she left Tristan...he might not be here when she got back.

"Ssssh, don't talk," said Kip, laying her fingers against his still warm lips. He couldn't die. He couldn't! "Remember, my place—2 A.M. Scrambled eggs and cheese? You promised."

He nodded weakly, a slight squeeze of her hand. "Looks like I'm —not going to make it tonight—Kell."

Tears flooded her cheeks and she wiped them back, her gaze not leaving his pain-filled hazel eyes.

"No! Don't you talk like that. You hold on! You hear me, Bowker? You show these people what Midwest boys are made of!"

A ghostly smile touched his lips, a weak nod, his face so pale. Like that woman in the morgue. She let out a whimper, unable to hold everything inside.

Persephone laid her hand on Kip's. "It's not over yet. You've got to believe that."

"Thorpe!" St. James called from one of the petunia bunches as he rolled back the sod. "Need some help here."

The voice shrieking *help me* was painfully familiar.

Sarah!

She staggered up from the sod and ran around the hole as St. James pried at the lid with the shovel. She grabbed hold, pulling until St. James knocked the lid free.

She picked it up, throwing it into the brush.

Sarah lay in the box, face pale and tear-stained. Cuts and bruises dotted her face as Kip grabbed hold of the twine, cutting it with a pocketknife that St. James handed her until Sarah was free.

"Oh my God! Kelly!" Sarah shouted, throwing her arms around Kip.

Something shattered inside her and the aching sobs bubbled up from Kip as she and her sister cried on each other's shoulders.

"I knew you'd save me," Sarah whispered. "I knew you cared. I knew it." A sob shook through her again. "He was going to kill me tonight. He told me so. Then the fight started and I was praying someone had found me—and the others."

Kip helped her up from the box and St. James slid an arm around her, reassuring her.

"Can you help me locate the others now?" he asked in a quiet voice.

Nodding, Sarah leaned against him, moving to the next batch of petunias as Kip rushed back to Tristan.

25

2:55 A.M., September 3rd

PERSEPHONE HELD her hand against Bowker's wound, trying to control the bleeding. It was so close to his heart.

It was a mortal wound. She was certain.

But Tristan Bowker would not die this night. Not if she had any sway left on the underworld, any narrow path through Hades' bitter indifference.

With a hand raised into the night, the ebony moon a black hole in the starry sky, she called to Hecate—and to Hades.

"The hour is late," she whispered into the warm breeze. "Dear Hecate, hear my voice and come to me. You loved me once, Hades. If you still have love for me, help me save this young man's life tonight."

In an instant, Hecate was at her shoulder, slender and regal, her eyes wet with kindness and generosity.

"I've been watching from the crossroads. My heart aches for this young man and the young woman who fought so hard." She shook her head, her wavy hair falling over one eye.

Persephone turned toward Hecate, her hand still pressed hard against Bowker's wound as she tried desperately to stop him from bleeding out.

He was fading. She felt it. Saw the shimmer of his life force appear then disappear in the darkness.

Stay or go, his soul fought with that decision.

And her heart ached for him. To face such a decision was brutal, even though she knew what awaited most mortals on the other side. But she also knew what he would leave on this side.

"Is there nothing you can do? No spell? No rite? Nothing to heal his wound?"

Hecate shook her head, the sadness obvious in her expression. She had no power over the dead, Persephone knew. Hades—only Hades had that power.

"Hades is still very hurt, Persephone—and angry—over your decision."

"So, he chooses to hurt me back by allowing such an injustice to unfold? Where's his passion? His intensity? Those were part of the man I loved once."

Hecate shrugged, laying her hand on Persephone's shoulder. "I'm here for you, my dear, even though I can do nothing."

Anguish swept over Persephone as she patted Hecate's hand and whispered on the wind for her husband's presence.

Hades had truly become like the gloom he'd fought so hard against all these centuries. That gloom had been the reason he'd sought her out that sunny day in Eleusis.

He was lost to her now.

Bowker gurgled, barely moving.

Where were the mortal doctors and their ambulances? Time—his life—trickled away.

They'd arrive too late.

Mortal medicine was so imprecise at best. The more time lost, the less likely Kip's intense, young detective would survive.

Brush rustled behind her.

She looked up, tears rolling down her face. Paramedics and police officers. Running toward the fallen officer.

But she already felt Bowker's soul in her hands, slipping through her fingers onto the ground.

Kip shouted, agony on her face as she rushed toward him. His heartbeat was slowing. Breaths fading.

Her breath hitched. Bowker wouldn't be here when Kip reached him.

"Hades, please!" Persephone shouted. "If you ever loved me, prove it by saving this man! These young lovers!"

A flash of white in the brush, smoke surging on the breeze.

She glanced around her. Nothing.

"We'll take it from here," a paramedic said, trying to move her back.

She held her hand firm against the wound, moving aside, but not withdrawing her hand.

As Queen of the Underworld, she had some power. The power to keep him from those gates, even if it was for only a few minutes more.

Casting all her thoughts onto Tristan Bowker, she held fast.

They tried to move her, both paramedics.

But she held on as a ghostly white stallion reared through the brush.

Wind chimes clattered. Wind rose.

Hades emerged like a spirit through the thick darkness, so tall and determined on the stallion's back, hair so pale blond and brown eyes luminescent.

He leaned down, reaching toward Bowker.

Her mouth fell open. After all her pleading, he appears to her, ready to carry the young man's soul away to the underworld.

"I'll never forgive you!" she shouted with a snarl, glaring at Hades.

Hades' warm gaze never left hers as a white mist rolled from his hand and onto Bowker.

Only then did she realize that he was returning the young detective's life force.

Returning it to his mortal body.

"Yes, you will," Hades said with a smirk, bowing his head. He wheeled the ghost-stallion around. "Because I love you."

She grinned, unable to halt her tears as he rode on the wind into the night on that white stallion.

Only then did she let her hand fall from Bowker's chest.

She rose to her feet, Hecate beside her as the paramedics flooded over Bowker.

Kip fell down beside him, eyes wet, hand on his brow, stroking. Someone's watch beeped and she smiled.

"It's three A. M.," said Kip to Bowker, a hand on his face. The weariness in her cut and bruised face was evident despite her smile. "I was so afraid you wouldn't be here."

Bowker took her hand in his. "So was I," he whispered.

The paramedics loaded him onto a transport board and carried him out of the woods, Kip beside him, as the other paramedics moved toward the women emerging from their underground prisons. St. James led Sarah to her sister then grabbed blankets to wrap around the shoulders of three exhausted women he and Sarah and unearthed from the sod.

"I think it's time I came home," Persephone said to Hecate in a quiet voice.

In a day or so. After Kip and the others were safe.

"So do I," said Hecate, her image fading. "Spring isn't far away. Not much time to spend with your beloved."

Her beloved. Persephone smiled, laying a hand against her stomach and the pomegranate seeds tattooed there. A sign of permanence. A sign of her love for him.

He'd found his passion again. And he'd proven that he loved her.

For the first time in a long while, she was glad for those seeds, more than she'd ever felt before.

And she couldn't wait to be back in his arms again.

26

2:41 P.M., September 4th

FOR THE FIRST time in days, Seattle felt cool and sleepy again, the temperature barely sixty-two. A fine mist had rinsed the air all morning, making it smell clean and new.

Like it had almost washed away Steven Platt's evil. Almost.

Kip wore a green chenille sweater over a white t-shirt and jeans as she stood on the sidewalk by Sarah and her mother's taxi. She'd been up all night with Tristan at the hospital, only leaving an hour ago to see Sarah and her mother off. They'd stayed at Kip's place, but their plane left Sea-Tac around five today.

Back to Idaho.

Sarah smiled, setting down a small shopping bag, and moved toward Kip. Her face was all cut and bruised, but she was still able to smile, despite what that bastard did to her. She glanced at the bootcut jeans she'd given her little sister. Illegal in most states now, but hey, she liked pissing people off. The jeans were a little too long, but otherwise they were a close fit. If not a decade or so out of fashion.

Kip gave her a purple University of Washington sweatshirt and a barrette to hold her hair out of her face.

She looked thinner than Kip had expected and the distant stare colored with fear bothered her. Sarah wasn't okay. She knew that. On top of the kidnapping and being kept in that box for a week, her little sister had been assaulted.

Kip felt rage every time she thought about that sonofabitch, but Steven Platt would never hurt anyone ever again. She'd seen to that.

Still, Sarah needed help to get through this and she'd be there for her. Mom had already arranged for counseling in Idaho.

Kip slid her arms around Sarah and felt her trembling.

"You're going to get through this, Sarah," said Kip in a soothing voice, tightening her hold. "I promise."

Tears dripped down Sarah's face and she wiped them away. "I hope you're right."

"I know you've been through hell," said Kip, holding her out at arm's length. "And nothing I say will ever change that, but I'm here for you. No matter what." She cast a glance at her mother who was no more than an arm's reach from Sarah. "Mom's gonna be here for you, too."

She glanced at her mother. The angry woman she'd once known had aged more than Kip had expected, making her look frail and tired. Her oval face was lined deep around her mouth and between her dull blue eyes. The anger that Kip always remembered was absent, replaced with an expression she couldn't quite read.

Her mother went through a lot since Sarah disappeared. That could age anyone. She still wore her hair in a bob, but it seemed darker than she remembered, greying at the temples and around her face. She'd gained a few pounds, but it seemed right on her somehow.

"You lied to me, Kip," said her mother, a hand on her hip.

Kip bristled, her jaw tightening. *Here we go.* She was worried sick about Tristan and didn't feel like arguing with her mother. It was never a discussion. Always an argument.

With a sigh, she stared at her mother, waiting for the woman to launch into her *you know what's wrong with you, Kip* speech.

"You knew all along Sarah had been kidnapped by that killer and you never said a word." Her mouth was pressed into a tight, angry line.

Kip nodded. "Yeah, you're right. I didn't figure it would do you any good to know that. You were worried enough without knowing about a killer."

The line softened, her eyes kind of glassy.

"That's the first time you ever told a lie to protect someone else from pain. Thank you."

At last, she smiled and Kip felt her muscles relax. Her mother stepped forward until she was right in front of Kip.

"Detective St. James told us you bleached your hair and put yourself out there as bait." Her bottom lip began to quiver. "To draw this guy out, so he'd—he'd take you to Sarah. That was so dangerous, Kelly. He could have killed both of you."

Kip felt the sting of moisture in her eyes at her mother's use of Kelly.

She shrugged. "It was fastest way to find him."

Her mother laughed and laid a hand on Kip's face, just under the stitched-up cut on her cheek.

"Only to you. It terrifies me every time I think about it, but I thank God you and Sarah got out alive."

Her mother stifled a sob and put her arms around Kip in a quick hug then turned away.

"Thank you for that," said Kip. "Mom."

She turned around, a hand to her mouth, but her eyes...they said it all. She'd forgiven a lot of things in that gaze and the pride that hovered there made Kip smile.

She'd never seen that look before. It was kinda nice.

"They said you killed him," said her mother, not a trace of revulsion in her eyes.

Kip nodded. She wasn't sorry for it either. He was a predator and he would have killed her in another moment.

And the rest of those women.

"Good," said her mother, a hardness in her eyes now. "Is your cop friend going to be all right?"

Kip felt her insides twist and burn. He'd been in surgery for hours after the attack. He'd nearly bled out, they'd told her. They weren't sure if he'd survive. His mother and brother were on their way out here. Wouldn't get here until tomorrow. She bit her lip to keep it from trembling.

Tristan had to pull through—he had to.

"Oh, God," said her mother, reaching out a hand to her. She stroked Kip's hair. "He's more than a friend, isn't he?"

She nodded, her eyes rimmed with tears. "He took a blow meant for me. And I'll never forgive him if he dies on me."

"He'll be okay, Kelly," said her mother. "He has to be."

Kip frowned, cocking her head at her mother. "Why does he have to be?" she asked.

Her mother smiled. "Because you and he gave a lot last night. Both of you deserve to be happy and together. I'll pray for him, Kelly." She planted a quick kiss on Kip's cheek and hurried toward the taxi. "You're a hero, you know? All the news outlets are calling you that. Call me when you have an update on him."

A hero? Kip frowned, the word making her uncomfortable. She wasn't a hero, she just did what she had to do.

Sarah held up her cell phone. "I've got your number, sis. I'll call you as soon as we're home." She managed a small smile. "We've got a lot of catching up to do."

"Can't wait, Sarah," said Kip, hugging her sister. "In a few weeks, I'd like to come out and visit you."

Her eyes grew wide. "Promise, Kelly?" her mother asked, opening the back door for Sarah.

"A promise," she answered and smiled.

"Bring your man, too. I'd love to meet him."

Kip sighed. She wanted to, she really did, but what if he—No! She gritted her teeth against that *what if*.

Tristan was going to be okay. Mom was right. He had to be.

"I will," she replied.

She waved at the taxi as it pulled away from the curb and disappeared down the street. When Kip turned toward the apartment complex, Seph sat on the bottom step, dressed in a short black skirt and gauzy white blouse. Those red pomegranate seeds on her stomach bled through.

"Hey, Kip, you look tired," she said, rising as Kip approached.

"I thought you'd already left for home."

Without a goodbye, she wanted to say but didn't. She was glad to see that Seph hadn't left the area yet.

"Not without saying goodbye. You going back to the hospital?"

Kip nodded. "I was gonna grab my jacket—"

Seph held out a jean jacket to her and Kip took it.

"Thanks."

"Why don't you come to the ferry with me? You can grab a bus from there, right?"

"Sure."

Seph motioned toward the pale pink VW bug beside the curb and Kip shook her head, grinning.

"Pink this week?"

She shrugged as she walked over and opened the driver side door. "I just had this sudden rush of femininity."

Kip rolled her eyes as she opened the passenger door and folded herself inside. She hated pink.

"If you say so."

Seph drove in her typical wild fashion, getting them to the dock in record time and into the ferry line. Kip checked her watch with the ferry schedule on Seph's dash. The ferry would board shortly. And she needed to get to the hospital and check on Tristan.

"You taking this thing with you?" She snickered, thinking about a pink VW bug at the Underworld gates.

"Just to the Crossroads," said Seph with a shrug. "Hades has seen worse."

She didn't doubt that.

"How's Tristan?" she asked.

Kip's jaw tightened. "He coded last night. Needed a transfusion, too, but he's stubborn. He's holding his own in ICU." She stared at Seph a moment as something clicked in her head. "He shouldn't be here right now, should he?"

Seph frowned. "What are you talking about?"

"You stayed with him the whole time he was down. Even when the paramedics tried to get to him, you held them back." She shook her head. "I saw the wound, Seph. It was fatal."

"You're right, the wound was fatal," said Seph, nodding. "But Hades and I kept him from the gates. I couldn't let him be taken like that. It wasn't right."

Kip shook her head. "There aren't any words, Seph...I—"

She smiled. "It's okay. I stayed here to help you and I ended up helping myself, too."

She leaned over and hugged Seph. "I can't thank you and Hades enough."

"You helped us more than you know, Kip."

The loud speaker announced the ferry was loading cars, so Kip stepped out of the car as Seph rolled down the windows.

"When will you be back?" Kip asked, leaning on the window.

"In April. Will you still be at Pacific Blue Tattoo?"

Kip nodded. "For now. Nick won't fire me now because I'm good publicity. Might even be a raise in there somewhere."

She and Seph laughed.

"Yeah, right. It's Nick you're talking about, remember?" Seph tossed a set of keys to Kip as she turned on the motor. Kip caught them. "Hey, wanna housesit for me while I'm away? Rent's paid up through April."

Kip's eyes widened. "You mean that penthouse?"

Seph nodded. "Just keep the plants watered and the parties to a minimum." She winked. "And a roommate's fine."

"Thanks, Seph. For everything."

Seph's lane started to move, so she nudged the VW forward. "Seeya in April, Kip."

"Bye, Seph."

She waved as Seph's pink VW inched forward in the line, disappearing aboard the sleek green and white ferry. The *Wenatchee*, Kip saw on the sign. She watched the ferry load and with one long blast, the ferry slid across Elliott Bay.

Kip watched it another moment then hurried out to the street to catch a bus to Harborview Medical Center.

27

3:23 P.M. The Crossroads

PERSEPHONE GOT out of her pink VW at the crossroads, glancing at the three paths that stretched into the twilight, the sound of Elliott Bay behind her, air cool and sweet.

"Hecate?" she called. "Hecate, where are you?"

The nicker of a horse made her turn.

A ghostly white stallion tossed its head, looking part mist and part spirt as Hades stared at her from the edge of the crossroads.

Silent. Motionless.

Her heart leaped at the sight of his faint smile, his hair so blond in the growing darkness, his eyes so piercing and blue. Encompassing her with a look she couldn't read.

Back there, as Bowker died beneath her hands, she'd shouted for Hades, demanding that if he ever loved her, he'd prove it by saving this young detective.

"You saved him," she said, her black stiletto Prada boots clicking as she moved toward him, arms crossed. "Why?"

"I already answered that question," he said, his voice like warm velvet.

She took another step toward him.

"Answer it again."

He slid off the spirit stallion, his body lean and strong, so tall and statuesque in his black leather armor. His footfalls were hollow against the crossroads as he stopped three feet from her.

"Come home, Seph," he said, an ache in his voice, his blue eyes watery.

"Has something changed?" she asked.

He nodded and took a step toward her. Gently, he laid his hands against her shoulders, fingers caressing.

"I have," he answered. "I've kept you every six months of your existence in darkness. In shadows. Because I ached for your love, your light. Never understanding what I'd asked of you. Never understanding the toll it would take on you. On us. Until you didn't come home to me."

A deep sigh rattled through him and he bowed his head.

"I've done a lot of soul-searching, Seph," he said, sounding weary now, something she hadn't heard in his voice until now. "You gave up everything for me and I refused to change anything for you."

His admission stunned her. Made her chest ache.

"What are you saying, Hades?" she asked.

His hands slid to hers and he stood only inches in front of her now, his beautiful face kissing-close.

"I am King of the Underworld," he said in a soft voice. "I am bound to oversee the dead, but I've forgotten my duty to the living." He sighed. "To my wife. And I was never bound to the underworld itself—just my duty to its souls."

She smiled at him. "What does that mean?"

He reached up and cupped her face, stroking. "It means I love you, Persephone, and without you, I am nothing. Being without you is an emptiness I never again want to face. How does winter in Greece sound?"

Her heart wanted to soar. "You would leave the underworld? With me?"

He nodded, pulling her close. "I will be at your side, come winter, come summer."

"Does that mean you'll return to Seattle with me in April?"

Again, he nodded. "Help me find my passion again?"

"Every day we're together, love," she said, her eyes misting.

He slid his arms around her, kissing her with all the heat and fire she'd ever wanted, that mortal heat and fire she'd always envied.

"I've already found my light," he said, cradling her against his chest. "It's you, Persephone. Always."

Just like that, she was home again. And for the first time, she looked forward to winter. In Greece. In Hades' arms.

3:51 P.M., September 5th

KIP SAT by Tristan's bedside, stroking his hand. The smell of antiseptic and cafeteria food hung in the air, an untouched food tray on the bed table of the light blue hospital room with wood-like vinyl flooring.

She winced at the memory of him coding and then needing a transfusion a few hours later. But he was holding his own now. He'd regained consciousness this morning in ICU, sleeping on and off until he awoke hungry and weak.

They'd moved him into a regular hospital room, so she knew he was doing better.

Definitely a good sign.

His face was porcelain-pale, sandy hair flat against his head. A thick white bandage wrapped around his chest underneath the white and blue hospital gown. Dark circles ringed his closed eyes. His hands were warm and smooth and she wanted desperately to feel them against hers.

His eyes fluttered open, giving her little glimpses of those bright hazel eyes, like sunlight through blinds.

"Hey," he said, reaching a bruised hand toward her, tubes tangling. A heavy sigh rattled his chest and his eyes turned watery. "Can't tell you how glad I am to see you." His eyes closed a moment. "I thought I'd lost you."

Kip choked up, staring at his pale, pale face, his beautiful hazel eyes dull with pain. He was still hot as Seattle's heatwave.

"When you took that hit for me, I hated you," she said, glaring at him, her jaw tightening. "I didn't want to lose you." She stared down at the floor. "Over the past few days, I've realized that I didn't want to be here without you, Tristan."

He laid his hand against the bandage on her face and cupped her chin.

God, his touch felt good! She closed her eyes a moment, losing herself in his warmth, so scared she'd never feel it again.

"Funny, I came to the same conclusion."

She smiled. "It's the most intense emotion I've ever felt." At last, she got the courage to look him in the eye. "I didn't think I could feel anything that deeply, but I do."

"It's not the chip, Kell. It's all real—it's all you. You're not a monster. That mask you wear over all of it, afraid we'll see this monster...that's not exactly true."

She frowned, her body stiffening. *What did that mean?*

His expression warmed. "I think you're afraid we'll see the real person beneath the mask, the one that's a good and decent person. The one that offered up her own life to save four women. Most of them strangers. That's the real you, Kell. That's what's under your mask. I hope that someday, you'll see what I see."

She hadn't had someone look at her like Tristan did in a long, long time. Maybe ever.

She squeezed his hand and held it to her lips, kissing his bruised, scraped fingers, grateful to feel the steady pulse of his heartbeat. Almost losing him nearly broke her into pieces. A puzzle that she wouldn't have been strong enough to put back together again if she'd lost him.

"There's also an incredible profiler hiding in there, Kell. St. James has been singing your praises to everyone in the department."

"St. James?"

He nodded. "He's telling everyone—including my family —how you located this guy with nothing but street smarts."

His family. They'd see something more than a felon. Maybe they'd even like her someday?

"Captain wants to meet you, too—soon as I'm well. There may be some freelance profiling work coming your way, Kell. The department was very impressed. And in need of another profiler."

Kip couldn't stop the grin. Kip Thorpe working for the police department. She'd never dreamed of something so crazy. Her mom would never believe it.

"Is Seph around?" Tristan asked, glancing around. "I'd like to thank her for staying with me like that. Paramedics said she kept me from bleeding out."

She did so much more than that, but Kip couldn't tell him. She owed Seph everything. Without Seph, she'd have lost him.

Forever.

Kip shook her head. "Seph went home for the season. Said she'd be back in April and she expects to see you back to your old self."

She imagined Seph sitting in that pink VW at that magical crossroads, summoning Hecate. She could almost see Hades himself meeting her there, picking her up in his arms and carrying her off into Elliott Bay's grey mist.

Seeya in April, Seph had whispered. *With your hot detective boyfriend back on his feet.* She couldn't wait.

She kind of missed Seph already, but she knew Seph was happier than she'd been in a long time. Enough to give Kip the key to that penthouse overlooking the Bay. She looked forward to winter by that fireplace and that view, Tristan on the couch snuggling with her. But she was putting up her Nirvana poster. End of story.

For sentimental reasons.

"How's your sister?" he asked.

"She's going to need a lot of therapy," said Kip with a sigh, rising to her feet and pacing around the bed, hands in her back pockets. "But she's going to be okay. She plans to come back next year and visit, but my mother won't let her come alone. My mom insists on coming with her. Says she wants to make sure Sarah's okay. And she wants to spend a little time with me. Get to know me again. I might even go out there soon—now that there's a ceasefire."

Kip felt her eyes sting. Her mother hadn't said anything good about her in a long, long time. It was a start and for once, she was grateful for the opportunity.

St. James strutted through the doorway, a big sloppy grin on his face, and a manila envelope tucked under his arm.

"How's our patient today?" he asked, stepping over to the bed, and patting Tristan on the shoulder. "Glad you're back, Thorpe," he said, still smiling. "He's been asking for you ever since they moved him to a regular bed. His desperation was getting annoying."

Kip cast a glance at Tristan who rolled his eyes and looked away from his partner.

"Mom and Eric get in yet?" Tristan asked, his voice only a ghost of its usual sound.

St. James shook his head. "Their flight doesn't get in until after six tonight." He squeezed Tristan's forearm. "Don't worry, I'll get 'em checked into the Edgewater and bring 'em on down."

Kip's eyes widened. "Wow, the Edgewater?" That place was one of the best places in town to stay—way out of her price range.

St. James got all proud-looking, sticking out his chest like a peacock. "It was my suggestion and it's the department's dime. Captain said it was the least we could do."

"You've got good taste," said Kip.

Okay, so the guy wasn't grating on her so much anymore. He'd actually been helpful, even getting her mom and Sarah booked on their flights.

"Thanks," he replied.

St. James laid the envelope on Tristan's stomach.

"What's this?"

"Just the loose ends on this one." He sighed, the smile falling away. "A confession from Mason among other things."

Tristan frowned. "Confession?"

St. James nodded and opened the envelope flap. "She confessed to running drugs through that cosmetics business. And—" He held up his finger. "Accessory to murder. Seems she's the one who set up her nephew with Carolee and some of the others."

"You're kidding me," said Tristan, casting a look at Kip. Kip wasn't surprised. She'd seen Freida's type before.

"What'd he do?" Kip asked. "Threaten her if she didn't keep it up?"

St. James' eyes widened a little, his lips parting slightly. "I swear, Thorpe, I don't know how you do that. But yeah, that's basically it. She set him up, hoping to keep him out of trouble and then she finds out one's dead and two are missing. She panics, afraid it'll expose her drug-running, and confronts her nephew. He threatens to kill her unless she keeps her mouth shut and keeps sending him girls."

Tristan shook his head in disgust.

"She had some conscience though. She didn't set him up with any more girls."

"That's what you think," Kip muttered. "She's just mad because she got caught."

Freida Mason was afraid of one thing: getting caught. She didn't care anything about those women. Kip saw that when they first met.

St. James patted the envelope again.

"So, what's in the envelope, Keith?" Tristan asked.

St. James picked it up and slid out what looked like a large photograph. "Check this out. Mason gave us a picture of Platt's mom."

He laid the photograph on top of the envelope and Tristan leaned forward, staring at it. Tristan's breath hissed out as he exchanged a surprised look at St. James then at Kip.

"Yeah, blew me away, too, when I first saw it," said St. James, crossing his arms. "She could be Carolee or even your sister. That was taken when she was about twenty years old."

A woman in a white tank top, cut short to show her belly button. A pair of butterfly tattoos fluttered on her shoulder, her blue eyes dark with makeup, her hair bleached blonde, roots clearly showing. She was standing in front of the Ballard Beauty Academy.

"Damn, Kell—" he said finally, staring at her. "You were spot on. Every detail."

She wasn't proud of how she knew those things, but she was proud that it helped catch a killer. She smiled.

"So, where's Platt's mother?"

"She had a prior for prostitution when Platt was nine. Spent two nights in the bullpen until Mason made her bail. She was arrested at a bar near Stewart. Bar's gone now. Replaced by The Midnight Hour."

The look on Tristan's face was nothing short of awe and it made Kip grin. No one had ever looked at her like that before.

"She died a few months ago, of cirrhosis."

"About the time the murders started," said Kip.

St. James nodded. "Spot on, Thorpe. You're an amazing piece of work. Glad you're on our side."

She poked him in the shoulder with her fist. "Pleasure working with you, St. James."

He shook his head, a sober kind of look on his face. "No, the pleasure was mine, Kelly. And I hope I get to work with you again." He nudged Tristan's leg. "With this lug as a partner, I'm sure I'll get the chance. Seeya later, buddy."

"Thanks, Keith."

St. James picked up the photo and envelope and left them alone again. Tristan held out his right arm and Kip snuggled into it.

"Hey, you still owe me scrambled eggs and cheese," he said with a weak grin.

Kip sat down beside him, leaning over, and kissing him. His mouth tasted like medicine, but she couldn't get enough.

"Soon as you make bail from this joint, I'll fix you anything you want." She smoothed the hair off his forehead. "I'm place-sitting at Seph's until April, by the way."

His eyes widened. "The penthouse?"

Kip nodded. "I'll bring the eggs. You bring the Pyramid."

"That'll do for next week," he said, suddenly looking all serious and brooding. "But what about next month?"

"Move into the penthouse with me and find out," Kip said with a wink.

"And after that?"

The smile faded off Kip's face. She shook her head, shrugging. "What do you mean?"

He took her hand in his, squeezing, his thumb stroking her knuckles. "I don't know. Maybe buy a houseboat in the Spring? Who knows—maybe even a ring?"

Kip sucked in a breath, the smile on her face widening. "From scrambled eggs to engagement rings—that's quite a jump, Bowker. Let's start with the eggs. See where it leads."

She could only imagine where it would lead and she looked forward to every minute of it.

"Okay, but I'm damned good at following leads," he said with a smirk, pulling her toward him, kissing her lips. Even weak and shaky, he was one hell of a kisser.

She pulled back, grinning. "I'm counting on it, Detective," she said and kissed him hard.

The End of PACIFIC BLUE TATTOO

While you're waiting for Lisa's next book...
Read Book One of the romantic paranormal fantasy, ***A Game of Lost Souls***:
THE CINDERELLA HOUR
—Currently FREE!—

Need a little more romantic suspense in your life?
ISABEL'S TEARS

BEAUTY: CAPTURED AND FRAMED

LANDFALL

NOVELS BY LISA SILVERTHORNE

Standalones:

ISABEL'S TEARS

LANDFALL

PACIFIC BLUE TATTOO

A Game of Lost Souls series:

THE CINDERELLA HOUR

THE PRINCE CHARMING HOUR

THE EVER AFTER HOUR

THE FALLEN HEARTS SEASON

THE RISING SPIRITS SEASON

THE ETERNAL SOULS SEASON

THE ROYAL WEDDING HOUR

THE HEAVENLY HONEYMOON HOUR

Haunted Portraits series:

BEAUTY: CAPTURED AND FRAMED

SCIENCE FICTION WRITING AS L.S. SILVERTHORNE

Standalone:

REDISCOVERY

Experiencing True Purple series:

RECOMBINANT, Book 1

HELIX, Book 2

COMING SOON!

A Game of Lost Souls series:

The Divine Newlyweds Show, Book Nine

The Celestial Couples Show, Book Ten

The Enochian Apocalypse Show, Book Eleven

The Angelic Anniversary Hour, Book Twelve

A Game of Lost Souls—Angelic Hearts:

Muriel's Spark

Kesien's Fire

Anahera's Flame

Azrael's Embers

SCIENCE FICTION WRITING AS L.S. SILVERTHORNE

Experiencing True Purple series:

Splice, Book 3

Cipher, Book 4

Renascence, Book 5

ABOUT THE AUTHOR

LISA SILVERTHORNE has published sixteen novels and more than 100 short stories and novelettes in many genres. Her short fiction has appeared in professional publications that include: DAW Books, Roc Books, *Pulphouse Magazine, Fiction River,* Wildside Press, and Prime Books. She lives in Las Vegas, Nevada.

Before you go, you are invited to please leave a **review of this book**!

Reviews are a wonderful way to help an author. They are also an exciting opportunity to share your honest thoughts with other readers, so **please post yours,** in as many places as possible!

9 781955 197236